ELEPHANT HERD

ELEPHANT HERD

A NOVEL

ZHANG GUIXING

TRANSLATED BY

CARLOS ROJAS

Columbia University Press   *New York*

Columbia University Press wishes to express its appreciation for assistance given by the Chiang Ching-kuo Foundation for International Scholarly Exchange and Council for Cultural Affairs in the preparation of the translation and in the publication of this series.

Columbia University Press
Publishers Since 1893
New York   Chichester, West Sussex

Library of Congress Cataloging-in-Publication Data
Names: Zhang, Guixing, author. | Rojas, Carlos, 1970– translator.
Title: Elephant herd / Zhang Guixing ; translated by Carlos Rojas.
Other titles: Qun xiang. English
Description: New York : Columbia University Press, 2024. |
Series: Modern Chinese literature from Taiwan
Identifiers: LCCN 2023044207 (print) | LCCN 2023044208 (ebook) |
ISBN 9780231211680 (hardback) | ISBN 9780231211697 (trade paperback) |
ISBN 9780231559034 (ebook)
Subjects: LCSH: Sarawak (Malaysia)—Fiction. | LCGFT: Novels.
Classification: LCC PL2837.K79 Q5913 2024 (print) |
LCC PL2837.K79 (ebook) | DDC 895.1/352—dc23/eng/20231024

Cover design: Chang Jae Lee
Cover image: © Shutterstock

CONTENTS

INTRODUCTION

CARLOS ROJAS

Born in 1956 in Sarawak, one of two Malaysian states in the northern portion of the island of Borneo, Zhang Guixing moved to Taiwan for college in 1976. He published his first story collection in 1980, the same year that he graduated from Taiwan Normal University with a degree in English. After college he remained in Taiwan, where he is now a naturalized citizen. Although his day job was teaching high school English, he also achieved considerable acclaim for his fiction. For instance, his 2018 novel *Wild Boars Crossing the River*—which explores the legacies of the Japanese invasion of British North Borneo during World War II—was awarded several major literary awards, including the 2019 Taiwan Literature Award and the 2020 Dream of the Red Chamber Award, further cementing Zhang's status as one of the Sinosphere's leading authors.

At a time when China is establishing itself as a major geopolitical power and literature from mainland China is increasingly attracting global attention, there has also been growing attention to literature from more marginal regions of the global Sinosphere—including Hong Kong and Taiwan, Sinophone regions of Southeast Asia, and the global Chinese diaspora. Seen in these terms, Zhang Guixing's literature originates from and is grounded in a region that is located at the margins of the margins. That is to say, although Zhang is closely associated with Taiwan, where he has lived most of his life, he is also viewed more specifically as a Malaysian-Chinese ("Mahua") author, given his roots in and continued focus on Malaysia. Even among other Mahua authors, however, Zhang occupies a marginal position in that he is not from the Malaysian Peninsula, but rather from the relatively underdeveloped Malaysian region of Borneo (also known as Eastern Malaysia)—which accounts for 60 percent of Malaysia's total area but only 20 percent of its current population. Moreover, unlike fellow Sarawak native Li Yongping, who similarly moved to Taiwan in 1967 for college and subsequently became a naturalized citizen, Zhang sets almost all of his fiction in Sarawak, with particular attention to the region's distinctive history, sociocultural characteristics, and natural environment. As a result, his works diverge significantly not only from mainland Chinese literature but also from mainstream literature from both Taiwan and (peninsular) Malaysia.

Borneo's rainforest figures particularly prominently in three novels that Zhang published between 1998 and 2002, including *Elephant Herd*, *Monkey Cup*, and *Siren Song*. In addition to their attention to the rainforest itself, each of the works in this informal triptych—which fellow Mahua author Ng Kim Chew has dubbed Zhang's "rainforest trilogy"—revolves around a male protagonist in the contemporary present, but they also include extensive flashbacks to events years and even decades earlier. These works give particular attention to the legacy of the mid-century communist insurgency in Borneo while also exploring the complicated interethnic relations between the region's ethnic Chinese, local Malays, and Indigenous peoples.

The main diegesis of *Elephant Herd*, for instance, begins in December 1973, with twenty-year-old protagonist Shi Shicai traveling up the Rajang River with his former high school classmate Zhu Dezhong. Shicai—or "the boy," as the narrative usually refers to him—is an ethnically Chinese Malaysian whose family has been living in Sarawak for three generations. Having migrated to the Malaysian region in multiple waves over centuries, ethnic Chinese currently make up roughly a quarter of the nation's overall population (down from around 40 percent in 1957, when the Federation of Malaya, as the nation was known at the time, achieved independence from Britain), and also make up a quarter of the population of the state of Sarawak. Unlike peninsular Malaysia, where Malays are the largest ethnic group, in Sarawak the largest ethnic group are instead the indigenous Iban people, who account for between 30 and 35 percent of the state's overall population. Also known as Sea Dayaks, the Iban are a subgroup of the Dayak tribal group and historically were known as warriors and headhunters. Although Shicai's classmate, Dezhong, appears to use a Chinese name, he is actually an Iban, though, unlike many of his relatives, he attended Chinese schools and speaks fluent Chinese.

Dezhong's family lives deep in the rainforest up the Rajang River from the town of Daro, where Dezhong and Shicai had been working after finishing high school. Dezhong offers to accompany Shicai on his journey upriver in search of his uncle, Yu Jiatong, the leader of a local communist guerilla group known as the Yangtze River Brigade. As the novel notes in a series of flashbacks, the Yangtze River Brigade was one of three guerilla brigades formed by members of the Sarawak Communist Party when they returned to Sarawak in 1965 from the Indonesian portion of Borneo, where for three years they had been receiving training from the Indonesian Communist Party. In Indonesia, the Sarawak communists had been training to fight the British, but after they returned to Sarawak their primary foes were the Sarawak government forces. After several years of pitched battle, one of Sarawak's three communist brigades agreed to lay down their arms in October 1973, and many members of the other two brigades quickly followed suit. In the novel's fictionalized version of this local history, Yu Jiatong and a handful of followers refuse to follow the other brigade's lead and lay down their arms, and instead they remain holed up in a base camp deep in the rainforest. When Shicai sets off in search of his uncle, accordingly, he is searching for this base camp, though the novel does not immediately specify *why* he is trying to find his uncle.

The world's oldest and third-largest rainforest (it is 130 million years old, which is twice as old as the Amazon's), the Borneo rainforest in which Yu Jiatong establishes his base camp and through which Shicai and Dezhong travel is also one of the most biodiverse regions on the planet, containing countless species of flora and fauna that are endemic to the island. The novel's very first lines, for instance, make reference to more than a dozen different animals, including snakes, lizards, dragonflies, butterflies, spiders, millipedes, scorpions, crabs, red-winged flies, scallion-green rain frogs, and waterbirds, while also alluding to assorted plants such as jackfruit trees, duckweed, and algae. Throughout the work plants and animals often function as vehicles for exploring the affective stances of the work's human protagonists while also being used to reflect on the region's delicate ecological web. Both of these approaches are evident in the work's portrayal of the titular elephants, which are alternately eroticized and abjected, and which are repeatedly described as being "positioned at the interstices of imagination and reality."

Like the rainforest itself, *Elephant Herd* is wild and inchoate. For instance, the work's first paragraph, which runs two full pages in the Chinese edition and spans the first five paragraphs of this translation, consists of an extended flashback (including another flashback embedded within the first) and features a combination of full sentences and assorted sentence fragments. The first set of animals referenced in the work's opening lines appear in a series of noun phrases separated by periods: "camouflaged scallion-green rain frogs. waterbirds. dragonflies. butterflies." In my initial translation, I had originally "domesticized" this opening passage by transforming it into a complete sentence with the noun clauses separated by commas instead of periods. However, a very helpful anonymous reviewer of this earlier draft of the translation suggested that it might be useful to preserve the fragmented syntax of the original, noting pithily that *Elephant Herd* "is a really weird novel, written in a really weird style, and the translation captures that, but it could maybe be a bit weirder."

Translation is inherently an exercise in compromise—of attempting to preserve the foreignness of the original while endeavoring to make it reasonably accessible to the new readership. Following the reviewer's suggestion, however, in this volume I have sought to retain as much as possible the weirdness of Zhang's original novel. For instance, I have kept many of his sentence fragments as well as much of the work's extensive use of onomatopoeia (except for a handful of cases, such as when I render the characters 嘎嘎—pronounced *gaga* in Mandarin, and used in the novel to describe the ducklike vocalizations of the protagonist's mute mother—as "quack" or "quacking"). This translation's largest concession to preserving the novel's readability, however, involves the work's paragraph structure. The novel contains multiple flashbacks, as well as occasional flashforwards. In the original work, these temporal shifts are not explicitly marked, and they sometimes occur in mid-paragraph.

In the early portion of the translation, I have introduced line breaks and double line breaks to help clarify the work's narrative logic, though as the novel progresses and readers become more familiar with the work's storyworld, I add progressively fewer of these breaks, to the point that in the final chapter—which is also where the work's different storylines are most tightly interwoven with one another—I have added no breaks at all.

One of the novel's dominant representational modalities involves camouflage. Throughout the novel, people, animals, objects, and even optical phenomena like shadows are repeatedly described as being "camouflaged" as other animals, plants, objects, or optical phenomena. One interesting variation on this theme of camouflage can be found in the passages where geckos crawling across a chalkboard filled with Chinese writing are described as merging with the Chinese characters themselves:

> A gecko, as pale as ash and with veins clearly visible beneath its skin, scurried onto the blackboard, running through that assemblage of Chinese characters. The reptile was transformed into one of the numerals already written on the board, replacing several of the Chinese character's original strokes. Eventually, it came to rest in a spot on the board that didn't have any characters, and in the process it became a new character in its own right.

Conversely, the novel also features several passages where Chinese characters come to resemble living beings, such as when Shicai imagines that he can see his own father "crawling through the Chinese characters like a bug," which inspires Shicai to continue writing "until the page appeared full of intestines and the Chinese characters resembled tender flesh." Camouflage here may be viewed as a form of translation from flesh to script, and from script to flesh.

As another very helpful anonymous reader pointed out, this interest in camouflage also extends to the novel's use of place names, several of which are slightly modified versions of the names of actual Sarawak sites. For instance, Shicai's hometown is rendered with two characters, 大鑼 (pronounced *daluo* in Mandarin), that are close homophones of the characters usually used for the actual Sarawak town of Daro, 達佬 (pronounced *dalao* in Mandarin)—located at the estuary of the Rajang River. Similarly, Dezhong's hometown is initially rendered with two characters, 畢加 (pronounced *bijia* in Mandarin), that are a precise inversion of the characters usually used for the actual Sarawak town of Kapit: 加畢 (pronounced *jiabi* in Mandarin), a predominantly Yiban community located along the Rajang River. In this translation, accordingly, I have initially rendered the town as "Pitka," but when the protagonists pass through the town again near the end of the novel and town's characters appear in the correct order, I similarly render the transcribed name correctly as "Kapit."

This circuitous process of taking the Chinese transliterations of local place names (many of which are derived from names that were originally in English, Malay, or other local non-Sinitic languages) and then retransliterating them back into roman script captures in miniature a key linguistic quality of the novel as a whole. For instance, although technically composed entirely in Chinese, the novel actually represents a linguistic environment in which several different Chinese dialects appear, including Hakka, Hokkien, Teochew, and Hokchew, which the novel silently "translates" into written Chinese. Moreover, some figures in the novel, such as Dezhong's relatives, speak little or no Chinese, meaning that their Iban speech is necessarily embedded within the novel's Chinese-language narrative (sometimes in the form of speech that Shicai is unable to understand), just as the novel's extensive use of onomatopoeia may be viewed as a process of "translating" an array of nonlinguistic sounds into Chinese. From a linguistic perspective, meanwhile, some of the most intriguing exchanges are the dialogues between Shicai and Dezhong's younger sister, Fadiya. Given that Shicai does not speak Iban and Fadiya does not speak Chinese, they instead communicate in English (which Fadiya speaks with difficulty). The novel silently translates their English-language dialogues into Chinese—and here, of course, they are retranslated back into (broken) English. This use of broken English in my English translation attempts to capture the broken English dialogue that the novel invokes but does not represent directly, while at the same time alluding more generally to the translational fractures that run through the original novel and, inevitably, through this translation.

1

The boy was six years old. He was sitting under a jack-fruit tree watching his distraught grandfather inside the animal shed. The lake behind the shed was covered in duckweed and was filled with camouflaged scallion-green rain frogs. waterbirds. dragonflies. butterflies. In front of the shed there was a well full of black, shiny water. Heavy. Heavy as metal. The tall jackfruit tree had a thick canopy, and its inky shadow enveloped the shed, the well, and half of the pond. Spiders. millipedes. scorpions. crabs. lizards appeared and disappeared in the haze. On cloudy days, the boy would sit under the tree, and if he held out his hand, in place of his fingers he would instead see his grandfather's tiny eyes like a pair of fluorescent mushrooms. Not long before the shed had housed a couple of pigs, and every morning and night the boy would take them two paint cans full of lavalike chaff. The chaff was sweet, sour, hot, bitter, and exceedingly foul, and it attracted a firelike swarm of red-winged flies.

The boy dished several hundred duckweed blossoms out of the pond and mixed them with the chaff, then pounded the mixture with a wooden board. A green snake leaped out of the bucket, while the rain frogs remained camouflaged and a butterfly with a broken wing fluttered through the air. Red flies buzzed around like sparks. As though someone were holding up a bowl of fire.

Every Tuesday and Saturday at noon the boy would use a small steel pail to draw water from the well, and then, still holding the pail, he would stand either outside or inside the shed to wash the pigs and rinse away their waste. Small clumps of animal waste would flow into the pond, saturating the duckweed and algae. The well water always carried a faint stench—like marinated chickens, birds, cats, scorpions, lizards, and rodents. During the monsoon season, the water was surprisingly clear, as though it had just been disinfected, and the inside of the well was extremely fragrant, attracting countless birds and animals to come drink. However, some of these birds and animals would periodically fall into the well, and within a month the well would begin to produce a faint stench. Apart from fetching water to wash the pigs and fertilize the vegetables and plants, the boy's family never used this well. The family had three wells in all— with the other two being located outside the bathhouse and in the garden, where they were used for bathing and irrigation. These other two wells had been there for a long time, from even before Grandfather settled in this area. By this point, however, these other two wells were already broken-down and overgrown with weeds, and their exterior resembled desiccated rafflesia blossoms. There were no other traces of humanity nearby.

Do you know when the two wells were dug? Or who dug them? When the boy's paternal and maternal grandfathers set about reclaiming this wasteland, the first thing they did was dig a pair of wells. In the process they dredged up an assortment of objects, after which they proceeded to dig even deeper while simultaneously fashioning the well's walls. As they did so they discovered tile and pottery shards, as well as numerous jugs, dishes, and pieces of blue-white porcelain, many of which were covered in indistinct dragon-like markings. There were also coins from some Chinese dynasty or other, and even an animal skeleton. Was it from a bear? A tapir? A bay cat? A rhino? In the end, the diggers confirmed that the skeleton belonged to a baby elephant, which must have fallen in either while trying to drink or when simply passing by. The boy imagined how anxious the other elephants must have been as they crowded around, reaching into the well with their long trunks. Or maybe at that point the holes weren't even actual wells yet? Maybe they were simply deep pits for hiding valuables? The people who previously came to retrieve—or perhaps one should say to steal—the contents of these pits must have taken the valuables and left behind this pile of worthless objects. The boy's two grandfathers then continued to deepen and widen the holes but made no additional discoveries.

The two old wells were now excruciatingly wide and deep, and their condition stood in stark contrast to that of the newer one next to the animal shed. The walls of the old wells were covered in thick moss and the wells themselves were filled with algae, mushrooms, ferns, and vines. Near the waterline you could find cauliflower-like clumps of frog and fighting-fish eggs. With the arrival of each monsoon season, the Shi home, which was located in a depression, would gradually become a marshland. Out with the old, in with the new! Inside the wells, however, the environment never changed. The wells contained some strange fish that had somehow managed to swim in from outside, which produced bubbles like a stone thrown into the water. The sound of these bubbles emerging from the deep night made the boy think that some animal must have fallen in again. He wondered what those large fish found to eat inside the well, until one day he observed them leaping a meter into the air and nibbling on the mushrooms and leaves growing on the sides of the well. The fish even devoured the lizards crawling along the sides of the well and the tiny birds perched on the railing. They also nibbled on the frozen melons and other fruits that the boy's mother and grandmother would often hang inside the well, to the point that all that was left was a few pieces of fruit rinds or peelings. The boy and his brothers would sometimes go fishing in the well, using worms as bait—and as soon as they pulled the fish out they would immediately cut the line with a sharp knife. By the next rainy season these large fish would have leisurely swum back to the wilderness from which they came. It was said that for a while after the two wells were first built, a Qing dynasty lady with pearly-white skin could be seen sitting on the railing, braiding rope. The boy's maternal grandfather claimed this woman would sell the rope she braided, then use her earnings to purchase jewelry. Eventually, however, a large fish leapt up out of the well and bit off all ten of the lady's slim fingers, where-upon she collected her basket of goods and departed. Where did she go? No one knows. When the boy was younger his parents would often warn him not to lean against the side of the well, saying, "You little radish-head, a fish could swallow you whole!" Despite these warnings the boy and his elder brothers would often loiter next to the well, fishing and using slingshots to hit the reptiles and amphibians climbing up the walls.

Raising pigs was the boy's first chore in life. When he didn't have anything better to do, he would lie on the pen's corrugated tin roof and stare up at the damp and sparkling tree canopy, as though gazing into a starry sky. He felt as though he were lying on a tree branch under the sun and rain, buffeted by wind and fog—awake and able to clearly distinguish the calls of various different vegetarian, carnivorous, and omnivorous birds. *Gugugu, gugugu.* The large magpie irrigating the shrubs was anxious but full of love. *Honghong longlong.* The crocodiles on the riverbank were full of fat. In the distance the boy could hear the sound of elephants running and fighting. . . . By the time the boy was two years old, he could already identify these various sounds. However, to say that he heard a herd of elephants was not entirely accurate. In fact, it was precisely on the day he was born that elephants ransacked his family's vegetable garden—trampling it to the point that afterward the garden would also flood when it rained. Some claimed that the animals in question were not elephants but rather wild boars. This incident occurred on December 20, 1954, and the northeastern monsoon brought torrential rains that continued uninterrupted for an entire week, adding another layer of devastation to the destruction brought about by the legendary elephants.

Grandmother had prepared a rope and stick to deal with Grandfather, whose opium cravings were starting to flare up again. However, three months passed in the blink of an eye, and although Grandfather was now sloppy and untidy his eyes still sparkled like phosphorescent mushrooms—such that he resembled a toad that, after having eaten its fill, digs a burrow to protect itself from drying up. There was nothing left at home for Grandfather to pawn, so Grandmother took her blade brigade and went to visit Daro's gambling and opium addicts—warning them that if anyone tried to offer Grandfather financial assistance of any kind, the blade brigade she had established with her descendants would chop him to death. Her brigade consisted of six people: the boy, his four elder brothers, and their grandmother. In addition to a cleaver, they also wielded a tomato knife, a trowel, and an ax—and because these implements had been repeatedly struck over a long period of time, their exterior was almost completely destroyed and was covered in glittering red blood, as though they had just been removed from the furnace. Grandmother took this brigade to slaughter all the garden's monkeys, pigs, dogs, and lizards, for which she received quite a lot of attention. The boy and his brothers treated these killings as a game and didn't give them much thought—though they were concerned that Grandmother might get bitten like a chicken by a large monitor lizard, get dug up like an abandoned grave by a wild dog, or get stomped like a pumpkin by a boar. By the time Grandmother murderously rushed forward, however, her enemy would have already disappeared. As she was running through the silvergrass grove chasing orangutans, the boy and his brothers found that they couldn't tell their grandmother apart from their primate ancestors. They couldn't even cut down the machins from the bean poles and melon sheds. . . .

One night after the rainy season had concluded—when the stars resembled water and the sky was like a tide—the boy's elder brother crashed through the dew-covered grass. *Xisu huala.* He was heading toward the town's Chinese cemetery where Grandfather had gone. Located next to a mountain road, the cemetery extended for several kilometers and contained the bodies of almost a hundred thousand Chinese immigrants. Grandfather was using a shovel to dig a grave behind the tomb, and Elder Brother was lying on the ground about ten meters away. The boy could hear Grandfather struggling for breath like a man starving to death, could see his mushroomlike eyes, and could smell his ferrous scent that resembled a mixture of tree bark and vegetable roots. Grandfather gradually disappeared into the pit he was digging, but after a while he climbed back out with what resembled a coconut shell stripped of its outer layer. He then straightened up the area around the grave, which took him even longer than it had taken him to dig the original hole. After he finished he knelt down in front of the tomb and loudly kowtowed, then departed with the shovel and the coconut shell. By this point Eldest Brother's hands and feet had gone completely limp, and he fumbled around for a moment before following Grandfather. As Eldest Brother was lying on the ground listening to the excruciating metallic sound Grandfather was making as he lifted the coffin with the shovel, he couldn't help peeing on a girl's tomb. Grandfather alternated between a brisk walk and a slow jog, and an hour later he entered a stilt house that had been rented by an English merchant named Christian.

Grandmother and her blade brigade tied up Grandfather with his back to the jackfruit tree. The tree was full of boils and other growths that poked into Grandfather's back, such that he cried out in pain and begged for mercy. By this point Grandmother already viewed Grandfather as comparable to animals that roamed the garden, and when she heard his cries she proceeded to chop him with the back of her vegetable knife, leaving his skin covered in purplish-red millipede-like bumps. This was how she had previously dealt with orangutans when they pulled people's hair and scratched their faces. "You dirty corpse. . . . The way you've injured us as we tried to follow you, you'd be better off dead. . . ." As the boy and his brothers were leaving, they heard Grandmother cursing while drawing water from the well and flinging it at Grandfather, as though trying to put out an endless summer forest fire. Attempting to escape Grandmother and her blade brigade, Grandfather spent five days wandering through the marsh, the rainforest, and the cemetery—and had he known he would encounter this sort of treatment if he returned home, perhaps he would have preferred to remain outside with the scabby dogs, with whom his appearance and odor had an ironclad identification. Christian, the English merchant, would seek out cheap elephant tusks, rhinoceros horns, hornbill skulls, animal pelts, rare animals, as well as Tang, Song, and Ming dynasty porcelain artifacts from the natives' longhouses, and secretly export them back to Europe and America. Legend has it that when he was younger he sold slaves in the American South, and more recently had received an order from a European medical society asking him to deliver a hundred Asian skulls. By this point he had already collected eighty-three skulls.

For three months and twenty-one days Grandmother kept watch on Grandfather under the jackfruit tree. On the twenty-second day of the fourth month, however, she, her sons, and grandsons used several dozen boards to construct an addition to the shed, creating a small fortress. The boy and his brothers excavated a pit under the floor of the new addition, then dug a ditch connecting it to the lake. That way, Grandfather's excrement could flow through the ditch and into the lake. Occasionally some climbing fish would swim up from the lake to consume Grandfather's fresh, hot feces. Intestinal worms up to twenty centimeters long occasionally appeared in the excrement, which would excite the fish to the point that they would spread their fins and almost impale Grandfather's butt. The fish's mouths were too small to bite these lively worms, which were each as thick as a man's pinky, and therefore they ultimately had no choice but to simply nibble at them, leaving the worms utterly heartbroken. Sometimes Grandfather would defecate directly into the pit, and sometimes he wouldn't. He frequently crouched in the corner of the room and, with his leisurely gaze full of phosphorescent mushrooms' poisonous light, would either peek out through a crack in the wall or else stare into space. When Grandfather finally left the jackfruit tree and approached Grandmother, his cravings were acting up again, and therefore he wasn't able to offer any resistance when Grandmother chopped the back of his skull with the side of a cleaver, as though he were a corpse that had been dumped in the animal shed. After this blow, Grandfather quickly came to—his swollen, bloodshot eyes now full of tears, his nose dripping with snot, and the corners of his mouth filled with mucus. Although his hair was soaked in sweat and his face was gaunt and emaciated, he nevertheless retained an elegant air, as though he were about to spread his wings and fly away. His trembling larynx made him resemble a comical pelican. After watching Grandfather for three months and twenty-one days Grandmother became seriously ill, after which the responsibility for looking after Grandfather fell on the boy's shoulders. Apart from raising the pigs, this was the boy's first job. Lying in bed, Grandmother told him, "I want you to look after your grandfather the same way you looked after the pigs."

Grandfather liked to eat live crabs. He would use his tongue to lick the foam from the crab's abdomen, and after cracking open the shell he would then place the crab in his mouth and bite into it. Sometimes when he stuffed his mouth with small crabs he would swallow them with a gurgle before his teeth even had a chance to react. The boy felt as though these crabs were still roaming around inside his grandfather's belly. He would take the crabs he caught outside the shed and toss them through an opening in the wall, then watch as Grandfather noisily devoured them as though they were thousand-year-old pieces of porcelain. Once the boy tossed a dead frog into the shed, and Grandfather devoured it as though it were a crab—using his thumb and second finger to yank off the frog's front legs as though they were a pair of claws. After finishing the frog legs, Grandfather tried to pry open the frog's belly with his finger, as though prying open a crab's abdomen. When the boy tossed in a half-dead grasshopper, Grandfather went through the same motions. Grandfather also chewed noisily on the shed's lizards, mice, scorpions, and even the fruit bats hanging upside down from the rafters. *Zizi-zaza.* The boy finally acceded to Grandmother's request and proceeded to look after his grandfather the same way that he would look after the pigs. When the boy found himself idle, he would climb the jackfruit tree and gaze out at the rainforest and the bushes, listening even more carefully to the cries of the coucals, the rumblings of the crocodiles, and the galloping of the elephants positioned at the interstices of imagination and reality.

Two months later Grandmother returned to the shed to continue looking after Grandfather, but after ten days Grandfather broke down the door and fled, never to be seen again. Grandmother also disappeared on the same day. A week later the boy was sitting in the jackfruit tree gazing out at the rainforest, and when he lowered his gaze he saw two egg-shaped orbs floating inside the well. Countless tiny fish resembling dog teeth were biting the orbs from below, pushing them back and forth. Occasionally a large fish resembling an oxhorn would push the orbs down to the bottom of the well, whereupon they were torn apart by the dogtooth and oxhorn fish—to the point that they came to resemble a mixture of sputum, fat, fish maw, and pheasant meat. The boy excitedly watched the scene then spat into the well. There was also another object floating in the darkness. At first the boy assumed it was either some sort of light or a reflection from the jackfruit tree, and therefore he kept his gaze focused on the two orbs. The other object continued to slowly float upward, as though it were a creature gradually evolving or a film being developed. When the boy focused on it, it was still floating upward but also appeared to be sinking. Later, the boy noticed countless dogtooth and oxhorn fish tugging at the object and congregating around it like ants, helping push it upward. When the object reached the surface, the dogtooth and oxhorn fish quickly tore it into pieces, so that it was unable to sink back down again. It turns out that the object in question was Grandmother's corpse—and the swollen face had two gaping holes. So the two egglike orbs were actually Grandmother's eyeballs, which must have been pried from their sockets by the dogtooth and oxhorn fishes. But Grandfather—a murderer? Whoa. The boy harbored an inchoate sense of guilt for his grandmother's death, feeling that he should have continued looking after his grandfather even after his grandmother recovered from her illness.

When the boy was fourteen, six Yangtze River Brigade troops delivered a couple of damp and rickety coffins to his home from the mainland. When the boy's uncle led some North Kalimantan People's Army troops into the rainforest to resist the government's forces, they saw Grandfather's coffin outside one of the natives' longhouses. By that point the coffin had already been closed for two years. It turns out that the year Grandfather died, the owner of the longhouse had taken in an unconscious old Chinese man, and after the man died the natives, according to their custom, were unable to bury the body because there was no next of kin to claim it. Uncle brusquely requested confirmation that the dead man was in fact the boy's grandfather, and when they opened the coffin Uncle saw Grandfather's body looking exactly as it had before he disappeared—his eyes still gleaming with a poisonous light, like phosphorescent mushrooms, his arms like bitter melons, gray hair growing down to his belly like fishbones, and his fingernails twisted like vines. When the natives originally closed the coffin, they had used resin, paraffin, and clay to seal it airtight, thereby creating a vacuum. Given that Uncle was unable to collect the corpse itself, he had no choice but to send away the entire coffin. The boy's second brother had assumed the position of brigade captain under Uncle's supervision and was responsible for transporting the coffin home. En route, however, the brigade was attacked by a group of natives, who chopped up Second Brother's body and kept his head for ransom. The other guerilla fighters told the boy's mother that the leader of the North Kalimantan People's Army would spare no expense to retrieve her son's head and ensure that this hero—who made such extraordinary contributions to the Sarawak Communist Party (SCP)—will be buried with his body intact. The boy didn't dare look directly at Second Brother in the coffin. His mother, however, knelt in front of the coffin and caressed her son's body, and it was only after caressing the body for a long time that she was finally able to recognize him. If it had only been his entrails in the coffin she would probably have been too heartbroken to recognize the body at all and instead would have numbly gathered the entrails into a pile. The boy once dreamed that his headless elder brother was trying to rearrange his own internal organs, but no matter what he did, he wasn't able to get them back in order and eventually had to summon the boy for help.

The boy was seven years old. He climbed the jackfruit tree and gazed out at the grassy fields, the bushes, and the marshland, searching for coucal nests. From the time he was four he had dreamed that one day he would catch a big, fat coucal hatchling that he could then give to his mother. Coucal hatchlings were first-rate medicinal ingredients. After they had been marinated for several days in rice wine or foreign wine, the liquid could be either ingested or used externally, and was useful for treating rheumatoid arthritis and other chronic ailments. Merchants and Chinese pharmacies were willing to pay top dollar for these hatchlings, and a chick that had just begun to sprout feathers could fetch ten or twenty Singapore dollars. Given that Father's carpenter salary was only about three hundred dollars a month, searching for coucal hatchlings became an important way for the boy to supplement his family's income, and his parents also occasionally leant him a hand. When the boy was four, he began climbing jackfruit, durian, and coconut trees, and also climbing onto the roofs of houses, in order to watch coucals seek mates and build their nests. He did this until it became second nature. Whenever he discovered a coucal nest, he simply needed to take a red ribbon with his name written on it and tie it to a nearby shrub or tree trunk, which would signify his legal rights to the nest. The boy searched the library and finally borrowed an illustrated anatomy book from the home of his elementary school principal, Teacher Shao An, from which the boy memorized the appearance and location of the body's various internal organs.

This was the boy's third job. His posture in the jackfruit tree resembled that of a leopard, his hair resembled the feathers of a night owl hiding in the shrubs, and his eyes resembled those of a monkey-eating eagle—meaning that he bore a resemblance to three different animals that all preyed on coucals. Nearby there was luxurious grass and clumps of shrubs, and the rainforest was lingering and sultry, with an abundance of moisture. The boy speculated that the animals were emerging to search for food. He saw two or three different species and could hear more than ten. Brilliant fur and feathers, ferocious scales and hoofs. Silent and loud. They used noise and odor to divvy up their respective spheres of influence. When the boy was feeling bored, he would hang upside down from a tree like a fruit bat, remaining in that position until he was dizzy and his limbs were limp—leaving him terrified that he wouldn't be able to return to normal. He would swing from one branch to another while making strange cries. From this height he could hear even more clearly the roars of the crocodiles on the riverbank, which resembled tractors driving through mud or driftwood floating in the current. The crocodiles spurted water vapor that formed clouds, and in the sunlight the dense mist formed countless rainbows that could be seen from a kilometer away.

The calls of five coucals seemed to come from all directions, but the boy could only see two of them. One was sunbathing and stretching its wings in a coconut tree, its tail feathers relaxed and its voice bright, while the other was perched on a shrub that had been reduced to a dead branch, its cries vaguely shy. Three days later, when the boy saw a coucal bring a first twig with which to make its nest, he tied a red ribbon with his name on it to a nearby shrub. As the ribbon fluttered in the wind, the boy's name resembled the title of a great general who, after a fierce battle, claims a new territory. The ribbon signified that from that point on this shrub and the surrounding land belonged to the boy, and not even the king of heaven could take it away from him. Satisfied, the boy returned to the tree and continued to observe as the coucal brought a second, and a third . . . twig. The boy searched for a second nest, swearing he would take his remaining dozen or so ribbons and tie all of them to shrubs in this wilderness area.

The boy was two years old when he first saw a crocodile spit out a rainbow. The rainbow flickered between a grove of redwoods then followed the fecund water vapor, oscillating between red and purple like a swarm of impetuous red locusts.

"Brother, what's that?" The boy was sitting on the back of a bicycle, holding a fighting cock. Breathing hard, the boy's eldest brother pedaled toward the cockfighting ring.

"A crocodile," Eldest Brother replied simply.

"Doesn't look like one," the boy said. "Do crocodiles really spurt water like whales? Let's go take a look."

"Stupid," Eldest Brother replied. "Don't go near it."

"I'm not afraid."

"Crocodiles can eat humans."

"I'm on land and it's in the water. It can't get me."

"Actually, eighty percent of a crocodile's prey is terrestrial."

As though responding to Eldest Brother's remark, the crocodile let out a loud roar. The roar was soaked in water—like thunder passing through dark clouds, as though the sound were emerging from the bottom of the river.

Three days later the boy inspected the bird's nest. The ribbon with his name it—together with the entire shrub to which it had been tied—had been removed, and instead now there was an even larger ribbon tied to a shrub next to the nest, on which there were three characters written in cursive script: *Yu Jia Tong.*

"Uncle, you already have plenty of nests. Why do you need to take mine?"

"Shicai, listen to me carefully." Yu Jiatong placed his hands on the boy's shoulders. "The Brunei People's Party is currently doing everything it can to retain its hold on power, and its efforts to combat the people's communist thought are in full swing. I need a lot of money, and therefore all the coucal nests on this tract of land belong to me. How about if I give you a pair of male fighting fish instead?"

After this incident the boy stopped looking for nests but continued to reminisce about coucals' love-filled songs. Overnight the surrounding shrubbery became filled with red ribbons inscribed with Yu Jiatong's name. Eventually Yu Jiatong wouldn't even bother to write out his name and instead simply used blank blood-red ribbons. It wasn't until later that the boy realized the significance of that bright red color.

The boy watched as one of his uncle's classmates, Wang Dada, grabbed a coucal hatchling, broke one of its legs, then returned it to its nest. The hatchling's breath resembled gossamer strands as its faint cries resonated through the wilderness.

"What are you doing?"

"Didn't you know?" Wang Dada walked toward his next target. "If a chick breaks a leg, its mother will eat a certain kind of medicinal herb and then regurgitate it and plaster it onto the broken leg. After the bone is healed, the herb's essence will enter the chick's bloodstream, and when the chick is then used to brew medicine, the herb's recuperative function will emerge. This kind of chick will therefore fetch a high price on the market."

The boy stared as Wang Dada broke another hatchling's leg.

As Wang Dada was leaving, he said, "Everything for the revolution."

When the boy was eight years old, he started his fourth job. . . .

The boy was six years old. He was in his Teacher Shao An's house, attending a Chinese class. He was the youngest student in the class. The Shao house was located next to the Daro Chinese public school—which is to say, it was positioned right on the school grounds. It was an old stilt house, built like a large, brittle crab shell. The living room was as wide as a basketball court, and the wall on the west side contained a large window, while the other three walls were filled with Chinese-language books and Chinese calligraphy scrolls. It was very hot inside the room and, given that during the day the room relied only on the sun for illumination, it was often as dark as a cage. As the sun emerged from behind clouds that were as thick as mountains, the room alternated between light and darkness, like the bottom of a lake. Two electric fans were whirring away like a pair of lawnmowers—spiraling like an open flame and blowing hot air that left everyone feeing deeply uncomfortable. However, the students were not at all anxious, and instead they listened attentively to Teacher Shao's lesson. The students included some instructors from the Daro Chinese public school, as well as the boy's brothers and uncle, while the remainder were in their twenties. Altogether there were usually more than forty students in attendance, but sometimes there would be more than sixty. The tables and chairs were ones the students had either brought with them or else had constructed using extra lumber they found at home. Some of the chairs were as rickety as rocking horses and the surface of some of the tables resembled chopping boards. Apart from the boy and his fourth brother, who were both too young to fully understand Teacher Shao's difficult lessons, everyone else was attentively taking notes. Every Saturday and Sunday afternoon from two to five o'clock Teacher Shao would offer a free lesson on Chinese cultural history. The lecture topics ranged from oracle bone inscriptions to the *Book of Odes*, and from Li Shizhen to Lu Xun. The course had no textbook and no predefined scope. Instead, Teacher Shao simply taught whatever he felt like teaching, and that's exactly how the students liked it.

Teacher Shao shook his head as he used a very precise pronunciation to read aloud Han Yu's essay "An Offering to a Crocodile," adding an explanation after every character: ". . . . in appearance, a crocodile has the head of a dragon, the claws of a tiger, the eyes of a crab, and the scales of a lizard. Its teeth are as large as saw blades, its tail is several *zhang* long, with hook-shaped thorns, and is covered in sticky slime. When a crocodile is submerged near a riverbank, people or other animals who approach may be struck by its tail and eaten."

Behind Teacher Shao there was a blackboard that students had wiped clean with their hands, on which were the following passages written, like strange new flowers:

Crocodile: a large type of animal with a dragon head, horse tail, and tiger claws. It can reach a length of up to four *zhang*, crawls well, and eats humans.

—RECORDS OF IMPRESSIONS OF ANIMALS

Crocodiles are more than two *zhang* long, have four legs, and resemble alligators. Their snout is three *chi* in length, with sharp teeth. When tigers and deer try to ford a river, crocodiles may attack.

—RECORDS OF EXTRAORDINARY THINGS

In the South Seas there are crocodiles, which resemble alligators.

—RECORDS OF DIVERSE MATTERS

Alligators: aquatic reptiles that resemble lizards. They can reach a length of about one *zhang*, and their hide can be used to make drums.

—EXPLAINING GRAPHS

Alligators . . . are shaped like dragons, produce an extremely frightening sound, may reach one *zhang* in length, and can spurt steam that forms clouds and rain.

—COMPENDIUM OF MATERIA MEDICA

Crocodiles: as large as a boat, have feet, and are classified as dragons.

—RECORD OF THE CUSTOMS AND GEOGRAPHICAL SURROUNDINGS OF ZHENLA

Dragons: long reptiles with scales.

—EXPLAINING GRAPHS

Dragons: live in the water, travel by means of the five colors, and therefore are divine. If they want to be small, they transform into silkworm pupae, and if they want to be large, they hide in the open. If they want to be high, they approach the clouds, and if they want to be low, they enter deep caves.

—GUANZI: CHAPTER ON WATER AND LAND

After Teacher Shao finished explaining Han Yu's "An Offering to a Crocodile," he proceeded—with spittle flying in all directions—to cover the blackboard with a series of passages, periodically pausing to add explanations next to them. He continued in this manner until the entire blackboard was covered with his "wild and unrestrained" handwriting. Teacher Shao's handwriting when he was using chalk was like when he was using a brush or a pen—and each Chinese character's joints and spirit appeared complete. Even if students didn't focus on the actual content of his writing and instead considered only the shapes of the characters themselves, that was still enough to make their blood boil, whereupon they would put down their pens and sigh. They would carefully copy Teacher Shao's text into their notebooks: *Mountains: rugged. Water: sparkling. Mist: hazy. Wind: whistling. On the mountain cliffs, there was a cluster of pampas grass. A line of waterfalls. A fallen leaf. A forking branch.* On the blackboard, the students saw the names Wang Yizhi, Su Dongpo, and Dadazi. The Chinese characters on the board contained pictures and the pictures contained characters. By the time Teacher Shao finished explaining the passages, the boy and Fourth Brother were about to doze off. "Crocodiles, particularly salt-water crocodiles, are ancient reptiles that have survived virtually unchanged for over two hundred million years, since the age of the dinosaurs. Salt-water crocodiles are one of the largest species of crocodiles. Crocodiles are a tropical species, and apart from a minority that can survive in temperate regions, most of them live in the tropics. . . ."

The boy's and Fourth Brother's eyes lit up as they waited for Teacher Shao to continue.

According to paleometeorologists, before the Xia and Shang dynasties, the climate of China's Central Plains region was similar to that of the Asian tropics, and this was particularly true of the middle and lower portions of the Yellow River and the corresponding alluvial fan region. This region was full of swamps and wetlands, with high humidity and heavy rainfall, and dense forests that were conducive to both herbivores and carnivores—thereby providing crocodiles with ideal living conditions. From the bones excavated from Yinxu, near the Yellow River, archeologists discovered tropical animals such as elephants, rhinoceroses, and bamboo rats. Abundant evidence reveals that in antiquity salt-water crocodiles were abundant in China's South Sea, East Sea, and the Bohai Sea, as well as the alluvial regions of the Yangtze, Huai, and Yellow Rivers. Many crocodile fossils have been unearthed in the Fen River watershed in Shanxi, and these archeological discoveries are corroborated by the pictures of crocodiles that can be found inscribed on many ancient Chinese jade, porcelain, and bronze artifacts, on stone chimes and on drums, bells, and silk paintings. Why are images of crocodiles so abundantly featured on these sorts of artifacts?

A gecko, as pale as ash and with veins clearly visible beneath its skin, scurried onto the blackboard, running through that assemblage of Chinese characters. The reptile was transformed into one of the numerals already written on the board, replacing several of the Chinese character's original strokes. Eventually it came to rest in a spot on the board that didn't have any characters, and in the process it became a new character in its own right.

. . . In Shilou, in Shanxi province, archeologists unearthed a Shang dynasty bronze cup containing a set of dragon-like inscriptions featuring two large crocodiles. One of the crocodiles was depicted from above and the other was depicted from the side. In this same location, archeologists also unearthed a Shang dynasty drum made from crocodile hide. The dragon inscribed on a large

Shang dynasty stone chime was actually a crocodile. Crocodiles in the form of dragons appeared in large numbers on ritual artifacts and musical instruments. Crocodiles could sense changes in air pressure and predict rainy weather, and before rainfall they would roar continuously. Like thunder. Luck drumming. They could summon the rain. In Chinese mythology as well as the views of the common people, crocodiles were gods of thunder, of rain, of drumming, and of music. The *Classic of Mountains and Seas* says . . .

Teacher Shao used an eraser to wipe clean a corner of the blackboard, then continued speaking as he wrote another passage:

Thunder River has a thunder god, which has a dragon's body and a human head. It sings while using its tail to beat its abdomen like a drum. . . . China has long had a practice of raising, hunting, killing, and eating dragons. Crocodile-dragons eat people. And when crocodiles eat people, a strong stench is secreted in their saliva, like salt, and after it dries up, it forms crystals. . . . During the Xia and Shang dynasties, however, the climate and ecology of the Central Plains region underwent a dramatic transformation. The region became colder, droughts became more common, lakes dried up, and crocodile populations declined until they disappeared entirely from northern China. Eventually, all that remained was a relatively small species of crocodile, also known as the Chinese crocodile or the Yangtze crocodile, which could be found in the middle and lower regions of the Yangtze River. From the Qin and Han dynasties forward, the Central Plains region became increasingly cold and the Chinese crocodile almost went extinct. Eventually all that remained were legends. These legends were gradually replaced by myths, whereby crocodiles became a primitive form of dragons. They became the mystification of dragons, the animalization of dragons. In this way crocodiles became secularized. Therefore—

The boy listened as the volume of Teacher Shao's voice increased dramatically. "The Central Plains dragons were indeed terrifying—they were man-eating crocodiles . . ."

With bowed heads, the students scribbled furiously in their notebooks, such that the sound of pens rubbing on paper drowned out the laughter of the children playing outside in the playground. Teacher Shao took a sip of tea and began discussing the symbolic meaning of dragons in Chinese culture. The students continued to listen attentively and take notes, as the Chinese characters in their notebooks grew like weeds, almost spilling out of their notebooks and onto the table. Even after completely filling a page, the students still weren't satisfied and would add additional explanations as though freeing wild animals, planting trees, or sowing flowers.

Father and Grandfather had already pawned everything of value in the house. Gamblers often came to bargain over prices, and eventually Grandfather even began considering the possibility of selling his granddaughter, Junyi. The night Junyi disappeared, Yu Jiatong and the boy's eldest brother, second brother, and third brother all rode their bicycles up and down the streets of Daro until finally, at two in the morning, they found her at the pier, aboard a fishing boat that was about to head out to sea. Junyi was just one year old at the time, and having heard Grandfather tell her that they were going out to sea to see whales and dolphins, she refused to return to shore.

Yu Jiatong taught the boy's eldest brother, Shinong, how to raise fighting cocks for sale. Shinong's cocks were a cross between local and Philippines pheasants and were as fierce as alligator snapping turtles. They were sold soon after they began to sprout feathers and before they'd had a chance to be trained. The boy felt that the only thing Eldest Brother had learned to do in life was raise fighting cocks. Jiatong acted as a comprador, and the Second Brother, Shishu, was his assistant and tag-along, observing as Jiatong purchased livestock at low prices from stupid locals who didn't understand simple math and then resold those same livestock at high prices to cunning overseas Chinese. This way, Jiatong could make enough money in a week to cover half the cost of another fighting cock. Jiatong introduced the Third Brother, Shiwen, to a foreign family's nightclub, where he could work as a "little brother." When Jiatong went hunting, Fourth Brother, Shishang, would help carry his hunting rifle or other items that weren't too heavy, and would also bring along a rare bird or animal to sell to Christian, the English merchant. At that point the boy was still too young to work, but Jiatong pounded his own chest and promised that as soon as the boy turned seven, he would find him a job as well.

"I want to work in the theater."

"That doesn't pay very much at all," Jiatong replied. "And you'll need to sweep the bathrooms, clean up excrement, and unclog toilets. It's very hard work!"

"But I can do it! Plus, I'd be able to watch movies for free. I love Japanese monster movies!"

"Japanese. Huh?"

Jiatong let Shishang carry his rifle, and then they—together with Shinong, Shiwen, Shishu, the boy, and his mother—headed over to the Li family's house. The dark yellow river water was flowing fiercely, and the riverbank was filled with verdant weeds and red, green, blue, and black dragonflies. Swifts mingled together and the sound of frogs croaking was so loud it seemed as though it would shatter your internal organs. The Li family home was located in a veritable Peach Blossom Spring—a remarkable place, but without remarkable people. Generation after generation could perform small tricks, like crowing like a cock or stealing like a dog. Every morning, the boy's mother would count her own ducks, and if there were less than thirty she would imitate the sound of duck's quacking and proceed to search the entire town for the missing fowl. She would inspect the Li family's hundred-odd ducks swimming in the pond to determine whether any of them were hers, whereupon the Li family would release its six dogs to chase her away.

"How do your Shi family's ducks differ from ours?" Li Yan led Yu Jiatong and the three brothers into the duck pen. Pointing at the hundred-odd ducks playing in the water, she asked, "Do yours have branded butts?"

"My sister would definitely recognize the ducks she raised." Yu Jiatong examined the Li family's pigpen and chicken coop.

"*Quack quack. Quack quack.*" This was the only sound the boy's mother was able to make. The ducks cocked their heads and peered at her. Dozens left the water and approached.

"*Quack quack! Quack quack!*" Li Yan shouted several times, as even more ducks left the water and approached. The Li family's three sons produced ear-piercing peals of laughter.

Yu Jiatong took the rifle from Shishang and, without even bothering to aim, struck a pair of amorous young ducks, sending their feathers and entrails flying everywhere. Then he reloaded and aimed at a terrified flock of turkeys standing next to the pigpen.

"Hey, hey, hey! Little Yu, you . . . have you gone mad?" The smiles of Li Yan and her three sons were wiped clean from their faces.

Xixisusu, zizigaga, jijiwengweng. It was as if there were two sets of interlinked sounds located a certain distance from each another—as though a howler monkey and a bamboo partridge were conversing with one another. Soon these faint murmurs were devoured by the cacophony of insects, beasts, and running water, to the point that not even their barren bones were left. The boy and his companions had to produce an ironlike sound, and only then would it be possible to discern their existence within the dark rainforest. The boy was carrying a small water jug on his back, and he had a *parang* hanging from his waist. On his head he was wearing a straw hat, on his feet he was wearing a pair of school-issued white cloth shoes, and he was dressed in a recently washed outfit. Together with his elder brothers, who were hauling tents, food, parangs, rifles, and other provisions, the boy confusedly entered the rainforest.

The boy was seven years old, and it was a month before he was scheduled to start elementary school. Under Yu Jiatong's direction the boy, his elder brothers, and Yu Jiatong's other sworn followers—more than twenty people in all—all went deep into the rainforest and proceeded to hunt for twenty-one days. As Yu Jiatong walked, he examined the compass in his hand. Nature released many different signs of danger, but the expedition was like an ant brigade marching in a single-file line, cutting through dense vines and earthen mounds. There were cliffs, swamps, rivers, lakes, and patches of quicksand. As the rainforest undergrowth was cut down by their parangs and trampled under their feet, it produced thick green, purple, orange, and clear sap that split open and resealed the twenty-odd men's wounds. *Zhizhizhazha, zhizhizhazha.* Nature moaned abjectly, as the members of the expedition felt its fragility and strength. They walked through the dark, wet mud, swinging their arms and legs to maintain their balance. The branches and vines offered the men some support, but they were neither orangutans nor mountain lions. Soon scholars who typically spend all their time working with ink and paper found their hands covered in blood. Mosquitoes, flies, and leeches surged forward like sand in a sandstorm, but the expedition's insect repellent had already lost its effectiveness. The loud and boisterous members of the expedition were reduced to whispers, then fell completely silent. It was as if a luxurious cruise ship had sunk to the bottom of the ocean. More than twenty pairs of eyes stared intently at the ground where their feet were about to step, attempting to calculate precisely how much force each foot had to exert, and whether the step should be tight or loose, weighty or fleeting.

When the expedition finally came to a stop, everyone looked up at the sky as though they had just received an amnesty, deeply envious of the pig-tailed macaque's ability to swing through the rainforest canopy. They looked back and saw that the wounds they had mercilessly opened up in the forest had healed miraculously fast, and the signs they had left to mark their path had already disappeared. The forest's protector spirits had transformed themselves into tender beasts and followed the expedition—licking their wounds and using grass and mud to cover their tracks. The members of the expedition saw many green plants and red flowers, all densely packed like vines. Like roots. There were also countless intertwined branches that were reabsorbed by the rainforest. With sharp fangs and shaggy fur, some animals were rushing forward to escape from predators. Each time the men took a step forward, they would rip out one of the rainforest's passionate kisses by the roots. Like a duck, the rainforest dug into its ears with its bill and teeth, and like a water bird, it extracted earwax with its long beak. The forest's maternal qualities inspired the men to entertain many dreams and fantasies. Her breasts resembled overripe wild fruit, waiting for them to pick and suck on. Her private parts were like cherries, with smooth skin and tender flesh, and they resembled a nepenthes pitcher full of nectar. Her phallus was transformed into a hairless, eyeless, sausage-shaped mole rat, burrowing through soil that was full of rotting vegetation. At night the boy saw dark shadows hiding in the vines outside his tent, ejaculating onto the dark, fertile soil.

The boy always hoped that night would quickly arrive, so that the brigade could set up camp and rest. He had developed red welts on his hands and feet, and his forehead was covered in black moles. One morning he missed the wake-up call and therefore failed to go out with the rest of the expedition. Instead he vomited on a fig tree and then lay against an old silk-cotton tree. He was lying on the tree's purplish-brown roots, which protruded from the ground like an elephant's trunk—as if the tree were about to use its roots to dig a hole in the ground where he was sitting and bury him. On the twelfth day the boy started running a high fever and spent the entire day riding on Yu Jiatong's back. He groped around inside Second Brother's chest, extracted a kidney, then pressed it back into its correct position. The kidney was transformed into a trilobite fossil. Second Brother passed the boy an artifact. It was a stone ax that had been unearthed in the rainforest.

Xixisusu, zizigaga, jijiwengweng. The boy lay on Yu Jiatong's back as his brain waves recorded countless sounds. *Huahua lala.* The rain enveloped the boy like a fresh bay cat pelt. His blood was still hot and his body ached. *Xixilili.* The drizzle resembled ferns growing on the boy's body, their roots penetrating his flesh, where they sucked out nourishment and left his organs painfully desiccated. When the boy opened his eyes, his gaze resembled a chick emerging from its egg. The sun, however, was so bright that he immediately had to shut his eyes again. The fern's teeth resembled larvae in a beehive. The boy had no energy to chew to solid food and could consume only liquids. His esophagus became as thin as a ureter, and his hands and feet became as soft as a woman's breasts. . . .

The boy tumbled off Yu Jiatong's back and fell into a deep gully. The other members of the expedition didn't see him fall, and therefore they continued forward. The boy tried to shout, but his voice was locked in by the rock walls, which produced startling echoes. The walls were so sheer that he had no hope of scaling them. Listlessly, he lay at the bottom of the gully as the rock walls closed over him like the lid of a coffin. A sharp sound suddenly emerged from above, as though dozens of horns were simultaneously sounding an attack. A long, soft, tube-shaped object descended from the top of the cliff and began sniffing him. It pressed his forehead and rubbed his belly. It was very loose, and he felt as though he were being embraced by dew from a lotus leaf. The object was wet and pliable, like a placenta, and it calmly lifted him up and placed him back on Yu Jiatong's back. The boy vaguely saw that this creature had a large body with four towerlike legs, a pair of thin ears resembling whale fins, and a long, funnel-shaped trunk that hung down to the ground, like a quiet summer tornado. Everything was jumbled together.

Before this mysterious creature departed, it emitted a cloud of vapor. As fragrant and refreshing as a drug, the vapor enveloped the boy, and his entire body felt soothed.

Kakajiji, xixisusu, dudugugu. That night, when the boy was lying in his tent, he heard his brothers sitting around the campfire talking, and when they reached the most exciting parts of the conversation their voices suddenly rose, like a man crying out just as he is about to be executed. They argued and sighed, expressing fury and passion. They read out loud, sang, then fell silent again. The song of the nightingales was beautiful and sorrowful, as male and female birds were filled with hopes of building nests and raising offspring. Male and female frogs croaked as loud as firecrackers. Owls sounded like manatees, and night owls resembled river dolphins. Or maybe these were calls produced by real manatees and dolphins in a nearby river? Sweat poured down the boy's back as he repeatedly groaned. He left the tent to relieve himself, releasing a pool of warm urine. The liquid pattered like raindrops, splashing on the mud like water pouring onto a cold pan. The boy gazed up at the sky and saw several stars sparkling through the tree leaves, like an array of ripe and unripe fruit. His head felt heavy and his feet felt light as the earth and sky spun around. The pain in his forehead left his entire body numb. He returned to the tent and lay down. Outside, his brothers were still arguing about matters that would never be resolved. The boy tossed and turned but couldn't fall asleep. He heard his brothers repeatedly mention three great men, discussing what these men had said and the immortal causes they had pursued. Drop by drop, the great men's accomplishments emerged in irregular spurts, like a patient with a urinary tract infection trying to relieve himself. When Teacher Shao lectured on Chinese cultural history, he always found time to introduce those same three great men whose portraits were hanging from the classroom's rear wall. These men had been abjectly relegated to a corner of the classroom, and their features were dark and indistinct—like clouds in an overcast sky, a mountain ridge covered in mist, or writing on a chalkboard that had yet not been wiped clean but that could disappear at any time. The portraits hung there surreptitiously—sometimes remaining in place for one or two weeks but other times disappearing without a trace for an entire week, like a temple's Buddha statue that has been borrowed to help support disaster relief. The boy knew that two of these great men were from Russia, while the third was from China. The one whose Chinese name began with the syllable "Ma" resembled a broken-legged captain of a whaling ship, the one whose Chinese name began with the syllable "Lie" resembled a bear-hunting mastiff, while the one surnamed Mao resembled a dragon-slaying, jade-faced god of war. Although the portraits the boy had seen in Teacher Shao's home were torn and frayed, that night they instead appeared well-illuminated and hyperrealistic, suspended above the campfire and his brothers' heads as they gazed down at this group of garrulous young men.

The day before the hunting expedition left the rainforest, the boy's fever finally broke.

"Brother, what did we catch?"

The boy saw that the cage was filled with an assortment of multicolored birds and oddly shaped monkeys. There were also squirrels, minks, badgers, and bay cats. The boars and rodents had already been disemboweled. This catch was rather modest and did not appear to be the product of more than twenty men's strenuous efforts over more than twenty days.

"Did I hinder you?" The boy looked at his uncle.

"No, not at all." Yu Jiatong smiled and rubbed the boy's head. "Stupid boy."

On the way out of the rainforest, the boy heard Yu Jiatong and the others discussing the real objective of the trip.

"Little brother, you missed a priceless opportunity . . . ," Fourth Brother bragged.

From their conversation, the boy was reminded of the enormous creature that had rescued him. The real objective of the hunting expedition, it turns out, was to find a herd of elephants that had been living and reproducing in Borneo for several centuries. Originally there were at least fifty or sixty elephants in the herd, but some claimed that there may have been as many as eighty or ninety. Because there are no reliable records it was impossible to determine the correct number. Over time, countless elephants were killed by hunters and natives, leading their numbers to decline precipitously. In a handwritten journal belonging to a seventeenth-century English explorer, which had been donated to the Sarawak Museum, however, it was recorded that the herd, at its peak, contained more than three hundred elephants.

"Little brother, don't feel bad," Second Brother consoled him. "As it turns out, we didn't see anything either."

Having just begun to recover from his illness but already feeling significantly more animated than before, the boy listened wide-eyed like a small lemur as his brothers discussed the elephant herd and their own journey over the preceding several days. Although the forest's cacophony of bird songs drowned out the cries of other animals, the several dozen birds in the cage were as motionless as preserved specimens. Each time the boy looked at the birds, they appeared dimmer than before. Meanwhile, all the mammals in the cage were either curled up into a ball or else were jumping up and down with a look of terror in their eyes. Their small bodies suggested that they had not yet been weaned. Their families had been destroyed, their parents slaughtered, and their kin lost forever. . . .

Towering trees frequently impeded the brigade's path. Some were growing in a row like a fence, some blocked the brigade's path like a towering cliff, some required that the brigade pass through enormous roots like a troop of ants, while others had already died or been split open by lightning—even as their carcasses continued to resist like a demolished wall. In some places the brigade encountered a pile of toppled trees like shattered battlements, while in others they encountered a single tree standing alone, its trunk only as thick as a man's leg, yet still managing to block their path with the spirit of an invincible army. The boy dashed back and forth, following whichever of his brothers happened to be speaking in the most animated fashion. Given that archaeologists had never found elephant fossils in Borneo, that suggested that the Asian elephants currently living in the region most likely descended from African elephants. Several centuries earlier Borneo had several thousand elephants, though later all but a few dozen were killed—to the point that in recent years no one would ever see more than a handful at a time. Local natives and visiting zoologists would occasionally glimpse an old elephant in the forest, like a prisoner serving a life sentence and waiting for death. Sometimes there would be countless birds perched on the old elephant's back, feeding on parasites hidden in the folds of its skin. When an elephant happened to glimpse a human it would respond by either attacking or fleeing, and in the process it might get bruised or stuck in a mud pit and would produce heartbreaking cries for help. Several centuries earlier, when the elephant kingdom ruled the entire island, even the young males that had left the herd would still receive the herd's support. . . . When Yu Jiatong patrolled the rainforest armed with a rifle and several rounds of ammunition, he didn't see a single bull elephant, though on countless occasions he did hear the few survivors of that legendary herd that had previously roamed the forest. It was as if he could hear their mysterious calls, smell their distinctive odor, and see their footprints, while also observing the traces where they used their trunks to pick up leaves, their tusks to strip off bark, and their heads to knock over trees. Tracking and waiting for them was always in vain.

Even among the natives, very few had actually seen this elephant herd. Sometimes the elephants' origins and their living conditions over the past several centuries appeared rather mysterious, but at other times they appeared as real as a housedog. By one account, in the year 326 India's King Potus had two hundred elephants, which carried archers to defend against Alexander the Great on the banks of the Hydaspes River. Later King Potus gave six of these war elephants to the king of Brunei as a symbol of the friendship between the two countries, and in return the king of Brunei gave him countless rare birds and animals. The king of Brunei, however, couldn't bear to keep the elephants in confinement, and therefore he released them into Borneo's rainforest. These six individuals became inseparable, quickly producing a large herd that has survived up to the present day. . . . By another account, during one of the southern expeditions led by the Ming dynasty court eunuch Zheng He, the tributary gifts Zheng He brought back from East Africa included numerous lions and elephants, leopards and rhinoceroses, great stags and kingfishers, celestial horses and albino monkeys. When Zheng He stopped in Borneo he exchanged some of his elephants for local peacocks, guinea fowl, wildcats, and other indigenous birds and animals. Because the elephants were difficult to domesticate, however, the Borneo locals eventually released them into the rainforest, where they developed into a large herd that roamed through the forest at will. Over the following centuries the exigencies of the local environment and food sources led the elephants to evolve into a more diminutive size than their African ancestors. The dense and humid rainforest and rivers decreased their need for large ears to dissipate heat, and consequently their ears became smaller as well.

Regardless of whether Borneo's elephants were descended from Indian war elephants, wild African elephants, or elephants from some other region altogether, this was a population that was very intelligent and had a strong sense of exclusion. The animals' enormous tusks were enticing treasures, and in the late seventeenth century a British hunting expedition carried out a mass slaughter of the animals in which more than a hundred cricket-sized bullets struck a hundred and twenty-six bull elephants. In the early eighteenth century, a Dutch hunting expedition carried out another slaughter, killing more than ninety bulls. There were also countless smaller hunts, and even in the beginning of this century numerous hunting expeditions still pursued and killed these elephants, offering the excuse that the animals had been destroying the rainforest and trampling people's homes and crops. Now, however, hunting expeditions can no longer find any elephants at all. Have they gone extinct? No one was willing to entertain this possibility. Instead, experts believed that after having been hunted for several centuries, the elephants managed to develop a variety of techniques for protecting themselves and avoiding humans. The elephants developed these techniques in response to their local conditions and passed them down from one generation to the next, such that they eventually came to resemble hermits in the rainforest, completely isolated from the outside world. Humans only heard about them, but rarely saw them. The elephants could only be found in some unknown location deep in the mountains, surrounded by clouds, where they enjoyed simple meals while reciting poems about the wind and moon. A powerful, old female elephant, which must have been over a hundred years old, led this herd of unknown size. These elephants became the world's most silent creatures, and only in moments of crisis would they emit a sharp cry, like an attack horn. They treaded slowly through the rainforest on their fleshy hoofs without producing the slightest sound or tremor. When food was abundant, they would restrain their greed and their needs, so as not to produce extensive destruction or leave behind excessive traces. They stopped pushing over trees and digging holes in search of mineral salt. They stopped playing in the river and instead would simply soak quietly in the water. They stopped mischievously rolling around in the mud all afternoon and instead would simply roll over once to give themselves a layer of mud to protect them against insects. They stopped devouring trees to the point that forests became reduced grassy plains, which had provided them with additional foraging grounds. They also stopped digging small ponds, which had given birds and other animals water holes from which to drink. Now they would wait for rainy days to move around, and when they did, they would try to walk along the shoals, and even when they had to go through the rainforest, they no longer opened up paths that could later be used by boars and muntjacs. They defecated directly into rivers and ponds and therefore stopped benefitting the rainforest with their excrement. They no longer remained in the same location for more than three days in a row, and their routes became very mysterious. They would wait for three to five years before taking the same route again. When they were on the move, two females would watch each flank of the herd, and two young males would bring up the rear. When they stopped to rest they each took turns standing guard and slept standing up.

"That's right. We didn't see anything." Eldest Brother consoled the boy. "All we saw was an enormous pile of bones."

On the third day after the boy came down with his fever, the hunting brigade discovered a large number of elephant bones in a dry lakebed. This was a clear day following a heavy rain, and a rainbow was hanging over the rainforest. Carrion-eating birds circled overhead, flying in different directions like a swarm of larvae. The elephant bones became a nest for hares. squirrels. rats. snakes. lizards. There were more than twenty skulls oriented toward the center of the lake, and behind them the ground was covered with an array of vertebrae and leg bones, which surrounded the dry lakebed like a site of worship. These bones were so neatly arranged that it seemed as though they had been placed there deliberately. Like a nest of bones. The skulls and other bones were riddles with bullet holes the size of dog pupils. Like sunken nipples. They had been killed while drinking water. Even more bones were scattered around the lake's outer perimeter. Some were half-buried in the ground, and bones of other animals appeared to be mixed in with them. From the orientation of the bones, it was clear that the elephants had been converging on the lake from all directions. When elephants are fleeing they usually all run in the same direction—but perhaps hunters had surrounded these elephants and were attacking them from all sides? A complete elephant skeleton was hanging from a tree branch four meters from the ground. The skeleton was covered in moss and vines, and sparrows were flying in and out of the skull. It resembled the remains of a giant prehistoric bird—a divine flying elephant that legend held had spouted wings. The dense foliage surrounding the site formed a natural tomb. The grayish-white trees resembled tombstones and had been there for at least a century.

The skeletons were enormous, but they all lacked tusks. There were also a few smaller skeletons of elephant calves. Some bones were located further from the lake, evidently having been dragged away by predators.

"This was a slaughter." Yu Jiatong looked down at the compass and the booklet he was holding in his hand. "It was a harvest. It must have been the work of Englishmen."

The men wandered around the bones, inserting their fingers into the bullet holes and gasping with astonishment. They used their palms to estimate the length of the bones, then measured them again with a ruler and recorded the results. They caressed the bones with their hands, kicked them with their feet, and struck them with other objects.

"These were a male and a female? From their appearance, it appears that they were doing that thing before they were killed."

"When it was killed, this calf was lying on its mother's chest, apparently nursing."

"They killed a female? But females don't even have tusks!"

"This one was even more pitiful. Its skull was struck by five bullets."

The men took photographs. They took photos from one side and the other. They photographed the entire scene. The boy was the only member of the group who didn't have his picture taken with the bones, since at the time he was still delirious from fever. Vultures landed on the bones, then spread their wings and walked through them. The men raised their rifles and shot at the squirrels, hares, lizards, and pangolins that were scurrying through the bones. In the process, some of the bones were shattered while the largest ones remained intact and simply acquired several small holes. Blood splattered all over the white bones, as the hunted animals struggled and cried out before dying.

"Enough, enough!" Yu Jiatong fired several shots into the air, and only then did the men stop the slaughter. That night they set up camp near the bones and roasted the flesh of the animals they had killed. The campfire burned brightly, as a wild smell spread through the wilderness. The flames burned blue and green, swinging back and forth. The moon and stars were not visible, the tree canopy was hidden in shadows, and the tree branches were soaking wet. The elephant bones, however, were magnificent, as humans declined and ghosts flourished. None of the men dared venture into the wilderness alone, and instead they lined up to relieve themselves directly onto the bones. They huddled together next to the campfire in groups of two or three—eating lizard meat, drinking snake soup, swallowing bird eggs, and singing about the legendary one-legged ship captain. The bear-hunting mastiff. The jade-faced god of war. Suddenly, an elephant calf skeleton stumbled toward the campfire, shoving people aside with its skull, its calls resembling a cross between laughter and crying. A burly fellow went over to the skeleton, moved some vertebrae, and lifted up the skull. Beneath the bones, he found the thirty-year-old Chen Sifa.

"Ah Fa, you nearly scared us to death!"

"Let's roast this calf and eat it."

Chen Sifa's actions animated the group, and they each grabbed a flashlight and went to play hide-and-go-seek amidst the elephant bones. Shinong, Shishu, and Shiwen went with them, while Shishang stayed behind in the tent to watch the boy. Shishang was not brave enough for this game, and instead resembled a mouse scurrying through an elephant skeleton. The flashlights flickered on and off inside the pile of white bones, as a foul-smelling white light was emitted from the elephant's butt, two rays of cold light were emitted from its eye sockets, and countless rays of green light emerged from the silvergrass grove. Over the course of the game, many of the elephant bones broke, collapsed, or were lost. The men used leg bones to fight each other and used other bones to make a peculiar nest—a cozy litter. Their hands were stuck, their waists were pinched, their feet were wedged, their bellies were pressed, their backs were crushed, their heads were locked, and their genitals were squeezed. The more they struggled, the more the bones hurt then and the tighter they became. Then the men helped free each other, and in the process they scraped off many layers of skin and bruised themselves in numerous locations. Eventually they counted themselves and discovered that one person was missing. It was Chen Sifa, the guy who had pretended to be an elephant calf. They eventually found him at the bottom of a pile of bones, and although they poked him several times, he didn't respond. They removed the bones one by one and massaged him until he regained consciousness. "No one has ever seen this pile of bones before," Yu Jiatong remarked before going to sleep. "After we return home, we mustn't mention this to anyone. This is a crucial clue in our search for the elephant herd."

Like a lemming hiding a piece of fruit, the boy kept a secret hidden deep in his heart. Based on the dream scene in which he was rescued by an elephant, the boy speculated that the hunting party must have passed very close to the legendary elephant herd, but he assumed that the clever elephants had easily avoided the humans. Given that the boy didn't have a chance to see the bones, he asked many questions on the way back.

"Do elephants have tombs? Where do they go when they are about to die?"

"No, they don't have tombs." Yu Jiatong said. "That's just an old wife's tale."

"Maybe they do, maybe they don't," Eldest Brother added.

"That's right," Yu Jiatong said agreeably. "It would be great if they did."

"If only we could track down the elephant herd, we'd be able to find them," said Wang Dada. "Just imagine, how many tusks!"

"Ay," Yu Jiatong sighed, his voice like a cat mewling for food. "If only I could hunt myself an elephant tusk, I'd die content."

The nepenthes pitcher plant sparked in the boy many associations. With flat roots rising up like pyramids, trunks standing straight and tall, and a canopy filled with vines and parasitic plants, a nearby tree resembled a miracle. Celestial footprints. Solomon's treasure. The boy fantasized that the tree might have a swing, on which his little sister would be sitting. It was as though the tree had neither hands nor legs, as its twigs and branches completely obscured the canopy, unlike other plants that might extend a tendril or something to tease people. The canopy also concealed many sensitive zones, and not even its features were visible—like a fox hiding in a foxhole or an elegant woman wearing luxurious clothing and a hazy veil. The boy dumped load after load of warm urine onto the plant's roots, creating a sort of connection between himself and the roots. He peed all around, filling more than ten nepenthes pitchers with urine. When he was finally finished, there were still several dozen—or even several hundred—pitchers proudly staring at him with their holy gaze. The human bladder is truly too tiny and is not sufficient to nourish even a single pitcher plant. There was a five-hundred-year-old silk-cotton tree that was completely covered in boils, holes, and odd angles, like the Great Wall of China. If you were to climb to the top, where would you end up? It was said that at the top there was a world that was completely different from the world on the ground. Up there, the air pressure was so low that people would secrete blood, sweat, and bloody urine. By the time the boy finished walking around the tree, areas previously hidden in shadows were directly in the sunlight. Various leaf insects were camouflaged by the green vegetation, and a great horned owl was camouflaged by the fallen yellow leaves, but fortunately it flew away before the boy could accidentally step on it. There were also katydids, cicadas, butterflies, and praying mantises. The toads were camouflaged, as was the boy. Pressed against a fig tree covered in enormous vines, the boy himself resembled a giant vine. When the boy's little sister Junyi couldn't find him, she squatted down next to a rotten log and wept, whereupon the boy emerged from behind the fig tree and said, "Junyi, Junyi, don't cry. I'm here." He peeled a rambutan and gave it to her.

The boy was eight years old. Shortly after this incident he began his fourth job: looking after his three-year-old sister Junyi. He often took her for strolls through the rainforest and taught her to recognize different plants and animals. He showed her which plants could be picked and which could be touched, which could be eaten and which could only be seen; and he also did the same for animals. The boy filled Junyi's hair with flowers and fruits, as bees and butterflies flew around her. She and the boy patrolled the perimeter of the rainforest for four days, until finally the boy was able to show her a troop of macaques eating wild fruit in the treetop. The boy picked up some rocks and tossed them at the monkeys, whereupon the monkeys screeched in alarm and some even threw pieces of fruit back at them. The monkeys mooned the boy and his sister, their butts resembling a "painted face" character in Chinese opera. Junyi laughed merrily, and the boy taught her a nursery rhyme:

> The monkey steals some oil,
> He dips his butt into the oil pot,
> And is enveloped in a ball of flames.
>
> The monkey doesn't recognize the dog,
> And with its butt toward a large dog,
> It is bitten until it becomes a giant sieve.
>
> The monkey is shameless.
> And with its butt toward my face,
> It is beaten until its face is black and blue.

"Shicai, don't take Sister into the rainforest. Take her to the riverbank," the boy's elder brother said.

Honghong, the river flowed toward the ocean.

Gonggong, the river flowed out of many tributaries.

The banks of the tributaries were filled with wildflowers and wild grass, which were growing toward the river. The tributaries were shallow, their shores were narrow, their water was very clear, and children often came to play. Sampans would frequently appear, piled high with fragrant yellow, green and red fruit, like a cage filled with colorful parrots. These sampans were heading to the market, and all that was visible were the oars, not the oarsmen. On the banks there were often people fishing, using fishing poles made from crooked tree branches that sometimes still had leaves and fruits attached. They would be using a fishing line that was as thick as a vine and would camouflage themselves and their fishing equipment to resemble a tree. The boy taught Junyi how to float in the water, and together they watched as grebes and other birds dove for fish in the shallows. Sometimes a bird would dive and remain underwater for a long time, whereupon the boy would teach Junyi a lesson, saying, *Don't overestimate your own strength, because if you fail to eat a fish, the fish might eat you.* The boy would take Junyi to the cockfighting ring and have her sit on his shoulders, but then all she could see was the back of his head. He would then take her to the front of the crowd, where could see not only the cocks fighting, but also Eldest Brother Shinong, who would be watching nervously, and Yu Jiatong, who would be leisurely smoking a foreign cigarette. The boy would also take Junyi to the seaside, where Second Brother Shishu would be romancing his girlfriends. Shishu's girlfriends were as numerous as feet on a road, and under the roar of the tide and in the dawn light Shishu would hug his girlfriends like a Malayan sun bear grasping a cornstalk. The boy would also take Junyi to Teacher Shao's house for lessons, where they would see Third Brother Shiwen wearing thick glasses and frantically reading Teacher Shao's books, as though those yellow pages might disappear at any moment or those desiccated characters might soon become unintelligible. Shiwen had a grand ambition, which was to read Teacher Shao's entire book collection before he turned twenty. The boy would also take Junyi to watch Fourth Brother Shishang practice his martial arts, and in the process might secretly learn a move or two. Shishang also had a grand ambition, which was to learn a set of exquisite martial arts skills that would allow him to "serve his country."

"Brother, how do you plan to serve your country?"

Fourth Brother didn't respond.

"Ah Cai and Junyi, wait a second. . . ."

On the side of the road, father stuffed some cash into their hands. Sometimes he reeked of alcohol and cigarette smoke, but at other times he smelled of scented soap.

"Pa, can I take Junyi to watch you gamble?" The boy asked.

"No." Father rarely engaged in child-talk, but even when he was cursing someone, he always remained very cheerful.

"Today is Pa's turn to be the banker, and he'll definitely win big!"

The boy had previously watched his father gamble. His father would sit quietly at the gambling table, like a long-tailed macaque waiting patiently for a crab to emerge from its burrow. Even when his father was losing, he would still maintain his composure—unlike a macaque, who would immediately start screeching as soon as a crab's pincers clamped down on its paw. Once, when it was drizzling outside, Father exclaimed excitedly, "Ah Cai, don't let your sister get wet. Where's your umbrella? Whenever

I win, I'll plaster the outside of an umbrella with money and give it to you, so that the empress will hold up the sky for you. These will be money umbrellas, and even Junyi will get one."

Father always sported shiny leather shoes, an entrancing gold watch, and scented hair oil. He had a leisurely gait and projected an implacable expression that resembled a cross between a gambler and a sloth. The monsoon season was about to arrive. The boy hid under the roof, looking for pigeon hatchlings and trying to escape the heat. He listened to the rain. *Dingding dangdang dingding dangdang.* As the raindrops landed on the galvanized steel sheet roof, they seemed to be devouring the metal. *Susuzizi.* After the rain stopped, the water in the well suddenly increased and the water tank overflowed. The vegetable garden, silvergrass groves, bushes, and fields gradually became marshlands, as the house became enveloped in a cloud of vapor. During this period the boy would frequently take Junyi out to play in the water, and they would play until the skin on their fingers and toes started to peel, and it appeared as though they were prepared to continue playing until their entire limbs were blistered. The river overflowed its banks, and the water was dark and deep. Fish gulped water in all directions, butterflies flew through the vapor, looking as though they were about to land directly on the water's surface, knocked over by the grass. Fishing birds perched motionless on branches oriented toward the river, camouflaged such that they resembled dead branches. Brown swifts skillfully skimmed over the water's surface, occasionally plucking a water flower. The mud, trees, sky, and water were all filled with the sound of frogs croaking. The boy felt as though his armpits, crotch, and his entire body were filled with tree frogs camouflaged as old scars and a wrinkled scrotum. Under a coconut tree the boy caught lizards, as well as a severed tail that was flopping around. He needed to pee and proceeded to unload an astonishing amount of warm urine against the coconut tree. His sister laughed happily, then toddled over to the river to watch some butterflies. The butterflies flew low and clumsily, and she almost caught some. After the boy finished peeing, he saw a tailless lizard dart out from behind the coconut tree and hide under a leaf. He picked up an empty milk can and placed it over the leaf. The can made a *hongdongdong* sound, and the boy confirmed that he had indeed caught the lizard. Just as he was about to turn the can over, however, he heard a *hualala* sound of water coming from the river. When the boy looked the river quickly calmed down, but Junyi was nowhere to be seen.

The boy rushed down to the riverbank. A whirlpool seemed to have formed in the river, and there were several eddies. An enormous black body appeared in the eddies. There was a long tail. Sharp teeth. A gaping mouth. Scales. There were small hands. Small feet. Black hair filled with wildflowers. A tiny pair of terrified eyes. A silent mouth. Junyi! Junyi was also in the eddy. *Hualala*, an even larger eddy appeared, and a shiny black body sank with Junyi into the water. Then the water became still again, and the eddies slowly drifted away. . . .

Shinong was watching his fighting cocks under a mango tree. The boy almost ran right into him, and exclaimed, "Sister . . . sister was . . . sister was taken . . . was taken by a crocodile . . ."

The monsoon season usually ended in February, but until then rain would fall hard and fast—sometimes falling continuously for one or two weeks straight. The magpies wouldn't even have a chance to dry their feathers. The Shi family was already accustomed to this long rainy season. During this season, Shinong continued feeding his cocks, keeping their cages a meter above the ground so that they wouldn't get flooded. When it rained, however, pythons and monitor lizards became very animated, and therefore Shinong often had to get up several times a night to check on the cages. Sometimes he would even sleep in a wooden shed he had built for this purpose. Each cock had its own "apartment," where it lived even more comfortably than its owner. Shinong had used a dagger to carve one of Teacher Shao's poems into the bark of the jackfruit tree next to the coop:

> On a dark and stormy night
> The roosters crow without pause.

Under Yu Jiatong's encouragement, Shinong would occasionally take some cocks to fight in the arena. He would keep some of his earnings for his own family and would send the remainder to support the People's Party that Yu Jiatong couldn't stop discussing. Meanwhile, Shishu continued to pursue Jiatong to do business and didn't have as much leisure time for flirting. However, he was naturally romantic, and therefore he built some swings in the orchard, and whenever he had any free time he would take girlfriends there to go swing—the same way that as soon as the sun come during the monsoon season, the magpies immediately emerge from their holes to dry their wings and play. Shishu noticed that Jiatong was desperately trying to make a profit, but although he had large numbers of transactions, the money he earned from each individual transaction was only sufficient to watch two or three movies. As for Shiwen, he had to hand over three-quarters of each month's earnings to Jiatong. Shiwen built a wooden shed in the orchard, which he called the Tower of Wind and Rain, and upon returning from Teacher Shao's house he would always go into the shed and study amidst the mosquitoes and the heat. The exalted sound of his studying sometimes resembled the martial crowing of Jiatong's fighting cocks. Finally, Shishang rarely had a chance to go hunting with

Jiatong anymore. However, hunting was still a means of earning money, and although Jiatong had his hands full, his loyal classmates would still take their rifles and accompany Shishang into the rainforest—though, in the end, Shishang only made enough from hunting to purchase a single pair of kung fu shoes.

While everyone else had a very garrulous mother, the boy's own mother was mute. She raised a flock of chickens and ducks—and sometimes the chickens would outnumber the ducks, while at other times the ducks would outnumber the chickens. The boy's mother could only quack like a duck, and not only did the ducks understand her, so did the chickens—meaning that she didn't have to worry about appearing partial to the ducks. She spent four weeks with the Shi family working in the orchards and fields, and every few days she would take a couple of baskets of mangos, mangosteens, pineapples, papayas, rambutans, jackfruits, and bananas to the market. Her fruits weren't any better than that of others, and some of her fruits even had worms. However, she was a mute who could quack like a duck, and she was able to peddle her wares well. The family's vegetable production was very modest and was sufficient only to meet the family's own needs. Most people are busy enough with these sorts of household responsibilities, but the boy's mother still somehow found time every day to do additional piecework, help the government dig irrigation ditches, cut the grass, and fill potholes. Sometimes she would also help rich people wash their clothes and clean their windows. She only had one breast, and when the boy was young, he noticed that female cats, dogs, pigs, and sheep had many teats, while other boys' mothers and elder sisters had a pair of fleshy mounds on their chests. The boy's maternal grandfather said that breast cancer ran in their family, and he noted that his own wife had died from the disease before the boy was born. Therefore, the boy's mother had her right breast removed before she gave birth to her first son, leaving the right side of her chest very smooth except for more than a dozen small red warts, like a rafflesia quilt. When the boy was young, he would often paw at his mother's chest until she laughed like a duck quacking. She walked like a duck, was as clean as a duck, and was short of stature. It was only after having five boys that she finally gave birth to a daughter, Junyi. The baby name Quackquack was passed down to Junyi from her brothers, since this was the only name Mother was able to call her children. After Junyi's death, Mother's face was drenched in tears, and she repeatedly raised her hand to slap the boy, but instead used that same hand to prevent Shinong from punishing him. Her duck sobbing continued, sometimes deep and sometimes sharp. From the middle of the night to early dawn, it was as if the Shi family had been under a spell for more than ten days.

The aquatic beast was as wide and deep as a sampan, but twice as long. It had a triangular crest on its tail, which could block and cut off a sampan. From its chest to its abdomen its body was full of fatty flesh, and when it rolled over it would create a wave like a storm. Its mouth was as long as a paddle, its back resembled a string of velvet-covered mountain peaks, and its body was covered in algae from head to toe. Sunlight and moonlight made the algae appear abundant, substantial, and dark green, like an array of vines, tendrils, or roots. The algae completely obscured the animal's original shape, to the point that the animal came to resemble a piece of driftwood floating in the water. The beast was holding Junyi in its mouth, and with its tiny eyes it was staring at the boy on the riverbank, as if planning to devour him too. Several of the beast's hooklike teeth had already penetrated Junyi's abdomen. Its lower teeth resembled a boar's tusks, and the river was filled with a putrid stench. . . .

"Uncle, help me . . . help me kill the crocodile . . ."

"There are thousands of crocodiles in the river. Do you intend to kill them all?"

"But I know this one. I know it. As long as I can find it, I'm sure I'd recognize it. . . ."

"Even if you can recognize it, where are you going to look for it?"

"I know I'll find it, if I'm are patient."

"How long do you plan to search?"

"I'll search for a hundred years, if I have to."

"I'm very busy, Shicai. Furthermore, previously I've only killed monitor lizards."

"Killing a crocodile is no different from killing a monitor lizard. Don't the Iban often kill crocodiles? Uncle, you're the best . . ."

"Shicai." Yu Jiatong placed his hands on the boy's shoulders, as his eyes filled with tears. "I feel terrible for you. No one feels worse about losing Junyi than I do. However, we must let bygones be bygones. No one will blame you for what happened. This is fate, and I have more important things to do . . ."

"What could be more important than killing that crocodile?"

"Ah, once you are a bit older, you'll understand. Shicai, you must persevere, and in the future Uncle will teach you all of his skills."

The boy chopped down some saplings and used them to construct an observation tower in a tree near the fork in the river. Then he lay there from dawn till dusk, holding a small parang that had been polished to the point that it was cold to the touch. The river was very animated, and turtles would periodically lift their heads out of the water and gaze toward the shore. After observing this area for a week the boy saw only a few large monitor lizards, but not even a single small crocodile. Therefore he headed further upriver and built another observation tower in a tree next to a different fork in the river. The Rajang is Sarawak's longest river, and both banks are full of forests and marshes. The area is full of a variety of different kinds of plants, flowers, and other wild species with tender leaves and bright blossoms, some of which hadn't even been named yet. This was a paradise for monkeys and birds. Here the boy finally spotted several medium-sized crocodiles, some of which were sunning themselves on the bank with their mouths open, like sleepy guards, while others were floating in the river with only their tiny knifelike eyes visible. Inside his observation post, the boy angrily hacked at branches with his parang while cursing under his breath. He wondered, if the crocodile really did appear, what would he be able to do with this small parang that was usually used for tasks like chopping wood and cutting grass, killing chickens and cleaning fish? . . . He continued hacking angrily at nearby branches.

Every few days the boy would pick a bundle of wildflowers, put on his plastic sandals, and walk a couple of hours to visit Junyi in the Chinese cemetery. Junyi's tomb was located next to her grandmother's, though the girl's coffin was empty. The day of the accident, the town of Daro dispatched virtually all its sampans, hunting rifles, water guns, javelins, and parangs. The townspeople scoured the river and the riverbank, and that evening they even hired a Chinese Taoist and a Malay shaman to assist in the search. It was said that a man-eating crocodile, after being subjected to supernatural suppression and necrotic induction, will venture onto the riverbank of its own accord, to stand trial. Meanwhile, people who hunt crocodiles say that after eating a human, a crocodile will always flee upriver. This is because the land upriver is vast, and the further the crocodile swims upriver, the easier it is it to disappear without a trace.

The boy snuck into his uncle's house and stole a rifle and twenty bullets. Then, outfitted with a small parang, flashlight, matches, water bottle, and half a sandwich left over from breakfast in a pouch hanging from his waist, and wearing shorts, a T-shirt, and white cloth shoes, he headed upriver. The rifle's wooden butt was smooth, cold, and as white as jade. The boy repeatedly caressed the gun's barrel, front sight, and trigger, then hugged it tight to his chest. The rifle, a repurposed Johnson automatic rifle, was about as tall as he was. After World War II the boy's maternal grandfather had bartered for it with an American soldier, ultimately costing the grandfather five exquisitely carved parangs and one Dayak battle shield. The rifle could shoot far and accurately, had only a slight recoil, never got jammed, and was effectively Yu Jiatong's third hand. On the left side of the wooden butt there was a carving of a crocodile twisted into a circle, and on the right side there was a dragon. The two images were partially worn away, like a dragon or crocodile hidden underwater. The rifle could be loaded with six bullets at a time, and Yu Jiatong had taught him how to load the gun, aim, and fire. On the banks of the Rajang River, the boy loaded the rifle and prepared to fire a test shot.

Each night, from his spot in the tree, the boy would shine his flashlight down at the river and then fire his gun at the space between a pair of red crocodile eyes. During the day he would follow the riverbank upriver. When it rained he would hide under a tree, protecting the gun with his body. When his water bottle was empty he would fill it with rainwater, and occasionally would eat some fruit to slake his thirst. He tried to kill some small animals to assuage his hunger, but before he could lift his rifle his prey would have already disappeared. Not having access to any meat, he simply ate whatever he could find, and in the process he became a vegetarian by necessity. During the day his body became covered in sweat, while at night he would shiver from the cold, as the rifle came to feel heavier and heavier. . . .

Exhausted, he lay on a tree branch, his head aching to the point that it felt like there was a wild beast pecking it open and screaming directly into his brain . . .

"I will not fail to speak of the crocodile's limbs, its strength and its graceful form. . . ." Teacher Shao read aloud from chapter 41 of the Book of Job:

> Who can strip off its outer coat? Who can penetrate its double coat of armor? Who dares open the doors of its mouth, ringed about with fearsome teeth? Its back has rows of shields tightly sealed together; each is so close to the next that no air can pass between. They are joined fast to one another; they cling together and cannot be parted. Its snorting throws out flashes of light; its eyes are like the rays of dawn. Flames stream from its mouth; sparks of fire shoot out. Smoke pours from its nostrils as from a boiling pot over burning reeds. Its breath sets coals ablaze, and flames dart from its mouth. Strength resides in its neck; dismay goes before it. . . .

The boy's mouth was dry and his body felt as though it were burning up. He felt as though a beast's beak had pried open his skull, or enormous fire ants were cutting his skin. In his sleep, the boy let out a scream like a tortoise's mating call. He tossed and turned, and several times he almost fell out of the tree. *Zizisusu, zizisusu.* An enormous animal was walking in the tree's shadow and was pressing down on the bushes and vines. With gentle eyes it gazed up at the boy. Its trunk swayed back and forth, as a geyser erupted toward the boy. The boy lay down on bridge of the animal's nose as though in a crib, then slid down to the ground. . . .

> The folds of its flesh are tightly joined; they are firm and immovable. Its chest is hard as rock, hard as a lower millstone. When it rises up, the mighty are terrified; they retreat before its thrashing. The sword that reaches it has no effect, nor does the spear or the dart or the javelin. Iron it treats like straw and bronze like rotten wood. Arrows do not make it flee; slingstones are like chaff to it. A club seems to it but a piece of straw; it laughs at the rattling of the lance. Its undersides are jagged potsherds, leaving a trail in the mud like a threshing sledge. It makes the depths churn like a boiling caldron and stirs up the sea like a pot of ointment. It leaves a glistening wake behind it; one would think the deep had white hair. Nothing on earth is its equal—a creature without fear. It looks down on all that are haughty; it is king over all that are proud.

The boy woke up. He was lying in the bed he shared with Shiwen and Shishang. The boy's head still hurt a bit, and Shiwen was sitting next to the window reading a book.

"You're awake," Shiwen said. He walked over and felt the boy's head. "Are you feeling better?"

"Who brought me back?"

"Uncle did."

Shiwen handed the boy a towel.

The boy silently wiped the sweat from his forehead, neck, and chest.

"You were lost in the rainforest for nine days, and after returning home you slept for five more days." Shiwen returned to his seat next to the window and opened the book he was holding:

Ci Lyrics at Baiyuzhai. "Your uncle and the others found you in a tree. You were lying there like you were dead."

The boy gazed out the window. When he slept, the window was always open, and the Big Dipper could often be seen above the dark trees, like a shattered blade.

"You're very bold," Shiwen said, still looking at his book. "You even dared to steal Uncle's beloved rifle."

"Where is Uncle?"

"There have been several major developments over the past ten days or so." Shiwen continued looking at his book. "The police came and detained many people, including Uncle, Wang Dada, Chen Qiang, Chen Sifa, Li Xiongwei, Yang Wenfeng, Huang Kuiying, and Qiu Xinru. . . . More than twenty more fled into the forest. Eldest Brother—he also fled. Teacher Shao is currently being held at the police station, and I hear that in a few days he'll be sent back to China. Little Brother . . . remember what Uncle said, that we must watch what we say. . . ."

Quack quack, quack quack. Mother walked in holding a bowl of Chinese medicine that resembled black ink.

It was the middle of the night—twelve o'clock, or maybe it was already one. The boy was lying in bed with his eyes wide open, and next to him two of his brothers were snoring loudly. The boy couldn't sleep, so he got up from bed and went to lie down in front of the window. Under the house's eaves the Big Dipper was still glimmering, accompanied by countless other stars whose names he didn't know. Some were hanging in the sky all alone, while others were clustered in groups. Some were moving, some were emitting an orange or red light, and some were so dim that it looked as though there were about to be extinguished. The stars resembled an infant's fingers. age spots. chicken claws. duck feet. a mother's tears. Teacher Shao's spittle. The sky was a celestial tomb, revealing and burying countless celestial bones. Periodically, the chickens, ducks, and pigs in the animal shed could be heard sleep-talking. Mother was feeding the pigs again. Can animals also talk in their sleep? *Kaleikalei, dididada.* Father went outside with his bicycle. Didn't Father, as soon as he woke up, always go directly to the gambling hall to fight? Following behind him there was another man, who was also pushing a bicycle. Both men were very careful, as their wheels made a soft *dididada* sound, and only after they had reached a certain distance from the house did they finally mount their bicycles and disappear into the darkness. The night was murky, and the lake water was imposing. In the blurred sight of the tree shadows caressing the wild grass, the boy noticed that the other man was much taller than his father and was riding his bicycle as though it were a small train.

The boy resumed feeding and washing the pigs. He would grab the pigs' hide with both hands, and sometimes would take the pig's bristle and scrub the two pigs until they gleamed. He used soapy water to wash the pig shed until the shed was filled with the sweet scent of olives. He hauled bucket after bucket from the well. A sow jogged around the pig shed, its cries lively and sweet, then swung its leg sideways and entered the shed. The boy caressed the sow's neck, back, and rear.

A neighbor's female mountain goat was grazing in an uncultivated area. The boy picked several bundles of fragrant and succulent grass and used them to lead the goat back to the field.

A fat female dog was licking the boy's hand, calf, and toes. The dog had more than ten teats dangling from its abdomen, and the boy had to use more than a dozen bones before he was able to dispel his nervousness. Eventually, however, he was able to pat the dog's head, and the dog wagged its tail in return.

2

The two oars slowly propelled the sampan forward. With the boy managing the left-hand oar and Dezhong managing the right-hand one, the sampan slowly made its way up the Rajang River. Soon Dezhong and the boy were breathing hard, and their backs were covered in sweat. When they grew tired, Dezhong found a shady spot on the riverbank and skillfully navigated toward it. Then he tied the sampan to a thick tree trunk and, panting heavily, retreated to a shady area. Both banks of the river were full of lush and verdant vegetation, and Dezhong and the boy would have loved to be transformed into a pair of birds so that they could soar through it. The trees were strong, stout, and as tall as cliffs. They resembled plants from the spectral realm, bones of giant beasts covered in moss and fungus, or a giant mass of algae that extended from the bottom of the river to the shore. The posture of the birds flying overhead resembled fish, and animals were roaring like whales or dolphins. The boy enjoyed listening to these sounds until his veins were filled with these calls—to the point that it seemed as though, without them, his blood might stop circulating, like a dancer without music or a river without a riverbed, like a beached whale without water or a spaniel without a burrow. Although the boy's hands were numb from rowing, he nevertheless felt completely relaxed. Perhaps this was because the air here was unusually pure and the oxygen was exceptionally wild, since no one had breathed it in more than a hundred days. Towering cliffs periodically appeared on either bank, and clouds either enveloped the mountain peaks or separated them from the mountain base. There were also many smaller hills in an array of odd and deformed shapes. The boy was reminded of the landscape paintings in Teacher Shao's classroom and felt as though he were entering ancient China.

Two figures appeared on the shore. One was sitting and the other was standing, and they were in the process of grilling something. On their chests, they were wearing North Kalimantan People's Army badges. The boy gestured for Dezhong to row over to them.

"North Kalimantan People's Army?" The boy asked as he grabbed a bush on the riverbank to steady the sampan.

Rail-thin, with bloodshot eyes and clothing that was completely in shreds, the men resembled husks of insects trapped in a spider web. They were in the process of eating some small animals they had charred to a crisp, and they devoured the creatures whole—skin, bones, and all. The men were ethnically Chinese and appeared to be about forty years old. Upon hearing the boy's question, they stopped eating and became as silent as a pair of walls.

"Are you part of the Yangtze River Brigade?"

Silence.

"The Flame Mountain Brigade?"

Silence.

"The Little Rhino Brigade?"

Silence.

Dezhong and the boy exchanged a quick glance. "Are you preparing to surrender?"

Silence.

The boy couldn't resist any longer, and finally said, "Regardless of which military unit you belong to, we're all communists, right? I'm the nephew of Yu Jiatong, leader of the Yangtze River Brigade, and my four elder brothers also joined that same brigade. Can you tell me where can I find my uncle? Where is the Yangtze River Brigade's base camp?"

Silence. . . .

Eventually, the boy untethered the sampan and prepared to continue upriver. Just as he was lifting his oar, however, he saw the two dark figures on the riverbank slowly remove their military badges and toss them into the river. A pair of fierce prisoner-like eyes continuously bore down on Dezhong and the boy, as a couple of dark shadows ruminated on them like cows. They rowed into those prisoners' eyes, into their shattered retinas. . . .

Half an hour later, another dark shadow appeared on the riverbank. Was this one of the earlier two men? The new figure was wearing a black shirt, and when he saw the sampan he immediately stood up. The boy went ashore and asked,

"North Kalimantan People's Army?"

The soldier removed his parang from his belt and held it in his hand. He stared at the boy for a long time, then said, "And who . . . are you?"

"I am . . ." The boy noticed that the parang was covered in blood. Was it animal blood? Or was his eyesight failing him? "I am . . . Yu Jiatong's nephew. . . ."

"Yu . . . Jiatong . . ." The man muttered under his breath. ". . . nephew . . ."

"I'm looking for news about my uncle," the boy said. "I'm Yu Jiatong's nephew. My four elder brothers . . ."

The blood-stained blade was raised and pointed toward the boy's chest. "Get lost . . ."

"But Uncle . . . I'm just asking whether you have any information . . ."

The parang swished through the air. "Scram. Leave. Get lost. . . ."

In December of 1973, the boy was nineteen years old. After graduating from high school, he had worked for a while and saved up some money, then piloted his sampan up the Rajang River to the SCP's liveliest Red area to search for his uncle Yu Jiatong. Zhu Dezhong, the boy's classmate and friend, was ethnically Iban but had received a Chinese education, and therefore could speak fluent Chinese. After finishing high school Dezhong had worked in a lumber mill for a stint, and now was returning to his hometown for the first time since graduation. Dezhong's family lived more than four hundred kilometers upriver from Daro, and the boy decided to travel with Dezhong. From Daro, Dezhong and the boy took a ferry three hundred kilometers upriver to the ferry's terminus, then continued forward in a sampan. The boy found it difficult to imagine how Dezhong was able to make this trip every year. The boy's belongings filled their sampan, as though he were a hoarder, but Dezhong was carrying only a small bag and his year's wages. The scenery on both banks appeared rather cold, as though covered in frost. Many Punan men were carrying blowguns to go hunting, and a rotting monkey carcass was hanging from a tree, its maggot-filled head suspended only a few centimeters above the water's surface. It was said that the monkey was crocodile bait, and its abdomen was filled with iron hooks. An otter was silently swimming back and forth, and in the distance beasts roared forlornly. Similar scenes kept recurring, which made Dezhong and the boy feel as though they were going around in circles. They continued rowing until their hands were numb, and the scenes in front and behind them became indistinguishable—making it appear as though they were rowing backwards. Whenever they reached a shoal they would have to get out of the sampan and push it forward, and whenever they encountered a fallen tree blocking their path Dezhong would hack it apart with his parang so that the pieces would be carried away by the current. At four o'clock they stopped on a shoal to rest. They watched as the sun sank toward the horizon, at which point, shirtless, they continued rowing upriver. Sunset appeared early in the sky above the forest. In the wilderness, sunset is always rich and prolonged, like the official title of the Malaysian empress. *Shashasha, chichichi.* A man was scurrying around on the riverbank full of knee-high silvergrass. Holding a parang and wearing a green shirt, with a green ribbon tied around his forehead, the man was hiding in the bushes. Another man with a parang was following the first. The second man stood in the middle of the field and looked around, whereupon the first man suddenly leaped out of the bushes and almost chopped the other man in half with his parang. They fought silently until one man's leg was sliced open, whereupon he turned and fled into the bushes. The other man pursued him, and soon they both disappeared from view. Dezhong recalled how, at the beginning of the twentieth century, a Chinese man had led more than a thousand Hokchew soldiers to open up the banks of the Rajang River and build a base in the wilderness. "At the time, these banks were our people's liveliest region." Dezhong put down his oar and looked around, then added, "But now the area is just a Chinese communist hotbed."

The river water was as cold and clear as well water—as cold and clear as well water excavated by Zheng He. . . . Dezhong stopped rowing for too long, and the boy was unable to maintain control over the sampan as it drifted toward the riverbank, where a jumble of branches and twigs was pointing at the boy. Some of the branches resembled nail rakes, while others resembled gill rakes. The boy put down his oar and parted the branches with his hand. Dezhong picked up his own oar and, after rowing for another kilometer, they came upon a man with a black shirt who was squatting on the riverbank and firing his rifle into the bushes. Each time the man fired his rifle he would then crouch down again behind a stone—as though there were an enemy hiding in the bushes. The man kept firing and reloading his rifle, but the invisible enemy never returned fire. When the man noticed the sampan approaching him from behind, he turned and looked at the Dezhong and the boy with surprise, then continued shooting into the thicket. *Bang.* The bushes suddenly stopped moving, and evidently whoever had been trying to flee must have escaped. Even after Dezhong and the boy had proceeded several more kilometers upriver, the sound of gunshots continued to resonate faintly in the distance. Eventually dusk fell, and the surface of the river became covered in fog. Beaks and claws emerged, sounding like metal as they hunted for food. Faintly, like a dog following a scent. A few tombs periodically appeared on the riverbank,, but it was difficult to make out the knife-carved characters on the tombstones: "The tomb of Li Chun (?) The light of the Chinese Communist Party August 14, 1968" "The tomb of Yangtze River Brigade member Jiang Guangping The soul of martial (?) combat (?) September 2, 1968" "The tomb of the wife Zhou Baoxia (?)" The sunset faded and fireflies blinked on and off, like the blood of savages. The boy felt as though their sampan had entered a wound in the body of Mother Nature herself—who had skin so dark that it seemed as though it was spattered with her blood. The boy turned on his flashlight, but Dezhong immediately told him to turn it off to conserve batteries: "If you row, I'll handle the navigation." As instructed, the boy turned off the flashlight.

At this point the moon was swaying back and forth overhead, like a skull. It was as though the moon were hanging under Grandfather's five fingers, locked in a cargo box that had crossed the ocean—which was now either suspended from the rafters of one of the natives' longhouses or tucked inside the hand of some government official about to offer someone a bonus. Second Brother—the knight on a white stallion who had been beating the gongs behind Yu Jiatong—was lying there decapitated. The boy fantasized about taking his brother's bloody head and using his brother's tender and affectionate lips to give all his adoring girlfriends a kiss goodbye. When Second Brother was still alive he would often fib to these girls, and then deflower them in the rainforest like honey bears and abandon them. But then he fell in love with Dai Qinyun, who worked in the ticket booth of the Daro Theater. At the time Qinyun was only sixteen, and sitting in the ticket booth she resembled a beautiful maiden that a beast had dragged away to its lair. Second Brother once took Qinyun to watch a movie. The movie was silent and black-and-white and was about ghosts or demons—and it appeared as though the movie itself had been produced by spirits. Second Brother was nineteen at the time and sported a stylish quiff haircut, Elvis sideburns, and bell-bottom pants. In the ticket booth Second Brother often engaged Qinyun in childish banter. Qinyun, however, simply wanted him to give her news about Yu Jiatong. She eventually left home and, wearing only light, casual clothes, she threw herself at the mercy of her beloved Comrade Yu Jiatong and joined the Yangtze River Brigade. Not long afterward, stupid Second Brother began pursuing another beloved: He responded to the summons of the Chinese Communist Party and became a general under Yu Jiatong. In the end, however, the natives brilliantly dismembered him, like meat paste. Now his lips were still slightly warm, and the girls could still kiss them. This time he would not be able to run away from them.

"Who is it?"

Several flashlight beams shined onto the boy and Dezhong, who squinted and stopped rowing. Two sampans holding seven or eight people drifted up to them.

"I'm from Pitka." Dezhong reported the name of his hometown. "I'm returning home to visit my relatives."

"And you?" Three or four light beams converged on the boy.

"I'm from Daro." The boy pointed to Dezhong. "He's my classmate, and I'm going home with him."

"Daro?" The man spoke with a thick voice, which sounded as though his throat were full of sores. "What is your relationship to Yu Jiatong?"

"No relationship. . . ."

"No relationship? Huh?"

The other sampans attacked theirs from both sides. *Xixisusu.* The other men took everything the boy and Dezhong had, leaving behind only their oars. The boy noticed that several of the men were wearing black shirts, and that one of them was wearing a Yangtze River Brigade badge.

"Actually, I'm Yu Jiatong's nephew. My name is Shi Shicai, and I've come to join forces with Yu Jiatong. . . ."

The beams converged on the boy.

"Really?"

"My four elder brothers all joined the Yangtze River Brigade. . . ."

"The Shi brothers."

"Why didn't you say so earlier?"

"Because . . . at first, I didn't know who you were. . . ."

"Have you also come here to die?"

"You're the Shi family's youngest son? Go back. . . . We wouldn't want the Shi clan to be left without any descendants. . . ."

"Dear uncles, you are all great Communist Party members and revolutionary warriors. I sincerely admire you. So, please tell me, where can I find my uncle . . ."

Was that the sound of laughter? Or of coughing? Or . . . of arguing?

"Boy, I'm telling you . . ."

"Let's go. Who knows whether he's telling the truth?"

"Why would I dare lie to you? My ID card is in my bag."

"Let's go, let's go!"

As the sampan was about to set off, one of the men suddenly asked, "Do you have any money?"

Dezhong and the boy looked at each other.

"Quick, take it out."

One man picked up his rifle, whereupon Dezhong and the boy each removed their year's wages, which were crumpled up inside a pair of yellow envelopes. One man reached over, took the envelopes, and opened them.

"This is not a small amount."

"Uncle, please be magnanimous. This is our entire year's wages." The boy pointed to Dezhong. "You can take mine, but he needs to give his to his parents. . . ."

"Take half, and leave them the remaining half," said the thick voice. "Little brother, I'm sorry. We don't have any money on us, so please lend us some."

The envelopes were tossed back to their feet, and then the other sampans departed like an arrow. Were they followed by the sound of laughter? Or coughing? Or arguing? . . .

"Uncle, please don't take my things . . ."

"Damn it, count yourself lucky that we didn't take every-thing." One man ejected a glob of spittle, which plopped into the river like a ripe fruit. "How tedious . . .."

The thick voice wafted over in the darkness. "Stupid boy, tell your uncle to stop dreaming. . . ."

Laughter. A long string of laughter. This time the sound was very clear.

"Dezhong, I'm sorry." The boy gazed at his classmate's face in the darkness. "They were wearing black shirts and were Yang-tze River Brigade troops. When I find my uncle, I'll ask him to return your money. . . ."

"Forget about it. At least they didn't take it all."

"Why don't you keep my half? After all, I don't have any use for it."

"I couldn't do that, because then you'd be left with nothing. Money can always be used. Keep rowing; we've almost reached my house."

In less than half an hour they arrived at Dezhong's family's home. Dezhong and the boy got out and headed toward the house, and Dezhong said, "Let's just claim that the sampan over-turned and all of our luggage fell into the river. My family already has a bad impression of the Yangtze River troops."

There were several fighting cocks tied up outside the house, a few dogs were lying on the ground, and positioned over the hallway there was a great hornbill. As soon as Dezhong and the boy appeared, the dogs and cocks—as well as the pigs, cattle, chickens, and ducks that were kept beneath the house—all began to produce a melodious racket. *Wangwanggege, aoaojiji*. Out of this weird livestock symphony, only the hornbill's calls were grat-ing on the ears. Dezhong's thirty-plus relatives were all stand-ing on the balcony to greet their guest. The house was over a hundred meters long, and although more than thirty people lived there, it seemed as though the humans were vastly outnumbered by the livestock, whose cacophonous calls drowned out the people's voices. That night Dezhong's family prepared a lavish banquet with abundant food and spicy wine. The women were warm and attentive, and the men were bold and strong. Having spent the entire day rowing the sampan, the boy didn't say a single word and instead focused on eating his food. Several glasses of wine entered his belly, until eventually he collapsed at Dezhong's feet. Early the next morning the boy got up from his sleeping mat, still a bit hung over. It was raining hard outside. The overdue monsoon season had finally arrived.

This strange downpour continued for an entire week, sucking up the sun, moon, and stars. The rain fell until the land was silenced and the livestock were voiceless. The jungle resembled algae, mountain rocks resembled eggshells, the sky resembled a cliff, and the raindrops resembled fish scales. Day was like night, and the longhouse's gas lamp stayed lit twenty-four hours a day. Occasionally sunlight would break through the cloud cover, but the downpour would continue and the rain would glow with an orange light. At night one could simultaneously hear the rain, see the moon, and smell the stars. Through the rain, the moon resembled a crystalline drop of water inside an old well. Through the rain, the stars resembled an inextinguishable meteor shower. Through the rain, the sky resembled water-soaked gunpower. The rain fell continuously onto the roof made from salt-wood chips and coconut leaves, onto the grain-drying area of the balcony, and onto the tree leaves, the muddy ground, and the river's surface. When the rain fell on the roof it sounded like tiny geckos, when it fell on the grain-drying area it sounded like tiny crickets, when it fell on the tree leaves it sounded like tiny grasshoppers, and when it fell into the river it sounded like tiny shrimp. *Dididada. Zizichacha.* The rain disappeared from view.

Eleven years earlier there had been a similar torrential downpour. In the hazy evening light, a swarm of termites had flown away, and the boy, after having run a high fever during the preceding crocodile hunt, was still passed out in bed. An old man wearing a raincoat and rain hat was going door-to-door to relay urgent news in a muddy-sounding voice: "The Brunei Revolt has failed, and the British government has now begun arresting members of the Brunei People's Party. All comrades should assemble immediately at the wharf on the estuary." The messengers spreading the news appeared as a range of different characters: An old man, a youth, a hunchbacked middle-aged man, a stuttering wife. These were disguises put on by Yu Jiatong and his followers, who were expert at using makeup and camouflage. The British government was bewildered. There were five or six hundred Chinese Communist Party members hiding in Daro, as well as countless government spies. In December 1962 the Brunei Communist Party launched an armed rebellion, but it was suppressed within a week, and the leaders subsequently fled the country. The British government, which had helped Brunei suppress the rebellion, began detaining all members of the SCP, and the town of Daro—which at the time was the community that was most supportive of the communists—bore the brunt of this new offensive. Yu Jiatong took more than five hundred men and women from Daro and led them into the rainforest. The group hiked through mountains and ravines, and on the border of Sarawak and Indonesia they received training from the Indonesian Communist Party and prepared to engage the British government in armed struggle. The torrential downpour completely erased their tracks, and when a few dozen bloodhounds and several hundred British soldiers arrived and saw the rainforest, they sighed in despair.

The downpour continued uninterrupted. Could it be that it intended to pelt the structurally unstable longhouse until not even a corpse remained inside? The boy stuck out his hand and used the rainwater to rinse his face. There were more than a hundred skulls hanging from vines tied to the house's eaves—testifying to the success of Dezhong's ancestors in hunting human heads. The rain pelting the roof leaked down onto these skulls, creating enormous column that resembled a tree trunk, with the skulls resembling tree cysts. Or desiccated fruits. Or beehives.

"Let's wait until the rain stops before leaving," Dezhong said.

"But it seems like it will never stop, . . . " the boy replied. "And in the meantime, I keep eating your family's food and enjoying your family's hospitality . . . while the gifts that I brought were . . ."

"What are you talking about? We Iban are the most hospitable people."

"I don't even have a parang. . . ."

"Don't worry. My family will provide you with whatever you need."

"But I have money. . . ."

"Keep your money. My father says that the Yangtze River Brigade headquarters is located about fifty kilometers upriver. I don't have anything else to do at the moment, and furthermore we're good friends. So, after the rain stops, we'll go together to look for it."

"You mean, go look for the six months of salary you lost?"

". . . my best friend always understands me the best."

Ten days later the rain finally began to taper off, and Dezhong's family predicted that there would be clear skies the next day. Dezhong and the boy prepared their bags, so that they would be ready to set off first thing in the morning. Dezhong's family gave the boy a parang—which had a raised engraving that looked like a black dragon on the blade and a strange animal that was neither a dog nor a deer on the handle. The wooden sheath was also inscribed with countless whorls. That night Dezhong's family organized a farewell banquet at which young women were banging gongs (these were bronze gongs that had been imported from China centuries earlier . . .), beating drums, playing zithers, performing dances, and singing the lyrics to the welcome guest dance. The boy did not have a very high tolerance for alcohol, but when eating meat he often couldn't resist the urge to drink. *Dingdingdongdong. Zhengzhengzongzong.* He groaned out an unintelligible version of the welcome guest song, followed by a series of weird variations: "Using alcohol as a song, what is life? . . . I have an esteemed guest, for whom I'm beating the drums and playing the flute. That young woman is either your sister or your cousin." Dezhong interjected, "Let me describe this song's lyrics to you: You have forded rivers and climbed mountains to come visit us. My beautiful wine and delicacies help you recover from your exhaustion. You arrived in a rush and now are leaving in a rush—like a wounded mountain lion that doesn't have a den. . . . She's my sister, and the most beautiful girl in our family. If you like, you could stay and become my brother-in-law." The boy replied, "I'm not blessed with this sort of good fortune. Also, I shouldn't drink any more. I'm afraid if I continue, I'll lose control . . . like . . . like my eldest brother. . . ." Dezhong said, "My friend, get up and let's go out to the balcony. My relatives will organize a cockfight for you to watch."

From the balcony, the boy saw that a crowd had gathered around the house, with two men standing in the center. Both of the men were holding a cock—one was date-red and the other was snow-white, and both cocks had tiny curved blades attached to their claws. When the men released their cocks, the neck of the white one was sliced open by the red one's blade. Blood immediately began to gush out and the white cock died, whereupon the red cock them spread its wings and crowed. Dezhong and the boy went back inside. The hand with which the boy was holding his glass was visibly shaking, and his face was as red as a date. He alternated between standing and sitting, and barely even knew where he was. The girl smiled sweetly, her eyes like water and her teeth like seashells. The cock suddenly leaped up, its blade shimmering in the light. *Bang!* Blade met bone. The boy said, "What's so great about these cocks? My eldest brother's cocks were truly first rate." Dezhong replied, "Your eldest brother also raised fighting cocks?" The boy said, "Yes. . . ." In the fog of the wine and the welcome guest dance, the boy began to miss his eldest brother, Shinong. Shinong used to live and sleep with his cocks, and would feed them centipedes, scorpions, spiders, bats, and snakes. His cock prices were the highest in Daro, but even so gamblers still competed with one another to purchase them. In the fighting rink, Shinong's cocks usually emerged victorious. One afternoon, however, two masked Malay men took advantage of the fact that Shinong was out looking for the boy, who had gone to the Rajang River to hunt crocodiles, and the men killed Shinong's two guard dogs with a parang, then reduced his flock of more than a hundred cocks to mere chicken tenders. Shinong was disconsolate and proceeded to erect a giant tomb for the slaughtered cocks. Several days later he decided to follow Yu Jiatong into the rainforest, but before leaving he went to a wooden wall in the market and wrote a phrase consisting of just six characters and two punctuation marks: "People of China, stand up now!" If his fighting cocks hadn't been killed, Shinong would never have been able to bring himself to leave them behind. When his cocks were still alive,

Shinong was alive; but when they died, a part of him died as well. It was said that Shinong wasn't actually a brave warrior, and instead was often so frightened by government troops' gunfire that he would wet his pants. Jiatong introduced a young Iban girl to Shinong, recommending that they establish a mixed Hua-native marriage so that communist thought might thereby permeate the Iban people. At this point the Yangtze River Brigade was still very powerful and was able to enter and leave the Rajang River watershed at will—as easily as though it were an uninhabited area. Whenever the army reached a town, the local Chinese would cook chickens and slaughter an ox while praising the troops' heroism. The boy went up to Dezhong and whispered, "If that Iban girl that Uncle found for Eldest Brother was as pretty as your sister, she must have driven Eldest Brother crazy. In fact, under the circumstances, even I would have considered marriage." When Jiatong, after several failed attempts, finally made the desired introduction, he invited both parties to drink and enjoy themselves, and Shinong proceeded to get drunk. That young Iban girl who received Shinong had been specifically arranged by Jiatong, and after the two of them were sent into a bedroom, that which was soft became hard and rice grains were cooked into rice. The Iban ancestors were valiant and martial— they hunted heads, killed pirates, and resisted the British naval guns with their own bodies—and this sort of valor circulated through the veins not only of the men, but also of the women. After Shinong was married his wife trained him to become a brave Iban warrior. He wore nail pants, went shirtless, and drank rice wine. He chewed betel nut and tattooed his body. He hunted monkeys with a blowgun and killed wild boars with a hatchet. In the end, however, he was disemboweled when a grenade exploded right in front of him. After his comrades-in-arms abandoned him, government troops had to carry his corpse back to the Shi household. It must be noted, however, that Shinong was a good man and died a soldier, just like his fighting cocks. Had it not been for his parents' opposition, the boy would have buried his brother's corpse next to the tomb for the fighting cocks. The boy leaned over and whispered, "Dezhong, you're not going to be like my uncle and take advantage of the fact that I've been drinking to have your sister ride my body, are you? You asked me why I'm looking for my uncle? Why am I looking for him? . . . Why am I looking for him? . . . I . . ."

The boy proceeded to vomit up a mass of filth, then collapsed at the feet of two young Iban women who were dancing the welcome guest dance.

Clear skies, breaking dawn. The sunrise over the rainforest was as bright red as a poisonous tree frog. The coconut trees resembled iron carvings, and large birds made a loud rustling sound as they soared through the air, like an aircraft that had run into mechanical difficulties and was about to crash into the forest. Several black pigs were feeding behind the longhouse, digging in the soil with their long snouts and occasionally unearthing worms that were as thick as a man's finger and as long as a man's arm. Each time they unearthed a worm, they would make a fighting sound. All the livestock were continuously eating and defecating, which was an indication that their digestive and excretory systems were healthy and fully functional. Dezhong and the boy bid farewell to the relatives who had come down to the riverbank to see them off, but before they had proceeded three kilometers upriver, they both had to squat down in the rear of the sampan and relieve themselves. Their shit plopped down into the river, like an infant's arm or leg, and accumulated along the riverbank, like an infant's corpse.

With one oar, Dezhong dexterously controlled the sampan as though it were his slave. It was as if there were a motor embedded in the sampan's rear. The boy felt a bit lightheaded and kept rinsing his face with river water, but the more he did so the dizzier and filthier he became—as though they were rowing through a cesspool. Thirty meters ahead a dark cloud was hovering over the water's surface. *Wengwengweng. Wengwengweng.* There was a swelling in the river, which repeatedly rose and fell. Dezhong and the boy both had to cover their noses with one hand as they continued rowing with the other, and only in this way were they able to slowly proceed forward. The black cloud floated overhead, and the swelling floated over to the side of sampan. The swelling was covered with layer upon layer of green-, red-, and black-headed flies and was surrounded by countless fish, large and small. The flies were startled by the waves produced by the sampan and formed an even more majestic black cloud. In addition to the flies, the swelling in the river was also covered in layer upon layer of orange and pink maggots, and before the wave had fully receded, the black cloud immediately covered everything again. The swelling, Dezhong and the boy realized, was a human corpse—its posterior was oriented upward, and although its limbs were still intact, the flesh had rotted away and the bones visible. Maggots formed the shape of the Chinese character 大. The corpse was still wearing a tattered green shirt. A green shirt . . . the uniform of the Flame Mountain Brigade. . . .

Dezhong and the boy rowed furiously, as their rhythm completely fell apart. The larger the splashes created by their oars, the slower the sampan advanced, and the closer the corpse drifted to them. One eyeball had abandoned the corpse, and the waves pushed it toward the sampan until it struck the boy's oar with a *plunk* sound. It was as if an invisible force were pulling the corpse, followed by the black cloud. Countless flies shot by Dezhong and the boy like bullets. Dezhong and the boy shouted and—no longer bothering to cover their noses—rowed as fast as they could. It was as though their lungs were filled with decayed air, their stomachs were filled with flies, and their bodies were covered in maggots. They rowed nonstop for twenty minutes, finally pausing under a tree to catch their breath. Then they rowed nonstop for another ten minutes. When they reached a shoal, they got out and pushed the sampan forward until the water was knee-deep again, whereupon they let go of the sampan, stripped off their clothes, and began furiously washing themselves with the river. However, it seemed as though the stench could never be washed away, as the corpse's beauty continued to spread in all directions. It was said that this kind of fly would lay eggs on humans' scalp and clothing, and even their genitalia.

"A little further upriver there's an elementary and middle school. The children in my family's clan all go there," Dezhong said. "The school has several Chinese instructors, and we can go ask them."

"I haven't seen your siblings attending class."

"It's still early, but if we wait for a while we might be able to run into them," Dezhong replied casually. "My brother Lachar and my sister Fadiya are responsible for taking them to school."

Dezhong and the boy placed their clothing on the roof of the sampan to dry and continued rowing upriver in their underwear. The school was located on a hill and had approximately two hundred students, the vast majority of whom were natives. There were only two wooden buildings on the school grounds. These were the classrooms, with the longer one being for the elementary school students and the shorter one being for the middle school students. As Dezhong and the boy approached the school in their sampan, they put their clothes back on and went ashore. In the middle of the playground, there was a bamboo flagpole, at the top of which there was a rope dangling from a pulley. Five or six native children were kicking a soccer ball in the green playground. The ball rolled over to the boy, who kicked it back. This was an imported brand of soccer ball. The instructors' dormitories were located about a hundred meters from the classroom—a row of squat, white structures. A man on a bicycle rode out of one of these buildings and approached Dezhong and the boy. He was about forty years old. He was frowning. He was Chinese.

"Are you a teacher?" The boy asked, as the bicycle passed them. The man stopped. "Excuse me, do you know Yu Jiatong? He's a member of the North Kalimantan People's Army. . . ."

"Why are you looking for him?" The man asked.

"There's something. . . ."

The man examined Dezhong and the boy, then gazed into the distance. "Yu Jiatong used to come here frequently, but we haven't seen him recently. He always comes and goes without leaving a trace." Without waiting for the boy to respond, the man continued down the hill. He sped away making such a loud racket that it seemed as though an entire bicycle-repair shop were rolling down the hill.

Dezhong and the boy watched as the man disappeared from sight. "In such a wild and undeveloped area, where is he going on that bicycle?"

"Some students live quite far away, so the teacher needs to pick them up in the morning," Dezhong explained. "And after school he takes them home again."

"He does this every day?"

"My people don't like to send our children to school, so if the teacher didn't come pick up the children, they simply wouldn't go at all," Dezhong said. "In fact, my elder brother had to lobby hard before our father finally agreed to let me go to school in Daro. My brother argued that the teachers there are relatively well-educated."

It was still too early for school to start. There was a longhouse located about half a kilometer up the hill, and Dezhong went to see if they had any news. The boy, meanwhile, stayed on the riverbank to keep an eye on the sampan and their luggage. Little crystalline crabs that looked like they were made of white jade scurried back and forth along the riverbank, periodically disappearing into burrows and reentering the water. The large crabs looked like tiny axes, and when they walked they resembled a Swiss Army knife with all its components opened. The crabs climbed onto a tree branch to kill their prey. Mudskippers skimmed the surface of the water, and occasionally one or two would fall onto a crab, whereupon they would recoil like a burned tongue. The teacher on the bicycle picked up two Iban children, one after the other, and dropped them off in front of the school. Then he headed back down the hill, still making a noisy racket. Some students began to assemble in the schoolyard. The boy originally had a Swiss Army knife in his luggage, but it had been stolen ten days earlier by the black-shirt troops. Now his only weapon was the sort of parang smelted from natural iron ore that the Iban people use, which had not yet been stained with blood or tree sap. A sampan quickly rowed up from downriver and moored on the riverbank. In the sampan there were four of Dezhong's siblings, including Lachar, who was seventeen, and Fadiya, who was sixteen. After graduating from middle school, Fadiya quit her studies and instead would shuttle her younger siblings to and from school every day. Fadiya—at the banquet, she had made the boy's imagination soar. She had the body and charm of a mature woman, her eyes were like the Rajang River, her smile was like a tropical rainforest, her voice was like astringent fruit, and her skin was like the night. Her fingers were delicate, like her long hair, and her waist was as curvy as her fingers. Her soles were fleshy and her toes were tender. She sat at the front of the sampan and smiled at the boy, then said several sentences in her native language. The boy smiled back but had nothing to say in return. After the two elementary school students got out of the sampan, Fadiya told them a few things and then slowly rowed away. The sampan rounded a bend and proceeded downstream. Fadiya waved and smiled at the boy. Lachar also waved and smiled at him. The boy followed them with his gaze.

By the time Dezhong returned, classes had already started. Dezhong and the boy headed toward the schoolyard. The principal was friends with Dezhong's father, and therefore he received Dezhong and the boy in his office. After classes ended, the principal introduced the school's teachers. The school had four Chinese teachers. The boy decided to fib:

"Following my parents' instructions, I've come to urge my uncle to surrender. My parents are worried that he may be killed by government troops, so if any of you have news about my him. . . ."

"It would indeed be good to surrender, it would be good to surrender," a Chinese teacher in his sixties intoned. "Those who surrender will be forgiven. The government is magnanimous, and would even be willing to advise him on finding new employment. This . . . is very good. This . . . is very good. . . ."

"Yes," a Chinese teacher in his forties said. "Virtually everyone else has already surrendered. . . . Only Yu Jiatong . . . oh, this is difficult. We have seen him, but he. . . ."

"When the Yangtze River Brigade was at its strongest, Yu Jiatong tried to change the Pitka elementary and middle school into a Chinese school, but eventually realized that this wouldn't be possible," the Chinese teacher who had been riding the bicycle said. "He didn't devote himself enough to doing ethnic work. However, he still donated money to the school, so that we might promote Chinese-language education. . . ."

"There was also Communism," a young Chinese teacher in his twenties added. "He gave the school several books by Marx, Lenin, and Mao Zedong. But we didn't dare display them. Besides, what would be the point? How could the students possibly understand these works? . . . "

"The students' Chinese proficiency is such that they have trouble reading even simple children's books."

"Eventually we simply burned the books he gave us."

"After the Communist Party lost power, Yu Jiatong never came around here anymore. . . ."

There was a silence, then the boy asked, "Do you have any leads?"

"Only senior party members know where the base camp of the Yangtze River Brigade is located," the teacher in his sixties said. "You should simply focus on continuing your way upriver. . . ."

The principal invited Dezhong and the boy to eat something before leaving, but first they wandered around the schoolyard, watching the children attend their classes. The sun was not very hot during the monsoon season, and furthermore half of the classrooms were in the shade cast by the trees. A water buffalo was grazing in the playground, and a white butterfly flew into the hallway, then proceeded into a classroom through an open window. When the butterfly reemerged through another window, it appeared full of color, which stimulated the children's imagination. Hanging from the building's eaves, there were several pots of wild orchids with blossoms that resembled butterflies, and when the children were reading aloud, the flower colors would change unpredictably. In the hallway, a troop of ants were carrying the desiccated body of a dead gecko. The gecko was as wrinkled as a dried leaf and had obviously been either crushed or stepped on. The water buffalo was grazing on wild grass outside the hall—and the more it grazed, the more it smelled like musty old books. As animals were roused from their sleep, the sounds of bird calls could be heard everywhere. . . .

The boy heard poems he himself had recited while in elementary school. Without realizing what exactly he was doing, the boy paused outside a classroom and peered inside. It was a sixth-grade Chinese language class, and the teacher who had been riding his bicycle that morning was now standing at a podium in the front of the classroom, earnestly explaining the meaning of some dipper-sized Chinese characters. The teacher would read a character out loud, and then the students would read the same character. The teacher would read a sentence, and the students would read the same sentence. The teacher would write a character, and the students would carefully observe him. The teacher would make a joke, and the students would all laugh. The teacher would wipe his sweat with the back of his hand and adjust his glasses with his index finger, as his pants legs became covered in chalk dust. Is this what Third Brother had been like? After Third Brother graduated from high school, he was assigned to teach in the Daro Chinese elementary school, and Principal Shao regarded him as one of the most outstanding teachers in the school's history. On afternoons when the boy didn't have class, he and Fourth Brother would sometimes climb the tree next to the elementary school and watch Third Brother teach. They would wave at Third Brother, but he would pretend he didn't see them. In the mid-1950s the Daro Chinese elementary school began promoting communist ideology to cultivate a new generation of communists, and this continued until Principal Shao left the school in 1962. Although the government subsequently began to exert tighter control, Third Brother still took the risk of communizing his classroom. From his perch in the tree, the boy had listened as Third Brother taught the children a poem by the jade-faced god of war, claiming that it was by the Han dynasty warrior and poet Cao Cao. At that point, officials from the education department happened to be standing outside the window. Next to the Daro Chinese elementary school there was the Daro English elementary school. The two schools had approximately the same number of students, and their campuses were separated by only a steel fence. Every weekday morning, each school would raise its flag and sing its school song and would compete to see who could sing the loudest. Sometimes one school would be overwhelmed by the other, at which point both schools' principals and teachers would join in. "Our Chinese school is located in Great China, and the source of knowledge is located there. . . ." Students from the two schools would often fight each other. Malays would fight Chinese, but the school principals didn't dare show favoritism, and therefore all the children would be spanked until their butts were black and blue. The Communist Party was like the sun in the sky, and communists were fighting guerilla battles in every town. Daro implemented a curfew, given that people who went out at night risked getting killed. Someone placed a burning torch in front of Daro Chinese elementary school. After Third Brother lost his job, he took several baskets of books and, in 1969, he followed in First and Second Brother's footsteps and joined the Yangtze River Brigade. The formal name of the Yangtze River Brigade was the North Kalimantan People's Army, and that year the troops were becoming popular in the Rajang River watershed. In 1963 Sarawak achieved independence from Britain and joined the Federal Republic of Malaysia. Then in 1965 there was the Indonesian military coup. Sukarno, the pro-communist prime minister, stepped down; Dipa Nusantara Aidit, the leader of the Indonesia Communist Party, died; and Indonesia and Malaysia joined forces to try to annihilate the communists. The two thousand SCP members who had been receiving their military training in Indonesia lost their support, and 1965 they snuck back into Sarawak, where they formed three armed brigades and established a secret base camp in the rainforest, from which they sowed Sarawak with revolutionary seeds of socialism and communism. . . .

After finishing lunch, Dezhong and the boy continued making their way upriver. As they were preparing to leave, the teachers at Pitka elementary and middle school wanted to speak, but they restrained themselves. The school's principal didn't know Chinese, but he had a warm expression. The boy suddenly became somewhat unsettled, because it occurred to him that when his four elder brothers left home to join the communists, they were all roughly the same age as he was now. . . .

As Dezhong and the boy proceeded upriver, the waterway became increasingly narrow, and the branches and leaves on the bank were like a fence that was so dense that even grasshoppers would have had trouble getting through. The branches formed a natural archway over the river. A large beehive was hanging from a tree branch, and the bees were like rolling yellow sand. *Wengweng yingying*—the bees sounded like a small tornado blowing through. On tree branches on both banks, spiders were furiously spinning webs, which made Dezhong and the boy's hair appear to turn gray. As they lifted their oars above their heads, they would cut a line through the webs. The trees were full of bats hanging upside from branches like dried fish or pork. There were green snakes on the green leaves, red snakes on the red leaves, yellow snakes on the yellow leaves, and purple snakes on the purple leaves. The result was like an agate diamond ring. a woman's dimple. a fat prostate gland. The sun searched for them, and they yearned for the sun. The leaves became increasingly withered, and the river became increasingly broad. On the right bank there finally appeared a field and a grove of short trees. There was a rambutan tree with red, furry fruits that looked as though large centipedes were sitting on a tree branch. When they saw the tree, Dezhong and the boy stopped rowing and stood up in the sampan to pick some rambutans. They used their oars to knock some high-hanging fruits down into the sampan, or else used their parangs to chop off an entire branch, and then they sat in the sampan, happily munching until their bellies were extended and the tongues were numb. The rambutan peels were like fireballs, but the fruit itself was as tender as lychees. Old-timers called rambutans "Yang Guifei fruit." In the boy's home, there were several of these trees. The boy's brothers would often climb them, and for every two rambutans they picked, they would eat one and pass the other down to Junyi, saying, "Junyi, Junyi, you should eat more, because that way you may become as beautiful as Yang Guifei. . . ."

This was the first time the boy had ever used a new parang. After a parang is used to chop a tree branch, its wooden handle and sheath usually acquire a smell of wood. Dezhong's blade, however, was different, and when it was removed from its sheath, the boy could immediately smell the stench of death. Dezhong cut branches as easily as slicing someone's finger, and he chopped at the rambutan tree until it screamed abjectly. His parang blade was twenty inches long, and each side had an embossed engraving of a crocodile, while on the back there was an embossed engraving of a beast lying in large waves. On the handle there was a deeply contoured carving of a man's head, and the entire handle was wrapped in long hair—symbolizing a hunter's head. When Dezhong grasped the handle, it was as though he were holding an enemy's head by the hair. This parang was more than two hundred years old, and Dezhong's ancestors had used it to protect their home and decapitate their enemies. During

World War II, Dezhong's grandfather joined the Chinese anti-Japanese volunteer forces and used this blade to decapitate four Japanese soldiers.

The uneaten rambutans were piled up in the sampan like a nest full of chicks that had just begun to spout feathers. Burping periodically, Dezhong and the boy continued rowing upriver. Soon it began to drizzle, followed by bona fide rain. The rain fell hesitantly but persistently. The sampan proceeded in starts and stops, as though brokenhearted. Several times Dezhong and the boy stopped under a tree, but then they felt they were making a fuss over nothing. Blood-sucking leeches were knocked down from the trees by the wind and rain and fell onto them. The boy remembered how it had also been during this sort of storm that Third Brother had bid farewell to the boy and his other brothers (while keeping his parents in the dark). That day the rain kept falling onto the thick lenses of Third Brother's glasses, and he had to keep removing his glasses to wipe them. When bidding farewell to his brothers, Third Brother didn't shed a tear until he got to the boy. The boy sensed that Third Brother was secretly hesitating, just like this rain—but he wasn't sure whether this impression was accurate. Third Brother reminded his two younger brothers that they mustn't follow him. The boy and Fourth Brother melancholically walked along the Rajang River to see Third Brother off— and they continued until a comrade from the Yangtze River Brigade came to meet him. In the boy's tear-filled eyes, Third Brother's skinny, hunchbacked, scholarly figure overlapped with that of a Yangtze River Brigade soldier braving untold dangers, as he became someone lost in the jungle.

The year was 1969, the communist forces were full of spirit, and the rainforest was filled with the sound of gunfire. The Communist Party had three armed divisions, each of which was

composed of six to seven hundred soldiers: the North Kalimantan People's Army, the Flame Mountain Brigade, and the Sarawak People's Guerrillas. The North Kalimantan People's
Army was led by Yu Jiatong, who had assumed command over
the Rajang River watershed, had an outstanding military
record, and was fearsome in combat. Government officials and
journalists often called the force "North Kali," but its formal
name was Yangtze River Brigade. When Yu Jiatong was studying geography in middle school, his left-leaning ethnically Chinese geography teacher would often draw the island of Borneo
in the shape of a begonia blossom, exclaiming, "If Mongolia
hadn't secured independence, look at how similar the territories
of China and Borneo would have been!" The instructor referred
to Sarawak's longest river, the Rajang, as the Yangtze, and to its
second-longest river, the Baram, as the Yellow River. Later,
when Yu Jiatong took control over the Rajang River, the Yangtze River Brigade was born. The Flame Mountain Brigade,
meanwhile, was led by Wang Dada, who assumed command
over an inland region in the second district. The Sarawak People's Guerillas were led by former journalist Huang Wenting,
who assumed command over an inland and coastal area in the
first district. The Sarawak People's Guerillas were also known
as the Little Rhino Brigade, because it was said that the troops
once killed a female rhinoceros, after which her orphaned baby
latched onto the brigade and became its spiritual symbol. The
Yangtze River Brigade troops wore black shirts, and their
emblem was a Chinese dragon. The Flame Mountain Brigade
troops wore green shirts, and their emblem was originally the
Chinese character for "mountain," 山, but later they changed it
to a red flame. The Little Rhino Brigade troops wore brown
shirts, and their emblem was a rhinoceros head. In the forest,
each brigade's shirts provided excellent camouflage.

The day Third Brother reported for duty to the Yangtze River Brigade, he was immediately appointed to the important position of assistant in the headquarters' textual propaganda department. Third Brother ended up composing or transcribing many of the pamphlets and propaganda fliers that circulated throughout Sarawak, and the boy could recognize at a glance his brother's long, thin handwriting. Less than half a year later, however, a Yangtze River Brigade soldier who was working undercover in Daro reported to the Shi family that Third Brother had died. The cause of death was unclear, and the brigade failed to issue a formal written announcement of his death. It turns out, however, that the Little Rhino Brigade did not support the Yangtze River Brigade's and Flame Mountain Brigades' diversionary tactic of using the rainforest as a permanent base area, and instead advocated engaging the government directly. Therefore, the Little Rhino Brigade kidnapped three Yangtze River Brigade cadres—including Shi Shiwen from the textual propaganda department—and demanded that Yu Jiatong either cooperate or surrender half of his weapons. Yu Jiatong, however, merely handed over a few broken pieces of copper and iron, which infuriated Huang Wenting, leading him to execute the three Yangtze River Brigade hostages. As Third Brother was about to be killed, he pleaded with Huang Wenting, saying, "Please don't shoot me in the head, but rather in the heart." Huang said, "Even when facing death, you're still worried about saving face?" Third Brother replied, "My head contains a bit of knowledge, and in the next life I'll still be able to devote it to the Communist Party." Two months later, the Little Rhino Brigade was chased down and defeated by government troops, thereby becoming the first brigade to be completely exterminated.

The drizzle continued, spurring the boy's endless recollections. Suddenly he began to feel somewhat homesick. The drizzle haunted people's spirits like death by a thousand cuts, rather than a clean blow. The boy's body was neither soaking wet nor completely dry, and instead he felt as though he had been licked by a dog. Even when passing through a densely forested area, he could still feel the silent torture of the ubiquitous raindrops. The rambutan tree that Dezhong had had savagely chopped up was shedding tears in the bitter rain. Lachar and Fadiya, to whom they had already bid goodbye, were picking up their younger siblings in the rain. The corpse of the Flame Mountain Brigade soldier, which they had avoided like the plague, was slowly drifting downriver back to the soldier's hometown. The random Yangtze River Brigade troops whom they had passed—and who had either ignored them and had treated them with open hostility—were now sheltering from the rain or else were fleeing for their lives. They were all either killing each other or attacking an imaginary enemy. The rain no longer hesitated, and instead it dispatched a regular army and hurled down knives and axes.

The rain gear the Iban people fashioned for themselves consisted of a cloaklike sheet of plastic, to which they attached a large hat made from bamboo and coconut leaves, known as a *dosa*. An hour later the current increased to the point that it became it impossible for Dezhong and the boy to continue their way upriver. Therefore, they tied the sampan to a tree, bailed out the excess water, then squatted down in the bottom of the boat to watch the rain. By this point the boy's head was soaked in sweat from rowing and his perspiration poured down like rain inside his raingear that was as hot as a steel plate. Meanwhile, the rain itself did not appear to be falling directly down, and instead curtains of water were flying in all directions, to the point that it was impossible to see anything more than two meters away. When the boy looked at the sky he saw it was almost dusk, and therefore he and Dezhong proceeded to erect the only tent Dezhong's family owned, ate a bamboo tube of sticky rice and a couple of bananas, and finally, with bulging bellies, they lay down shoulder to shoulder. Dezhong said, *Shicai, you can sleep without worrying, because, here, my parang is protected by the spirits of my ancestors.* That night, the boy rode a dream beast into the wilderness, searching for the bones of his lost siblings. Whenever he found a bone, he would pick it up with his mouth and deposit it into a sack that was already clattering with others. The dream beast was covered in fur and had a long snout that could suck up the boy's memories, like a mammoth. Fadiya was leaning against the railing of her house's balcony, and a date-red, shriveled-up fighting cock was pecking at her cornlike toenails. The next morning, the rain was coming down even harder, and the waterfall-like current was strong enough to shatter bamboo. Dezhong and the boy dragged the sampan onto the riverbank and flipped it over. Dezhong estimated that the rain would continue for another ten days to half a month, and suggested, "Let's wait three more days." He used his knife to cut down more than a dozen trees with trunks as thick as a man's arm, then leaned them around the tent so that their leaves would shield it. After chopping the nearby vegetation, he was able to clear an activity area. Three days later, they had already eaten most of their provisions, but the rain still showed no sign of subsiding. The river water surged forward, rushing toward the tent, and the ground became covered in a thick layer of water. Dezhong went out to observe the rain, then returned to the tent and said to the boy, "It was for your sake that we left my house at this time. I knew all too well that this was the monsoon season. . . ." The boy closed his eyes and moaned. Dezhong touched his forehead, and said, "Shicai, I think you're getting sick again. How about this: Let's return to my house and stay there for a while, then we can decide what to do next. We can wait for the rain to stop before heading off again. Moreover, since my house is located downriver, you won't even need to row. We can be there in a few of hours."

Bundled up in his hat and rain gear, the boy grasped the side of the boat, his head blank with pain. In a daze he drifted downriver, then climbed onto the riverbank and returned to Dezhong's house, where he lay down again. He kept waking up and falling back asleep. He heard people speaking in a language he couldn't understand. The sound of livestock. Apparitions. The sound of livestock exacerbated the animalistic quality of the boy's dreams, and he began moaning like a mammoth. This, in turn, further reinforced the apparitions' ferocious familiarity, as though he were a sack of bones on the chicken grave. A hand pressed against his forehead—it seemed to be his mother's hand. *Quackquack. Quackquack.* A duck sound . . . Mother. Grasping the hand, the boy opened his eyes and saw Fadiya smiling warmly. On the fifth day at around noon, the boy managed to partially sit up in bed and have a bowl of congee.

"Is it you who's been feeding me these past few days?"

With a smile, Fadiya said something in her native language, and the boy suddenly remembered she didn't know Chinese.

"Thank you." He said in English.

Fadiya's English was not very good either, but she replied awkwardly, "You're welcome."

"And your brother?"

"He's . . . working . . . with Father . . . in the fields . . ."

It was still raining crazily outside, and several sheets of galvanized steel were clanging on the roof as water poured down, completely demolished Fadiya's structurally incomplete language. There was the panicked sound of livestock, and the skulls hanging from the house's eaves emitted a *gelong gelong* sound, like Chinese porcelain. The boy thought he could hear Dezhong and his relatives walking barefoot through the garden that had become a marshland, as the melons and peas growing on the lattice plopped into the water below.

"When will Dezhong return?" The boy asked a rather mundane question.

Fadiya obviously didn't hear him clearly. "You . . . rest . . ."

"I feel much better today." The boy wanted to continue the conversation, and as he slowly ate his congee, he added, "This is very good. Is this rice that you grew yourselves?"

"Rice . . ." Fadiya pondered the English grammar. "Yes, we grow it. Lots of it. Eat."

After nightfall, the boy got out of bed and walked all around the longhouse. Given that the ground outside was covered in knee-deep water, the livestock had been moved inside. A black dog was in lying in the hallway nursing her four pups, her head resting on the ground like a lizard. Cats climbed on beams. Rabbits hid in crevices. Piglets and children climbed over each other. The piglets laughed sharply as the children crawled around searching for food. Chickens were fed and slaughtered. Ducks and geese laid eggs, and hens roosted. "Go back and get some rest." Dezhong suddenly appeared out of nowhere, patted the boy's shoulder, then disappeared again. The boy continued wandering around the house. The floor was covered with gold and silver dishes, together with musical instruments and ritual objects dating from China's Northern and Southern dynasties. Wooden shields. Parangs. Knife sheaths. Wooden paddles. Chinese-themed tattoos. "Every corner of the longhouse is full of China," Dezhong said more than once. "How do you expect me not to read Chinese books?" Everyone in the family gathered in the hallway and ate durians. One man offered the boy half a durian, but the boy waved it away, indicating that he was still recovering from his illness. In the end, however, he couldn't turn the fruit down, and therefore took a bite. Durians . . . when Zheng He embarked on his southern voyages, he stopped twice in Borneo and saw that an epidemic was raging, which he treated with durians. Zheng He named the fruit durians, *liulian*, because when he ate them he "missed," *liulian*, China— which is why Chinese love durians. The boy took a couple more bites, and before he knew it, he had finished them all. He repeatedly walked and paused, lingering in the longhouse. Several hundred kilometers away there was a world-famous grotto created between 450,000 and 500,000 years ago. The grotto's oldest artifacts include some forty-thousand-year-old flint-stone axes, and its youngest include some Tang dynasty coins and pottery. Many of the grotto's other artifacts also had ties to China, including boat coffins engraved with crocodiles or dragon heads, and murals resembling pictographs. At one point, Fadiya appeared in front of the boy and said with a grin, "Hungry? . . . We'll eat soon . . . there is a lot . . . of food . . ." The boy replied, "Thank you." Fadiya added, "I go work . . . busy . . ." With a charming smile, she disappeared again, like a paper kite on a clear day. Cooked rice. Rice grains. The longhouse's method of growing grain had been passed down from the Tang dynasty. Fadiya . . . Why was Fadiya so charming? Black hair, black eyes, and high cheekbones. . . . Like a Chinese . . . a Chinese woman's subtle charm. . . . Peking Man . . . Java Man . . . Our Asian ancestors. Four million years ago *Homo erectus* migrated from Africa to Asia. One million years ago Java Man was active in the Southeast Asian landmass of Sundaland (which extended from what is now the Malay Peninsula to Java, and from Borneo to the Philippines' Palawan Island). Eight hundred years ago Java Man migrated northward and reached southern China, becoming Lantian Man.

Six hundred thousand years ago Lantian Man migrated even further north, eventually becoming Peking Man. Meanwhile, in 1900 various members of the Shi clan migrated south from southern China, and settled in Borneo, thereby returning to the homeland of their Java Man ancestors. . . ."My friend," the Borneo native Zhu Dezhong said in fluent Chinese. He seemed to materialize out of nowhere, giving the boy quite a shock. "You haven't gone back to sleep yet?"

Durian fever. The boy ate too many durians, and that night he ran a high fever. By the next morning, however, the fever had subsided. Following Dezhong's instructions, Fadiya repeatedly entered the boy's room. Her forehead and nose were damp with perspiration, and several strands of her long hair were out of place. A few strands fell onto the boy's bed, and he picked up one of them and sniffed it. Once, when straightening up Fourth Brother's bed, the boy had similarly found dozens of strands of a woman's long hair. When a man and woman share a room for several nights, they may shed enough hair to make a ponytail. This was enough to make the boy daydream furiously. Fourth Brother was fascinated by Chinese martial arts and had borrowed several volumes on boxing and swordplay from Teacher Shao's library—though it was unclear from which master's heretical tradition he had taken inspiration. Fourth Brother hung a couple of sandbags from a rambutan tree and proceeded to pound them with his fists and feet from dawn to dusk. He would also run with iron bars tied to his ankles and would stick his hand into a pan filled with heated rocks. He did the former to practice light martial arts, and the latter to practice the iron palm technique. He would also sit cross-legged and meditate like an old monk while staring at a gas lamp two yards away, or he would place several hundred pieces of paper in a pile and then sit two meters away and count them one by one. The former was to train his gaze, while the latter was to train his eyesight. He would also grasp a sharp blade with his bare hands. In the fruit orchard there was a set of wood planks and wood stumps, and it was said that when Fourth Brother practiced his martial arts, he would often knock down some ripe fruits. The boy didn't know how good Fourth Brother's martial arts training was, but he did know that Fourth Brother was a strong as a tiger and as dexterous as a gibbon. Fourth Brother would frequently compete with monkeys to see who could climb a coconut tree the fastest, and in his school athletics competitions he was always the star. If Fourth Brother heard that any of his schoolmates or fellow Chinese were being bullied by Malays, he would immediately summon his friends to confront the perpetrators. Once more than a dozen Malays armed with clubs and iron rods beat him so savagely that he had to be hospitalized for more than two months. After being released he was determined to seek revenge, and ended up leaving countless bloody handprints throughout the forest.

The year was 1971, and the Yangtze River Brigade repeatedly attacked government troops in the Rajang River watershed. When the boy and Fourth Brother were in the streets, they often saw graffiti with phrases like "Chinese pigs, go back to China!" and would hear people shout "Communist pigs!" in Malay-accented English. When the boy went out, Malays would sometimes follow him. One night, Fourth Brother said, "Little brother, if I stay here, I'll just bring you trouble." Then he packed several tattered martial arts books and some simple luggage and went to the Yangtze River Brigade. By that point Eldest Brother and Third Brother had already been killed in battle. One day Fourth Brother and the rest of the Yangtze River Brigade were ambushed by government troops on the riverbank, and although the other Yangtze Brigade troops were killed on location, Fourth

Brother managed to escape into the rainforest with only minor injuries. One night more than ten days later Fourth Brother, running a high fever, climbed into the boy's bedroom. The boy turned on a flashlight and led his brother to a treehouse he had built in a jackfruit tree. The treehouse was large enough to hold a double bed and had walls, windows, and a tarp. Moreover, it was hidden by the tree leaves and not easy to see from the ground. Government troops frequently came to search the Shi home, and they even searched the barn and the outhouse, but they never noticed the treehouse. The day after Fourth Brother's arrival the boy sent their neighbor Xiaofu to visit him in the treehouse. Xiaofu was Fourth Brother's childhood girlfriend. Although Fourth Brother often claimed that a man who was training in martial arts should avoid women, however he and Xiaofu would often make out in the orchard. The boy took his brother food and water, and Xiaofu would see how he was doing. Three days later, however, Fourth Brother hung a horizontal bar from a tree branch, and that night he pushed away Xiaofu, who was embracing him while asleep, and then, behind the boy's back, he rejoined the Yangtze River Brigade.

Fourth Brother truly had awful luck, and at noon on the day after he left the treehouse, he was again attacked by government troops and was almost captured by three Punan youths who were skilled trackers. He resisted furiously, however, and managed to escape the Punan youths by diving into Rajang River, but as he was entering the water the youths threw a couple of spears, one of which missed him, while the other hit him in the thigh. Fourth Brother entered the water with the spear impaled in his leg, but by the time he emerged he was holding it in his hand. Before he had a chance to throw it, however, the government troops opened fire and wounded his right hand, and he once again dove underwater. Wanting to capture him alive, the government troops kept pursuing him. It was reported that Fourth Brother submerged and reemerged five times, and each time he reemerged he was shot in another noncritical part of his body as the government troops tried to avoid delivering a lethal blow. In the end, however, he succumbed to excessive blood loss and died in the river anyway. Afterward, Xiaofu would often go to the treehouse and sing like a little bird, as though conversing with Fourth Brother's spirit. When she did this, it disturbed the Shi family dog to the point that it would bark furiously at the jackfruit tree.

The boy's journey was delayed by the rain, but Dezhong's family attentively looked after their guest. During his stay, the boy taught Fadiya some Chinese, and in return she taught him how to make wicker baskets. Occasionally the skies would clear up for a while, and the boy would begin to resume his activity after his long rest, but then the rain would start again and continue nonstop for another ten days. The boy wanted to help his hosts with the housework, but they adamantly refused. When the weather cleared up the boy wanted to go hunting with Dezhong's family, but his hosts were even less amenable to this proposition. The house's family dynamics were very complex, but the thirty-odd family members took turns looking after the boy, and he therefore became an expert in the art of drinking rice wine. During the day, however, he often had nothing to do, and would simply shuttle back and forth through the house.

An elephant tusk . . . a curved, gray elephant tusk that was three times as long as the boy's parang was hanging from the wall in the house. More than two centuries earlier, the ancestors of the house's current residents had cut this tusk from the body of a dead bull elephant in a region on the border of Indonesia. When they found the carcass, it was lying on its side in silvergrass grove, and its flesh was already rotting and full of maggots. Several monitor lizards and crows had already consumed so much of the carcass that they could no longer crawl or fly. The elephant had no visible wounds, and it was unclear whether it had succumbed to disease or had died of natural causes. Another tusk had been obtained from an Englishman in exchange for a Mauser rifle. The Iban residents of the longhouse had only seen five or six small herds of elephants, and no one had ever glimpsed the enormous herd that is described in legends. The boy remembered the two times in his dreams that he was rescued by a long trunk. In the interstices of reality and fantasy he heard the galloping sound of the elephant herd and remembered the time he was seven and went with Yu Jiatong to hunt elephants, but missed the opportunity to see the elephant bones. For years afterward the boy remained entranced by elephants and would often go to the library to look up information about them. For instance, he was surprised to learn that elephants, whose life expectancy is comparable to that of humans, also have similar behavior and emotions. Each elephant has a distinctive personality and temperament, they are wise and logical, and they use different calls to communicate with one another. They rescue companions who have fallen into a pit or become sick or injured, and they may even euthanize those companions who were seriously ill. They roam through the wilderness without a fixed home, relying on their discipline and group support. When old elephants leave the herd to live alone, they often became neurotic and aggressive. . . .

When Yu Jiatong was leading the Yangtze River Brigade into battle, he never forgot his earlier love and dreams, nor did he forget that first elephant tusk he never succeeded in capturing. During the initial period after the military brigades were established, and before they began infighting, their leaders would often take their troops to hunt elephants, with their ultimate objective being the legendary enormous elephant herd.

Traversing peaks and fording rivers, they covered all of Sarawak and even repeatedly crossed the border into Indonesia. When hunting elephants, they would often fall into the government troops' fire net. Even when facing a forest of rifles and a torrent of bullets, however, Yu Jiatong made sure to remind his subordinates to conserve their bullets and keep their ears pricked for foraging elephants. Even at the peak of the conflict, from 1970 and 1972, Yu Jiatong and Wang Dada occasionally had time to leave the battle and, surrounded by smoke, were able to discern elephant tracks. After Yu Jiatong tracked down several pairs of tusks, he complained that had it not been for the government troops' obstruction, he might well have already found that legendary enormous elephant herd and solved the centuries-old mystery of its existence. The media dubbed the three communist armed brigades the "elephant-hunting brigades" and suggested that the government troops could simply pursue the elephant herd itself. The Chinese merchants who covertly donated money to the communists expressed considerable dissatisfaction with these developments, remarking, "We originally said we would provide money if you would supply the effort, and in this way we could establish a socialist heaven on behalf of the homeland. Now, however, you're taking money that was earned with sweat and blood and using it for purely hedonistic purposes. In doing this, how are you honoring those comrades who were sacrificed in battle?" Jiatong's response was that of a hunter and a soldier: "We don't have sufficient weapons, and if you don't quickly supply the funds we need, we'll have no choice but to sell elephant tusks to raise money. We're currently balanced on a razor's edge, attempting to extract teeth from a tiger's mouth. As Chairman Mao put it, when the enemy advances, we retreat; when the enemy sets up camp, we harass; when the enemy tires, we attack; and when the enemy retreats, we pursue. We swallow bullets as though eating food, bleed as though pissing urine, and slice our flesh to remove carbuncles as though simply taking a shit—all for the revolution." Initially this dialogue was conducted via secret letters, until the government's arrest operation targeting Chinese merchants was made public, after which news of the "elephant-hunting brigade" spread like wildfire.

Even though the rice wine was fiery hot, the boy had drunk it as though it were well-aged liquor; and even though the food was not very appetizing, he had eaten it as though it were a delicacy. He had already mastered the flute music to the point that he could play it easily, and he had already memorized the lyrics, which were as astringent as bestial grunts. He was shirtless and was wearing a loincloth with a traditional ceremonial costume. On his head he was wearing a bowler hat with a hornbill tail feather stuck in it. Holding a parang, he was learning the welcome guest dance. That night the boy got drunk. He regarded the roasted suckling pig as though it were a young Iban, and he stared as it started dancing. The more he ate the suckling pig, the smaller the pig became, and the eventually the boy said, "The more you dance, the more graceful you become." The boy was drunk for three straight days, and vomited as though he were peeing and shitting.

During the day he didn't have anything to do, and therefore he simply wandered through the longhouse.

"Are those four Japanese-devil heads?"

"Yes, four black ones."

"Why are they black?"

"When we captured them, we didn't have time to return to the longhouse, and if we had taken them with us, they would have stunk and developed maggots. So, we smoked and dried them on location."

"No wonder they have such strange expressions. And those two?"

"Those are Englishmen."

". . .?" The boy uttered a silent interrogative.

"When the British colonized Sarawak in 1841, they formed a field force and used their strong navy to assert their power. My ancestors fought for freedom and dignity, and in the process they chopped off quite a few Englishmen's heads." Dezhong pointed to a long string of heads, and added, "Many of the field troops were Chinese and Malay, and some of their heads are here as well."

"Can't you tell them apart?"

"Sometimes I can and sometimes I can't. The field troops were greedy, and therefore the British used them as human shields. If you notice a greedy expression on one of the faces, that would be one of them."

"Greedy. . . ." The boy murmured. He examined one head after another. "How about this one, which is split into several pieces?"

"During World War II my clanspeople raised elephants. One day one of them led Japanese soldiers to arrest several Chinese anti-Japanese troops who were hiding the longhouse. After a fierce battle the Japanese troops dispersed, and many of my clanspeople were wounded or killed. The elephants were also slaughtered, and only one survived. When our patriarch rode the remaining elephant to execute the informant, the elephant stomped on the informant's head with its front foot."

"And what happened to the elephant?"

"It wept day and night, and several days later it managed to escape its chains and return to the wilderness."

The boy suddenly remembered the baby rhino that had lost its protectors. By now it must have already grown into an adult. Was it still alive?

"There are three main reasons why my clan's resistance efforts failed: first, we were outarmed; second, our clan was dispersed; and third, other clans and outsiders, particularly Malays and Chinese, didn't support us and acted like jackals. In this respect, they were similar to the Communist Party. . . ."

The Communist Party. The boy looked for a head with a "communist expression" . . .

"Compared to the British, who massacred my clan countless times, what does that one accomplishment amount to . . . ?"

Massacre. Great massacres. In 1603 the Spanish massacred more than twenty thousand Chinese on Luzon Island in the Philippines. In 1740 the Dutch massacred more than ten thousand Chinese on the banks of Java's Hongxi River. And who knows how many Chinese died in 1969, in the crackdown following the Kuala Lumpur riots? . . . In 1973, during the season when fruit ripens, wild boars gathered and Dezhong's tribe slaughtered them in large numbers. That night they held a banquet to celebrate their gains and roasted thirty suckling pigs.

"Female (女). The first character in the word 'woman' (女人). Three strokes. Most Chinese characters are pictographic, and this one represents a woman bowing and kneeling. Here are her knees, and here are her hands. Female. You. Woman . . . I. Man. Male (男). Seven strokes. Man labors, plowing the fields. The character for male has 'field' (田) on top, and 'force' (力) on the bottom. I'll teach you how to write your Chinese name. *Fa. Di. Ya.*"—"The character '*di*' (蒂) is difficult to write," Fadiya interjected, furrowing her thick brows. —"You can also leave off the grass radical (艹) on top. Or else use the character '*di*' (娣), which is a homophone. Which do you prefer? Write it with me. Let me hold your hand as you write. Let's write a sentence. Let's make a sentence. *Fadiya . . . is a . . . beautiful . . .*

woman. . . ."—"The word *beautiful* (美麗) . . . is difficult to write."—"The two characters in *beautiful* belong to you." The boy held her hand. His wrist pressed against hers, and her hair tickled his chin. Breathing in unison, they wrote Chinese characters stroke by stroke. Fadiya was almost as tall as the boy, her breasts were like green coconuts, her butt was like a jackfruit, her shoulders were like durians, her lips were like mangosteens, her fingers were like snake gourds, her arms were like tubes of sticky rice, and her legs were like barrels of spicy rice wine. Her ancestors originally circulated through steep mountains and wild fields, carrying parangs with which to chop off their enemies' heads. Legend has it that if a woman's hair was caressed by a pair of hands that had hunted human heads, the hair would become beautiful and luscious. Fadiya's great-great-great-grandmother, great-great-grandmother, and great-grandmother all had beautiful, luscious hair. Fadiya's own hair didn't need to be caressed by a pair of stinking headhunting hands, however, since it lived up to its pedigree and was already sufficiently beautiful and luscious. At the banquet, when she danced the harvest festival dance, Fadiya's blood was full of romance, and when she performed the welcome guest dance it was coquettish and seductive—as though her great-great-great-grandmother, great-great-grandmother, and great-grandmother were all performing a sacrificial head dance.

That night, Dezhong's clan once again performed the welcome guest dance, and the boy once again got drunk. Dezhong sat next to him, taking advantage of the boy's incoherence to offer a gorgeous narration of how his ancestors, more than a century earlier, hunted human heads. Before going out, the headhunters carefully observed many prohibitions. For instance, they couldn't sleep the night before the hunt, to avoid having nightmares. They also regarded bird flights as omens, because it was considered auspicious if birds flew from left to right, but it was considered inauspicious if they flew in the opposite direction and meant that they should postpone the expedition until the next day. Eventually the troops retreated to a longhouse after nightfall and, in front of the sleeping enemy troops, the leader held up a tiny figure made of glutinous rice and broke it in half, shouting, "This is how fragile your necks are!" He then proceeded with the execution, chopping off the enemies' heads as though chopping vegetables. "That pig's head was staring at me! I want to consume its ears, its nose, its eyes. . . ." Afterwards, the warriors lifted the heads in triumph, as the women, heroically and flirtatiously, sang a hero's tribute in the hallway of the longhouse while the warriors appeared intoxicated, lifting their parangs to hack at trees, as though unable to resist the impulse to chop off even more heads. The women picked up the heads, and either one woman would lift a head by herself or several women would lift one head together, and then they would all dance crazily. They punched the heads until the noses were broken and the eyes were crooked, and until the heads were grinning and putrid black blood was dripping out. They tried to feed the heads various delicacies, but as soon as they stuffed the delicacies into the mouths, the food immediately fell out through the open throats. "Was that good? Was that good? If so, then have some more." Ears, noses, and eyes were all stuffed with rice. After they finished, the women placed the heads in the oven, and while the heads were roasting, they sang, "Give me more human heads! Give me more human heads! Stinky and fragrant, beautiful and ugly. For seven days and seven nights, the women ate, drank, pissed and shit. They either opened their boudoirs to entice men to enter, or else they stayed on-site to search for men's love. . . .

Ah, you are visiting our longhouse for the first time,
My beloved!
Let's have a toast.

"I want to eat that pig's head! I want to eat that pig's head. . . ." The boy lurched toward one of the dancing women and fell to her feet. "It's been staring at me all night. . . . I want to eat it whole, bones and all. . . ."

The boy was helped away from the banquet table, then he vomited in the hallway. He lay down on a reed mat and gazed up at Fadiya. He held her wrist with one hand and stroked her hair, face, and neck with the other. He pulled her close and sucked on her forehead, nose, and lips. . . . Fadiya moaned, like a weeping willow licking the river rapids. . . . The boy then pushed her away and vomited over half of the mat. He continued vomiting until dawn, ultimately ejecting the equivalent of an entire pig from his guts. Fadiya watched over him all night. "Fadiya, you're a good girl. . . ." The boy didn't care whether Fadiya could understand him, and instead proceeded to serenade her incoherently. "I've been lazy and glutinous, and have devoured at least ten pigs. . . . I . . . what am I doing? Regardless of whether or not it rains tomorrow, I definitely need to leave. . . . I still have things to do . . . important things. . . . Please tell Dezhong . . . that tomorrow I'm definitely leaving. . . . Fadiya . . . you're a good girl . . . have I been rude to you? . . . When I return, I'll make sure to come and see you . . ."

The rain continued falling on the coconut leaves and salted-wood shingles. *Dididada, dididada,* like a wave continuously striking the shore, like the Rajang River tirelessly flowing from the interior toward the South China Sea, like Mother's monotonous quacking, like the sound of some never-identified animals or objects in the depths of night, or like the never-ending sound of galloping elephants positioned at the interstices of reality and fantasy. . . .

3

The monsoon season finally ended, and in mid-February Dezhong and the boy quickly continued their trip upriver. The further they went, however, the faster the current became. They passed what resembled a centuries-old stone stele standing in the current, a treacherous beach, and a large whirlpool, but the speed of the sampan continued to increase. It was as if all the energy that had been stored up in their bodies over the preceding two months somehow transformed the sampan into a youthful river dolphin. After nightfall, Dezhong and the boy set up camp on the riverbank but remained as lively as fire ants. The moon resembled a marbled slice of meat positioned on a slab of fat, while the sun resembled a sleeping pig lying in a mass of dark clouds and dirty light. Early the next morning Dezhong and the boy continued their way upriver, and it was only after two days and three nights of continuous exertion that they finally began to exhibit the first signs of fatigue. As they were setting up camp on the third evening, the moon was beautiful and charming, and they predicted that the following day the sun would appear slim and flirtatious.

Xixisusu, ziziyaya. Just before Dezhong and the boy were about to go to sleep, they stepped out of their tent with parangs in hand. Outside two men in black shirts were standing beneath a durian tree. The men were holding rifles, and their faces were covered in black dirt, so that only their eyes and mouths were visible.

". . . Shi Shicai? . . . " The shorter of the two men said in non-standard Chinese.

"Yes, that's me." The boy replied.

"You're looking for Commander Yu?"

"Yes," the boy replied. "Yu Jiatong is my uncle. My four elder brothers all joined the Yangtze River Brigade and were heroically sacrificed."

The two men silently looked at the boy, then the shorter one said, "Get your bags and come with us."

"To go where?"

"We're taking you to see Yu Jiatong."

"Who's the aborigine?" The taller man asked.

"He's my classmate. He's attended Chinese schools ever since elementary school, and his Chinese is very fluent," the boy replied. "He lives in Pitka, and we're . . . good friends, and he was taking me to look for my uncle."

"He can't come with us," the shorter man said.

The boy returned to the tent to pack his bags, and as he was leaving, he said to Dezhong, "My friend, if it weren't for you, I'd already be at the bottom of the Rajang River by now. But after escorting someone a thousand *li*, eventually the time will come when it is necessary to bid farewell. You should sleep well tonight and then go back to the longhouse tomorrow morning. . . . When I return, I'll definitely go to the longhouse to see you and your family."

"You should depart soon, so as to return early, safe and sound." Dezhong examined the glass bead and boar-tooth necklace that Fadiya had given the boy, which was now hanging from the boy's neck. It was said that this was a good-luck amulet that Iban women often gave to men before they went to hunt or to battle. "Our good wine and fine food will be waiting for you. My sister will dance to welcome you back."

Some enormous nocturnal animal was hunting for food up in the trees. *Susuchichi.* Branches were broken and leaves were torn, and the animal's prey had already been trapped in the top of the tree.

"Ordinarily, when troops from outside the Yangtze River Brigade are taken to see our leader, they have to be blindfolded," the shorter man said. "However, given that you are the leader's nephew and that your elder brothers made such enormous contributions to the organization, we will therefore treat you with great hospitality."

The two men turned on their flashlights and entered the dark forest, and the boy also turned on his flashlight and followed them. The three of them didn't exchange a single word for the rest of the night. After a while the boy lost his sense of direction, and therefore looked up at the sky to try to find the seven stars in the Big Dipper. Because of his hesitation, the boy fell behind the two black-shirt soldiers. The circuitous path went up and downhill, winding through fields and forests, but the entire night the boy kept his gaze down to watch the path. Even so, he stumbled many times, as the black-shirt soldiers continued forward without ever looking back. In the pitch-dark night the boy's flashlight beam became the only thing he could rely on. The soldiers, on the other hand, knew the path like the back of their hand, and it made no difference to them whether it was day or night. At some points where the path was somewhat more open they would even turn off their flashlights and rely only on the moonlight, like Malaysian black panthers running through bushes, shrubs, or a marsh. Eventually the boy could no longer keep up, and called out several times, "Uncles. . . ." He wandered around lost for more than ten minutes, until eventually he stepped into a mudhole. *Shashasha lalala.* Something was hiding in the bushes. Was it a person, or an animal? At first, the boy thought it was the black-shirt soldiers, so he called out a few times. Then he turned off his flashlight and, holding his breath, stood in the bushes that were almost as tall as he was. The sound finally stopped. Dark clouds covered the moon, and the stars rose and fell, as though a diamond ring had fallen into quicksand. Soon the boy was covered in sweat, and as he wiped his face with his clothing, his jaw rubbed against the ice-cold class beads of his necklace, as though rubbing against Fadiya's pitch-black skin. He fondled the boar's tooth, as though fondling Fadiya's pert nipple. He grasped the knife handle as though grasping his own erection. The parang, invisible in the dark night, was quickly removed from its sheath, and the boy, his heart pounding, listened carefully. There was another sound coming from the bushes to his right. *Shashasha lalala.* The boy turned toward the sound, and it appeared to be some sort of enormous animal that was pressing the silvergrass stems, which made them look like they were cut off in the middle, and was jostling them such that they looked like they were ablaze. *Shashasha lalala.* The animal moved toward the boy's right-hand side. . . . Meanwhile, the boy kept turning in the direction of the sound until he had completed a full 360-degree rotation. Was the animal going in circles around him? . . . The boy grasped his parang with both hands and held it in front of his chest. The ice-cold boar's tooth rubbed against his ribcage, as though Fadiya's fingers were stroking his nose, eyebrows, and forehead. A drop of sweat rolled down his belly and into his navel. *Shashasha lalala.* The animal completed a full loop around the boy, then another half-loop. The boy stared into the bushes and lifted his parang. He could sense the animal's presence, like a prey sensing its predator. . . . Seemingly full of ulterior motives, the animal walked back and forth, left and right, estimating the boy's size. . . . Was this an attack strategy . . . like Fadiya circling the boy while performing the welcome guest dance? . . .

"Hey, what're you doing? Let's go!"

The two black-shirt soldiers finally reappeared, and without waiting for the boy's reaction they immediately turned and walked away. The boy followed them but turned around several times to stare into the bushes. He waited for more than half an hour before returning his parang to its sheath, as Fadiya's image lingered in his mind's eye. The boy's entire body was filled with the memory of her touch—sometimes he caressed her, and other times she caressed him. As soon the morning light first appeared, the two black-shirt soldiers continued forward, their black shirts clearly visible in the dawn light. They seemed to have eyes in the backs of their heads, and no matter how far the boy fell behind, they never once turned around to look for him. A sense of hostility radiated like spider web strands from their buttocks. The boy felt like a prey falling into a trap set by a predator. Occasionally he would deliberately slow down, and after about ten seconds the soldiers would slow down as well. It was as though an endless vine with countless tendrils was constantly monitoring him.

Eventually the three of them sat down on a boulder on the riverbank with several strings of wild rambutans, and then, like macaques, they silently peeled and ate the fruits. The shorter of the two men handed the boy a string of rambutans. By this point the man had already washed the dirt from his face, and the boy realized that it was none other than the Chinese teacher at Pitka elementary and middle school, who had been picking up students on his bicycle. "Oh, it's you. . . ." The boy's mouth was dry, and he noisily ate his rambutans.

The teacher looked at the boy, then returned to his rambutans. After finishing a handful, the soldiers stared at the Rajang River. They remained silent for a long time.

"My name is Mao Guoxiong." The teacher finally looked at the boy. "I taught during the day and fought guerilla battles at night. This is Wu Zhaoping, and we both joined the Yangtze River Brigade in 1963. It has now already been ten years, which makes us the most senior members of the brigade."

"If my eldest brother were still alive, he would be even more senior . . .," the boy said quietly.

"Shi Shinong?. . . ." Ma Guoxiong laughed drily. "That's right, if Shi Shinong were still alive, our Yangtze River Brigade would be even stronger than it is now, and it would still include all of its original leaders. Could we have managed to stay together—the six strongmen? . . . "

At first the boy didn't fully register what the soldier was saying. His mouth full of rambutans, his speech was stilted, like a spaniel. "Six—strong men? You mean that the famous Yangtze River Brigade now only has five soldiers left?"

"Five old and decrepit soldiers—five old crows who have been pursued by government troops to the point that they have nowhere to go." Ma Guoxiong spit a rambutan pit into the river. "Zhaoping, when the Yangtze River Brigade was at its strongest. . . ."

"Sir! Reporting to the brigade leader, sir!" The tall and strong Wu Zhaoping said in standard Chinese. "When the Yangtze River Brigade was at its strongest, it only had seven hundred and sixty-two soldiers, including six hundred and seventy-nine men and eighty-three women. The eldest was fifty-two years old, while the youngest was only sixteen."

"Haha," Ma Guoxiong laughed drily again. "So, now you're also a brave soldier? How many government troops have *you* killed?"

"Sir! Reporting to the brigade leader, sir!" Wu Zhaoping replied, blushing slightly. "I . . . haven't killed a single one. . . ."

"Damn it, you've been following me for ten years, and now it turns out that you haven't managed to kill even a single enemy soldier! You are truly an embarrassment to the Yangtze River Brigade! You're an embarrassment to all Chinese! If my mother, who is now in her seventies, had joined the brigade, I'm certain that countless Malay pigs would already have been slaughtered by her cleaver! . . ."

Wu Zhaoping silently bowed his head.
"Stand up straight and sing! Sing me a song!"
Wu Zhaoping straightened his waist and stood with his legs together. . . .

Arise! Those who don't want to be slaves!
Let our flesh and blood forge our new Great Wall!
As the Chinese people have arrived at their most perilous time.
Everyone is forced to expel his last cry.
Arise! Arise! Arise! Our million hearts beating as one,
Brave the enemy's fire.
March on! March on! March on!

"Dammit, if I'd seen you singing 'March of the Volunteers' like this at the time, I would have immediately sent you over to be chopped up by the government soldiers." Ma Guoxiong spat two more rambutan pits into the river.

Wu Zhaoping stood blankly on the riverbank, with tears in his eyes.

"Shicai," Ma Guoxiong called out tenderly to the boy. "Your fourth brother was killed by government troops. The final time he emerged from the river, he sang this song with his last breath.

Those Malay troops had no idea what he was singing, and they shot up both of his hands."

The boy stopped eating and stared at Ma Guoxiong.

"At the time, Commander Yu and I took more than a dozen troops and hid in the forest. Our opponents had significantly more troops and firepower than we did." Ma Guoxiong indignantly peeled an unripe rambutan. "Our opponents had at least three or four hundred troops and were clustered on both sides of the river. Each of their soldiers was carrying an automatic rifle, a submachine gun, several hand grenades, and a mortar launcher, as two helicopters were hovering over the river. We could only threaten them from the safety of the riverbank, and no one dared to go into the water to rescue your fourth brother. Those blasted snipers humiliated your brother in a hundred different ways. Their bullets rained down on the river's surface like transplanted rice seedlings, though not a single bullet managed to strike your brother's head or heart." Ma Guoxiong chewed on a rambutan with a strange, bitter expression. "All we had were hunting rifles, half of which were jammed and useless. Our soldiers were most adept at hunting boars and bears."

Both men were silent for a while, then the boy asked, "Is Uncle OK?"

"Yes, he's doing well. He's doing very well."

"Both banks of the Rajang River are situated such that we didn't even need to post sentries to guard our camps," Ma Guoxiong murmured. "Chairman Mao said, 'What is lost for a while is the empty city, and what is saved is strength.' Shicai, . . . "

The two men fell silent again, then the boy asked, "So, you're not teaching today?"

"I've resigned. I was previously stationed at the school by the brigade to serve as a lookout. Why would I have stayed?"

"What about the children in the mountains?"

"They can go to hell!" Mao Guoxiong stared at the boy. "Shicai, so you want to convince your uncle to surrender?"

The boy nodded.

"Then let's go." Mao Guoxiong stood up, stretched, and picked up his rifle. "The commander is waiting for you."

Wu Zhaoping led the way, with Ma Guoxiong in the middle, and the boy picking up the rear. The two black-shirt soldiers scurried right and left, increasing their pace to the point that the boy fell further and further behind. Over the course of the night, the boy had nearly mastered the soldiers' marching rhythm, and when he was following them closely he could correctly predict which direction they would go next. Even when he fell so far behind that he completely lost sight of them, he could still sense the sound of human breath behind some grove, under some tree, or next to some boulder. He might go for a full half hour without seeing any trace of the black-shirt soldiers, but he continued confidently, relying on his intuition and subtle clues to stay on the path. Around midday he finally realized why they needed to march so quickly. It turns out that when Fourth Brother was in the treehouse recovering from his illness, he had complained that when Yangtze River Brigade troops were leading the way, they were too hesitant and chose only existing paths, which is why they were always quickly spotted by the government troops.

Fourth Brother made this observation back in 1972, and although at the time the government and the party were still engaged in fierce battle, it was nevertheless rare to find youth like Fourth Brother who are willing to leave home to join the communists. Six to eight years after the Little Rhino Brigade was eliminated, the SCP once again faced a crisis—lacking grain, munitions, and local support. After a prolonged period of combat, the party found itself in a precarious situation in which its very survival was uncertain. Former supporters of the SCP gradually abandoned the party, and the people's strength was completely exhausted. Those who came over were forgiven, and no questions were asked about their past. Malaysia and Indonesia together eliminated the communists, while the Sarawak communists fought among themselves . . . to the point that the party ultimately had no choice but to use the rainforest as a natural shield and fight back against the government troops like a cornered animal. On October 13, 1973, the leader of the Flame Mountain Brigade, Wang Dada, signed a peace agreement with the government, thereby finally bringing to an end the twelve-year armed conflict between the SCP and the government. Wang Dada then ordered the Flame Mountain Brigade troops to lay down their arms and rejoin society. Out of the more than four hundred troops who surrendered, over a hundred were members of the Yangtze River Brigade. Afterward the remaining members of the Yangtze River Brigade either surrendered to the government as well, or else they abandoned the brigade and disappeared into the rainforest. In this way, the once-powerful Yangtze River Brigade effectively ceased to exist.

Dusk. In the glow of the setting sun, the boy arrived at the Yangtze River Brigade's secret base in the rainforest. The pink clouds in the sky resembled fish roe about to hatch, and the rainforest was bathed in the sunset glow to the point that it resembled coral. The mountains resembled nautilus shells, and the rocks resembled colorful conch shells. The grass resembled pottery glaze, the river resembled molten lava, and the jungle resembled a cracked retina. The clouds in the sky facing the setting sun were shaped like whirlpools, like an enormous eyeball that seemed to wake up after they appeared and stared at them like a scorpion. A grandmother's eyeball. The huge award that the government offered for the leader of a destroyed rebel brigade served only to burnish Yu Jiatong's inextinguishable prestige.

*　*　*

In the jungle there was a small, majestic mountain. It rose two hundred meters above sea level, and at its base there was a stream that originated from a mountain lake and emptied into the Rajang River. The sides of the mountain were so steep that not even wild monkeys could scale them. About a hundred meters up there was a tropical rainforest, and although the forest did not appear at all unusual when viewed either from above or from the riverbank below, hidden beneath the leafy canopy there was the famous Yangtze River Brigade base camp. A suspension bridge leading to the mountain was lined with tree branches as thick as a man's leg. The bridge was a hundred meters long and was suspended three meters above the water's surface. One end of the bridge was attached to a tree with a trunk the width of fifteen people. The black-shirt soldiers and the boy went onto the bridge, from which they could see several crocodiles in the river below, and when they arrived a nightingale perched on the bridge suddenly flew away and then alighted on a small bush on the mountainside. The other end of the bridge was attached to a pair of enormous boulders, but if the weight of the people on the bridge exceeded that of the boulders, the entire structure would collapse and bring the boulders down with it. After crossing the bridge, the soldiers and the boy climbed a series of stone steps that had been chiseled by hand out of the mountainside, winding their way through the forest as though they were in the Jiangnan countryside. The forest was the size of about four or five soccer fields and was surrounded by several dozen wooden houses and animal pens. In the center there was an empty plot with two bamboo flagpoles, on which were mounted the five-star flag of the People's Republic of China and the black-dragon pennant of the Yangtze River Brigade. The boy heard the sound of chickens, ducks, and pigs. Two sleepy dogs were lying at the base of the flagpoles, as though loyally guarding the flags. When the dogs saw the boy and the black-shirt soldiers, however, they merely shook their heads and flapped their ears. A flock of pigeons was walking back and forth near the dogs, cooing loudly, *gugululu*. A handful of chopped trees were scattered throughout the area, but most of the large trees had been preserved, to provide cover. The central clearing was dark without a hint of sunlight, and the five-star and black-dragon flags were very humid, resembling a pair of large bats hanging from a branch. On the trees there were several shooting targets and arrow targets. There was a hanging rod tied to the tree, and in a clearing there were several dozen overturned wooden target dummies—some of which were missing hands or feet, some were lying on the ground, some were covered in bird shit, and others were spread-eagled like crucifixes. The branches and leaves were rotten, there were animal droppings everywhere. There were millipedes, snails, ants, aphids running around. This clearing had previously been used by the brigade for its exercises. Ma Guoxiong led the boy to the largest wooden building, which resembled a turtle shell and reminded the boy of Teacher Shao's residence, and said, "Please have a seat in the hallway and wait for a while. The commander may have gone out hunting but should be back shortly." Before leaving, Mao Guoxiong added, "Inside you'll find some tea. Please help yourself." As the boy was entering the hallway, he couldn't resist remarking, "Teacher Ma, you should return to the school and continue teaching." Ma Guoxiong glanced at the boy with a blank look, his lips trembling slightly. Then the two black-shirt soldiers disappeared into the night.

In the hallway there were several benches and a recliner. Hanging from the wall there was a wooden board that appeared to be used as a bulletin board and that had several pins stuck in it. There was also a gas lamp inside the room. The boy walked into the room, and he felt as though he were returning to Teacher Shao's living room. Three of the walls had bookcases, and on the fourth there was a blackboard. Several dilapidated wooden tables and chairs were piled up in the corner of the room. Mounted on the upper corners of the blackboard there was a pair of five-star and black-dragon flags, below which there were three enormous portraits. Several Chinese calligraphy scrolls were hanging from the walls. The boy leafed through some of the books. The same calligraphy, the same books, the same photographs, and the same atmosphere—it was as if Teacher Shao's entire Chinese culture pulpit had been transplanted here! The only difference was that here there were far fewer books, the scrolls and photographs were more indistinct, and the classroom and blackboard were larger than before. The blackboard tray still had chalk and erasers, like before, and although most of the writing on the blackboard had already been erased, the classical phrase "When the angry lion kicks aside a stone, the thirsty stallion can then drink from the spring" was still visible in Teacher Shao's handwriting.

In front of the blackboard there was a large desk with a pile of white paper and two piles of graph paper for practicing Chinese characters—the sheets in one pile were already filled, while those in the other were still blank. There was also a cup of pencils, a pile of months-old Chinese and English newspapers, several Chinese books, an ink stone, and a gas lamp. In the left-hand corner of the desk there was a pair of elephant tusks, beneath which there was a black-and-white photograph of Yu Jiatong holding a rifle on his shoulder, with one hand on his waist and one foot resting on the rump of a recently killed bull elephant, as though he had already walked through the indefatigable Borneo rivers and mountains. Written in small Chinese characters on the back of the photograph there was the line: "July 18, 1971, at 3:11 in the afternoon, at the headwaters of the Rajang River, on the border of Sarawak and Indonesia, I successfully hunted my first pair of elephant tusks. Isn't this delightful?"

In the dark of night, the hands of the clock on the wall indicated that it was 7:50. The boy lengthened the wick of the gas lamp. In the flickering light landscape paintings, Chinese characters, and portraits all around him appeared either hazy or clear, either skinny or fat, either blushing or jaundiced. Books of different heights and thicknesses were piled up everywhere, like a Great Wall covered in blood-written Chinese characters. Several geckos used their thin bodies to create different sorts of calligraphic pictographs on the blackboard while producing a *xix-isusu* rubbing sound. Swarms of moths, termites, and mosquitoes flew into the lamp's glass lamp shade, and as they did so they either made a *dingdingding* sound or else they produced no sound at all—resembling either a thunderbolt or a beautiful woman's cosmetics. The boy put down his bags and his parang, reverting to his appearance as a student. He observed and walked around the room. A strange bird call sliced through the night sky like an ax chopping wood, and there were also numerous sharp, clear monkey cries, like the sound of a finger flute cutting through the bushes. The sound of the boy's footsteps produced a melancholic feeling.

Like the elephant from his dreams, a large, burly being suddenly appeared before the boy's eyes, so close that he felt as though he were pressed against Fadiya's bosom. The boy instinctively stepped back and looked up, and he saw that this large, burly being was actually an enormous landscape painting. In the center of the painting's cloud-covered mountains there was a herd of peaked, rugged, and cascading elephants walking through clouds of yellow dust that extended for who knows how many miles. The elephants looked up and pressed toward the boy. There was a path to a temple, and in the trees and streams there might or might not be some embellishments. Next to the painting there was a line of calligraphy the boy had never noticed before, which recorded the final lines of the poem "Snowscape, to the tune of Spring Garden Show" by the jade-faced god of war. The boy instantly recognized that this inscription was written in Teacher Shao's handwriting:

This land, so rich in beauty
Has made countless heroes bow in homage.
Alas, Qin Shihuang and Han Wudi
Were lacking in literary grace;
Tang Taizong and Song Taizu
Had little poetry in their souls;
And Genghis Khan, Proud Son of Heaven of his age,
Knew only shooting eagles, bow outstretched.
All are past and gone!
For truly great men,
Look at this age alone.

A series of *honghonghong honghonghong* sounds were shaking the entire mountain forest. The boy guessed that these must be the mating calls of the crocodiles in the river. The gas lamp dimmed, and outside the window the wind began to pick up, blowing so hard that the room's hanging scrolls made a *geleigelei* rattling sound, and Teacher Shao's ink-filled handwriting suddenly began to resemble the row of black skulls in the hallway.

A dog barked half-heartedly a few times. Was someone coming? The boy went over to look out the window and saw that there was no one there, only dogs. Two dogs were walking down the hallway, then lay down near the doorway. In the forest's darkness the other wooden buildings resembled a group of female tortoises weeping and laying eggs on a beach. The boy didn't know where the two black-shirt soldiers had gone, since the entire base area had only that single gas lamp on the table for illumination. The boy sat at the table and looked around the room. Eventually his gaze came to rest on the scroll hanging from the wall, and he suddenly straightened his back in surprise. Upon seeing the scroll from a distance, he realized that what he had previously assumed was a series of ridges was actually a single mountain, and the clouds covering the peaks made the mountain appear as though it had been sliced into several dozen fragments. No wonder he had felt oppressed and suffocated! At this point the cliffs that had been hidden in the clouds began to come into view, like a female elephant standing alone in a wasteland quietly gazing down at the boy at her feet. The boy remembered having seen this intimidating landscape painting on Teacher Shao's lecture podium, and although after twelve years the boy's recollection of Teacher Shao's face and features had grown hazy, he nevertheless still remembered Teacher Shao's lectures very clearly. Now he felt as though Teacher Shao's raised hand, large body, and standard Chinese enunciation were positioned right in front of him.

"China was originally an agrarian nation, and even today it still retains strong and resilient emotional ties to the earth and to the landscape. During the Wei, Jin, and Northern and Southern Dynasties, mountain forest literature was promoted. This is why Chinese artists have long been partial to landscape paintings, which developed into a self-contained landscape painting tradition within global art history." From the

Five Dynasties' Jing Hao, Guan Tong, Dong Yuan, and Juran to the Qing dynasty's Wang Shimin, Wang Jian, Wang Hui, Wang Yuanqi, Wu Li, and Yun Shouping, Teacher Shao introduced numerous giants of ancient Chinese landscape painting. He discussed each of the artists in detail, from their biographies to their artistic style. He picked up a piece of chalk and demonstrated several different painting styles on the blackboard, such as raindrop strokes, ox-hair strokes, skull strokes, cirrus-cloud strokes, and so forth—they all materialized under Teacher Shao's hand as though they were the real thing. Like chickens pecking for rice, the students made a *zizisusu* rustling sound with their pens as they recorded every last detail of the lecture in their notebooks. Whenever Teacher Shao reached a new master, he would pull out a replica or imitation of a painting by the artist in question and hang it in front of the blackboard. The students would then immediately stop writing and join Teacher Shao in his appreciation of the work, emitting gasps of admiration that may or may not have indicated that they actually understood the work in question, but they were nevertheless very sincere. Eventually Teacher Shao earnestly hung up a landscape painting that lacked a signature, and instead merely had the words "Landscape of Wind and Rain" inscribed in the upper right-hand corner. Before lecturing about the painting he asked the students to quietly appreciate the work. It turned out that this landscape painting was precisely the one that the boy was now observing in the light from the gas lamp.

"Think carefully, whose work do you suppose this is?" Teacher Shao had said.

The students fell into deep contemplation. Some leafed through their notebooks, attempting to deduce the identity of the great master from his style or technique. A string of artists' names rattled off their lips.

"You're all just guessing. You're simply guessing!" Teacher Shao exclaimed. "Although you won't be able to guess the artist, at least you should be able to determine the dynasty in which the work was produced."

The students rattled off the names of several dynasties from the Five Dynasties period up through the Ming and Qing.

"That's nonsense, utter nonsense." Teacher Shao's smile vanished. "Actually, it's no surprise that you don't know. This is by the Southern Song artist Wu Jian. He specialized in landscape paintings, but often didn't sign his works. Therefore, although he produced many paintings, he is not very well known today, and many art histories don't even mention him at all. This *Landscape of Wind and Rain* is a one of our Shao family heirlooms, and after having been inspected by numerous experts it has been confirmed to be an authentic work by Wu Jian. I brought more than ten landscape masterpieces with me from China when I came here, but I donated all the rest to help establish a newspaper, pay for education, and contribute to the party. The only one left was this *Landscape of Wind and Rain*, because I couldn't bear to part with it. Every time I see it, I'm reminded of our homeland's magnificent scenery. . . . I will give this painting to whichever one of you achieves the most success in the future."

Everyone gazed quietly at Yu Jiatong. Finally, one student raised his hand and asked, "Teacher, how does one distinguish between authentic works and forgeries?" Teacher Shao replied, "It's not as difficult as you might think. Apart from issues of technique, the most important criteria are one's own individual aesthetics and cultural cultivation. . . ." Using *Landscape of Wind and Rain* as an example, Teacher Shao then launched into a detailed discussion of several important factors that one should consider when attempting to differentiate between authentic works and forgeries.

One of the dogs in the hallway suddenly stood up and barked several times into the dark night, while the other merely lifted its head and looked outside without getting up. Eventually the dog that had stood up lay down again, while the one that was still lying down leaped to its feet and ran down the hallway and into the night. Standing in front of the window, the boy turned on his flashlight and aimed it outside. Instantly, the second dog returned to the hallway and lay down next to its companion, then began scratch the wooden floor with its claws, making a metallic rasping sound. The boy turned off the flashlight and sat back down at the desk.

Teacher Shao was a mysterious character of indeterminate age. He had attended college in the Chinese homeland, then worked as a reporter and editor at two different newspapers. In the early 1940s he moved south with a group of other leftist intellectuals and shifted his attention to South Seas education and media, advocating the Red Communist ideology that was gaining popularity at the time. In *Labor Daily*—a newspaper published in the Sarawak capital, which received financial support from ethnically Chinese businessmen—he promoted nationalist and anti-Japanese movements. However, an increasingly obvious leftist slant in his coverage eventually resulted in his being driven out of the press, after which he established a Chinese elementary school in the town of Daro, on the banks of the Rajang River. In 1962 he was arrested by the colonial government and was repatriated to China on charges of promoting communist toxins and attempting to overthrow the local government. In 1964 he snuck back to Sarawak and advised members of the SCP to establish armed brigades. It was said that after the creation of the three brigades, Teacher Shao became the brigades' first general commander. In 1968, after his health had begun to deteriorate, he snuck back to China, where he used his status as the chairman of the Central Committee of the SCP to direct the revolution remotely from Beijing. It was said that the authorities in Beijing thought very highly of him, calling him a "great overseas Chinese Communist Party comrade and fellow soldier." When Wang Dada and the government signed their peace agreement, Teacher Shao published an anguished critique from Beijing, calling Wang Dada a traitor and an opportunist, while at the same time praising Yu Jiatong's loyalty and his refusal to compromise, together with his efforts to preserve the People's last revolutionary fortress.

The boy read in the newspapers how, after surrendering, Wang Dada had appeared in a variety of public settings. In these public appearances Wang Dada was always glamorously dressed and chatting happily, and you would never have guessed that he had once been a revolutionary who had spent twelve years in the rainforest and on the battlefield. When reporters asked him whether he had any opinion about Teacher Shao's critiques, Wang Dada initially tried to avoid the question, but eventually he became angry and—with the sort of cold expression that he had previously used when breaking the legs of coucal hatchlings—retorted, "That old man is certainly living it up in Beijing. What right does he have to criticize us!"

Landscape of Wind and Rain was filled with driving rain, which appeared both near and far, and it bore the dark and calming glow from the gas lamp located outside the scroll. This seemed to be an elusive landscape. Confused, the boy felt he was seeing someone using a pen to draw directly on a mountain cliff, using skull strokes to transform the cliff into something extraordinarily delicate. There were holes everywhere, like a pile of skulls in the middle of a field of rubble, offering a distant echo of Teacher Shao's writing. . . .

The boy glanced at a small clock. It was 9:20. The two dogs were neglecting their duty and had fallen asleep in the doorway.

As the boy's belly was rumbling with hunger, the original two black-shirt soldiers appeared outside the hallway, each of them holding a flashlight.

"The commander hasn't returned yet?" Ma Guoxiong shouted into the room.

The boy went out into the hallway.

"Don't worry, just wait a little longer," Ma Guoxiong said. "We've already hunted and consumed all the wild game in this immediate area, so this time the commander may have had to go further away to find more. Are you hungry?"

The boy nodded, so Ma Guoxiong handed him a tin box containing some cooked rice and meat. "This is monkey meat. It'll do. Go ahead and eat."

The boy accepted the box and said thank you.

"Next to the blackboard there is a door that goes to the commander's bedroom, where there is a bed and water for tea. If you get tired, you can go lie down for a while. The commander might not return before dawn." After Ma Guoxiong said this, he and Wu Zhaoping turned to leave, saying, "Don't worry, it's very safe here."

"Where are the two uncles going?"

In the darkness, Ma Guoxiong laughed several times. "We live at the base of the mountain. The commander doesn't let us to stay up here."

The boy sat down on a bench in the hallway and wolfed down his food. Then he took the lamp and went into the bedroom, poured some cold water from a kettle into a tin cup, and proceeded to take several gulps. In the bedroom there was a bed with a bamboo mat, a wooden table, and a wooden chair. On the table there was a kettle, a hot water thermos, a tin cup, and a plastic cup. The wall next to the table had a window, and on two of the room's remaining three walls there were maps of both Borneo and China. In the Sarawak section in the northwestern corner of the Borneo map, a red crayon had been used to draw a series of dotted lines, wavy lines, arrows, stars, and triangles, most of which were concentrated near the Rajang River watershed. Each of the maps was so large that it covered virtually the entire wall. Meanwhile, the fourth wall contained a large grid, in which a calligraphic brush had been used to write the jade-faced god of war's "Ten key principles of military strategy." This grid covered three-fourths of the entire wall, with each square on the grid containing one character. Next to this text there was another poem by the jade-faced god of war. The poem was about plum blossoms and was titled "In Memory of Comrade Aidit, an International Communist Fighter." It read:

> Sparse branches stood in front of my windows in winter,
> Smiling before hundreds of flowers
> Regretfully those smiles withered when spring came
> There is no need to grieve over the withered
> To each flower there is a season to wither, as well as a season
> to blossom
> There will be more flowers in the coming year.

This poem was also composed with one character per square. The principles of military strategy were written neatly, and the plum poem was written simply, and neither of them appeared to be in Teacher Shao's handwriting. Up to that point the boy had been traveling day and night, and before he had finished reading the first three principles of military strategy he suddenly found himself yawning nonstop. Therefore, he extinguished the lamp and went to sleep.

The boy woke up in the middle of the night and hazily saw someone sitting in the chair. The visitor was smoking, and the red tip of the cigarette resembled a red agate. When the visitor sucked vigorously on the cigarette, the glow from the cigarette illuminated a face that appeared deeply contemplative. "Uncle, is that you? . . . " The boy asked hesitantly. The visitor's face remained hidden in the darkness. Without realizing it the boy inhaled smoke, making his throat itch and his eyes burn. Just as it was about to get out of bed, a hand gently pushed him back down. "Go back to sleep. We can talk tomorrow." As the boy was falling back asleep, he was unsure whether that hand was still pressing against his chest or whether the visitor had already left. He woke up the next morning at 7:00, and in the hallway he saw Uncle Yu Jiatong feeding the chickens and ducks.

Shirtless and wearing a pair of black pants, Yu Jiatong had just poured two buckets of dead fish into the chicken and duck pens. There were about a hundred chickens and fifty or sixty ducks. Their feathers were filthy and saggy, and many of them had bare thighs and butts, while the feathers on their abdomens and necks were very sparse, and the flesh on their butts was as warped as a rotten watermelon. The boy walked silently over to his uncle, who was using a wooden rod to mix water cabbage, water spinach, vegetable ferns, wild fruits, and dead fish. His uncle then poured the mixture into the pig trough, and more than a dozen large and small pigs immediately buried their snouts in the trough and began eating. Yu Jiatong was still as strong and burly as before, and apart from the fact that his hair was somewhat longer, his skin was slightly darker, his back had numerous scars, and he now had a mysterious long, thin red pepper-shaped scar on his chin, in general he looked just as he did twelve years earlier, when he was still in his thirties. He had thick eyebrows and large eyes, full lips and an aquiline nose, though his chin and cheeks were now covered in stubble. The boy felt an ineffable sense of complexity and melancholia.

"Did you sleep well?" Yu Jiatong was holding a bamboo basket containing four chickens and four ducks.

"Yes. . . ." The boy relied.

"You've grown," Yu Jiatong examined the boy from head to toe. "Soon you'll be as tall as me."

The boy . . . stared at the veins on his uncle's wrist, which resembled the embossed carvings on a parang handle.

"Are you hungry? Breakfast will be ready in a moment."

Holding his basket in front of his chest, Yu Jiatong headed toward the suspension bridge. The boy followed him and saw that his back appeared to be composed of the sorts of large stones that create whirlpools in the Rajang River. The boy remembered the time he had run a high fever and his uncle had carried him on his shoulders through endless mountains and rivers. At the time Yu Jiatong's pace had been steadier and faster than the others, while the boy kept dreaming, like the noisy chickens and ducks his uncle was now carrying. The boy followed his uncle down the steps, while beneath his feet there appeared a deep cliff. It was as if his uncle were once again carrying the boy on his back. The boy remembered a story his uncle once told him about a young plant growing parasitically on a hundred-year-old tree, and how a century later the younger plant absorbed and cut off the tree's nutrients, thereby becoming a hundred-year-old tree in its own right, while the original tree ultimately withered and died. When Yu Jiatong was young, he could never bear to leave his maternal grandfather, and one day he asked his grandfather to carry him on his back, but his grandfather unexpectedly fell downstairs and proceeded to play dead. Yu Jiatong's grandmother assumed that her husband had really died and proceeded to box Yu Jiatong's ears. After growing up, Yu Jiatong often remembered his father with his atrophied crotch area and felt as though his own muscular abdomen and limp member were being painfully crushed by his father's skeleton.

Yu Jiatong placed the basket in the middle of the suspension bridge, then removed two of the hens and tossed them into the river below. The hens squawked desperately and flapped their wings as they bobbed up and down in the water. Suddenly five or six crocodiles approached from all directions, and as they faced the hens they opened their mouths almost simultaneously. Yu Jiatong tossed down the other two hens, followed by all four of the ducks. More than ten crocodiles gathered in the river below, their bellies like deep gullies, their snouts like quicksand, and their claws like undercurrents. The water plumes and splashing sounds they produced gave the boy a sensation of having pins and needles. Each time Yu Jiatong tossed down a bird, it was as though he were tossing a grenade. The four ducks attempted to escape and walked on the crocodiles' heads and backs, then they spread their wings and attempted to fly to shore. Before they were able to reach the shore, however, they were devoured by the crocodiles. The reptiles lingered beneath the bridge, unwilling to leave. With their tiny eyes like secret darts, they stared up at Yu Jiatong and the boy on the bridge. Yu Jiatong waved his hands in a show of strength, appearing to toss something down, and the crocodiles immediately rolled over as though struck by a cannonball. One salt-water crocodile was mistaken for food and was chased away by several of the others.

"These bastards are used to us feeding them, and therefore they simply loiter here and refuse to leave," Yu Jiatong mumbled.

The boy glanced at his uncle. After a long pause, Yu Jiatong waved and said, "Let's throw Wang Dada into the river. . . . Let's throw Huang Wenting, who executed Shiwen. . . . Let's throw the government soldiers who killed your brothers. . . . Let's fucking throw them all into the river. . . ."

Like a mob, the crocodiles used overwhelming force. The boy felt bitter and excited as tears appeared in his eyes. He turned to peek at his uncle, and a long-suppressed idea slowly emerged. It hesitantly formed a fork, like a snake hissing.

"Shicai, let's go get some breakfast."

They went into one of the wooden buildings in the forest. This building also contained a small hallway, and inside there was a wooden table and several chairs. On the table there was a pot of hot congee and a cup of chopsticks. Yu Jiatong said, "Ling Qiao, please bring out the food." A woman not yet in her thirties walked through the door on the left-hand side of the room. She had long hair, was wearing a black shirt, and was holding a plastic tray containing several dishes in tin pots.

"This is Comrade Ling Qiao. She's been with us for eight years and is our brigade's heroine." Yu Jiatong wiped his face with a wet towel and spit out a globule of sputum. "This is my nephew Shi Shicai, son of the Shi clan, which has sacrificed so much on behalf of the party." With a smile, the woman placed the food on the table. "I've heard a lot about you from the commander and from your brothers. It is indeed true that you are handsome. We are out here in the wasteland, so I'm afraid all we can offer you is bitter tea and thin gruel." The boy replied casually, "Don't mention it. . . ." Yu Jiatong gestured for the boy to sit down. "My nephew is not very comfortable with women. Ling Qiao, you can go do your thing. Shicai has just arrived, so why don't you slaughter a pig, and tonight we can arrange some festivities for him." The woman indicated her agreement, then disappeared through a doorway.

Yu Jiatong went through the same doorway. There was a *hua-lala* sound, as if he were peeing. The boy heard the woman laugh and say something in a low voice, followed by sounds of rustling and grunting. When Yu Jiatong reemerged he had a foreign-brand cigarette dangling from his mouth, and he proceeded to sit down in a chair. "Do you smoke?" He offered the boy a cigarette. The boy accepted the cigarette and lit it by holding it up to his uncle's. Yu Jiaong then served some congee in a tin bowl and used bamboo chopsticks to serve some vegetables and proceeded to eat noisily. "This is venison, and this is carp. These two wild flavors can keep me satisfied all night. We have more than ten fish, so eat as much as you want. The rice was planted by the earlier regiment. It is tasty and crisp, and it was grown from revolutionary seeds. At the base of the mountain there used to be a field, and one season's rice harvest was enough to last the entire town of Daro for three months. Is my elder sister doing all right?"

"She's doing all right," the boy replied.

"Is she still raising chickens and ducks?"

"More than ever. . . ."

"That was back when the Yangtze River Brigade enjoyed the people's greatest support. People would donate rice and wine, cigarettes and oil. They would also send their sons and daughters to contribute to the revolution. How is my brother-in-law doing?"

"The same as always. . . ."

"Does he still gamble?"

"More than ever. . . . He is infamous in Daro for his gambling. . . ."

"Has he brought my sister any trouble?"

"It's all right. I think he recently won some money."

"After the revolution succeeds I'll have gambling legalized, and we'll then open an international-style casino in the rainforest. That way your father can come and manage it."

"Isn't gambling a product of capitalist society?"

"Times have changed. I used to tell people that the object of revolution is to make things new. At that time, when I walked along the banks of the Rajang River, people treated me like an emperor and viewed my brigade as though it were the imperial army. Whenever we reached a new town, people would fete us with good food. Newspapers reported that the Yangtze River Brigade was the 'underground government' of the Rajang riverbank. 'Underground government?' That sounds awful! Our troops are the people's nanny, and whenever the people encounter any difficulty, they simply need to go to the Yangtze River Brigade for help, and everything will be resolved. Why have you come?"

"I came to see you. . . ."

People treat me like an emperor? Our troops are the people's nanny? . . . Did uncle really just say these things? . . .

Yu Jiatong fell silent. After a while he asked, "Would you like to join the Yangtze River Brigade?"

"I . . . I don't have the guts. . . ."

"Oh, so you must be the least brave of the five Shi brothers." Yu Jiatong wiped the corners of his mouth with the back of his hand. "Shicai, don't be in a hurry to leave. Why don't you stay here for a few more days? I have to go check the traps I set yesterday, and while I'm out I'll collect some more wild food. I won't be back until evening, but you can look around here while I'm away. There are several books in the room where you slept last night. Just don't go down the mountain. At noon Ling Qiao will bring you some lunch. I know you must have many questions, and at tonight's welcome dinner we can discuss things further."

Yu Jiatong went into the house, and when he reemerged he was wearing a black shirt and a straw hat. He was holding a rifle and had a parang and a water bottle hanging from his waist.

Zizizaza, he stepped on the old branches and decayed leaves in the courtyard, then disappeared down the stone steps leading to the suspension bridge. The power of his stride, the dexterity of his movements, and the intelligence of his gaze—all of this gave the boy a sense of mixed feelings, and when that thought emerged, the sense of bifurcation was even more prominent than before. The boy sat motionless in the chair and didn't leave until Ling Qiao came to collect his bowl and chopsticks. The two dogs were once again under the flagpole, guarding the flag. Both flags were covered in dew, and occasionally would flap in the wind, as though the dogs sleeping at the base of the flagpole were sticking out their tongues. A small woodpecker was energetically pecking at the flagpole, seeking insects that existed only in its imagination—like Yu Jiatong pursuing the animals that had fallen into his traps and the enemies who were watching vigilantly in the dark. Wild pigeons flew back and forth—when they were in motion they had a paperlike texture, and when they were still, they were as immobile as pieces of wood. The rings on the wooden stake and the arrow marks on the target formed an interesting contrast, as though guns were being fired back in time at the tree's swaddling age. A board nailed to the tree was inscribed with a variety of different slogans, including: "A decapitation produces only a bowl-sized scar," "Don't fight battles for which you are unprepared, and don't fight battles over which you don't have mastery," "We can grasp the moon in the ninth heaven, and seize turtles swimming through the five seas," and "Women hold up half the sky." A seasonal northwestern wind blew over, rustling the tree leaves and rattling the tree branches. A group of trees were growing on a mound. The boy went back inside, and holding his scabbard, he went to look for Ling Qiao.

Ling Qiao was hanging some clothes out to dry, and when she saw the boy walking toward her holding his scabbard, she momentarily felt as though she were seeing the boy's brother Shi-shu. She stared at the boy's muscular body. The boy walked over but didn't see her, whereupon she realized she was wearing all black, leaving her perfectly camouflaged while standing amidst the soldiers' black shirts that had been hung out to dry. Just as she was about to pick up the steel bucket and depart, she heard the boy's hesitant voice behind her.

"I want to do some actual work . . .," he said. "All I've able to do here is eat and sleep . . . I'm bored to death. . . ."

"You look like you're about to kill someone," Ling Qiao replied. "There are many books in the library. The commander says you like to read."

"I'm not . . . I'm not in the mood. . . ." The boy waved the hand with which he was holding his scabbard. "Hauling water . . . chopping wood . . . cutting grass . . . I like doing all sorts of hard work."

The boy spent the rest of the morning chopping a couple of piles of lumber the size of small mountains. He also chopped down a tree with a trunk the size of a man's waist, then used his parang to trim the small branches and green leaves. He performed these tasks under the hot sun as sweat poured down like rain, leaving his pants and shirt completely soaked. His body became covered in sawdust and tree sap, and as while eating lunch he noticed a strong smell of mud. In the afternoon he used a nail rake to rake up the old branches, decayed leaves, and over-turned wooden dummies in the courtyard, then burned them, such that the smoke made many insects fall from the tree. He used his parang to cut down all the weeds he could find and to chop up all the wood for lumber. The parang's new blade was difficult to handle, and he developed several blisters in his palms. The handle became increasingly slick, but the more he used it the more adept he became. The knife became covered in tree sap and grass residue, becoming as fragrant as sugarcane. The boy rinsed the parang with water. The back of the knife was dark green, and the blade was silver, like a fast-swimming ribbon fish, or as though a secret he had been holding in his heart had just been forged. In the evening he removed his shirt, and with the parang hanging from his belt he helped Ling Qiao feed the animals.

"If there are so many chickens, ducks, and pigs, then why does Uncle . . . have to go hunting every day?"

Ling Qiao's nostrils flared slightly. "The chickens and ducks are not for human consumption. They are reserved for feeding the crocodiles. The same is true of the pigs. It was not easy for you to visit us, which is the only reason we are now slaughtering a pig. We don't have as many chickens and ducks now, but in the past the commander would feed the crocodiles more than a dozen chickens and ducks, and one or two pigs, every day."

". . . The crocodiles eat more than the humans? . . ."

Ling Qiao's face and palms were the color of old leaves, but her feet were as slick as the fleshy inside of a rambutan. The boy stared at Ling Qiao's feet as Yu Jiatong came toward the animal pen, carrying his rifle and several fish and small animals. The boy pressed down on the parang blade with his hand.

4

The boy was twelve. He was sitting under the jackfruit tree observing his deranged father locked in the animal shed. After more than ten years of ingesting nutrients from livestock manure, human feces, and the carcasses of wild animals decaying at the bottom of lakes and wells, the jackfruit tree had grown to the point that its roots now covered the bottom of the lake and the sides of the well, its trunk was now as wide as a truck tire, its leaves were as large as the ears of African elephants, and its fruits ranged in size from small olives to the sandbags that Fourth Brother used to hang from the tree. Rain or shine, several thousand branches were always open like umbrellas, leaving the shaded area under the tree cool, dry, and mysterious, like a separate universe. The only illumination came from a few mushrooms, which resembled Grandfather's eyes whenever his opium cravings started acting up. The boy would occasionally climb the jackfruit tree, part the leaves that were growing tightly together like fish scales, bristles, and gills, and then gaze out at the rainforest, the bushes, and the silvergrass grove. He would listen to the coucals' love-filled songs and wait until they were outnumbered by the roars of crocodiles in the river. From his youth, he remembered the sound of elephants galloping through the interstices of reality and imagination.

Every hour or two, Father's cries would emanate from the shed, attracting the attention of some rural children walking along the road on the other side of the chain-link fence. The children climbed the fence and gathered around to peer into the shed. At this point Father was wearing only a tank top and shorts, and he alternated between sitting up, lying on the ground, and peeking out through the cracks in the shed wall. Initially the children were careful to maintain a safe distance, but eventually they scaled the wall to peer directly into the shed. They thought they saw something inside. Was it a great ape? A Malaysian sun bear? A Malaysian boar? A mountain lion? The children made strange sounds as they poked bamboo poles through the cracks in the shed wall. The next time they came, they brought slingshots and water guns. There were several hundred fruit bats hidden in the jackfruit tree, so the children tossed various objects into the tree to dislodge them, and as the bats were flying away the children waved the bamboo pole through the air to knock them to the ground. There were also many centipede and scorpion nests around the shed, so the children tied a rope to the end of a pole and used it to sweep up the bats, centipedes, and scorpions, and then inserted the pole into the shed, dangling the insects as bait for the bats. A bat flew in, but just as it was about to hang from one of the rafters, the children swatted it down. Father was squatting in the middle of the shed, cradling his head in his hands, his sobs sometimes resembling a nun chanting sutras, and sometimes resembling a lion roaring furiously. The children played to their hearts' content while Father resembled a shooting target, offering them no resistance whatsoever. Periodically he would lift his head and gaze straight ahead, like a tortoise peeking out from its shell. In his delirium, Father was probably struck in the head by the pole more than a dozen times, and although he didn't dare resist, his cries clearly revealed his anger, like an old lion struck by lightning. Actually, the children weren't really trying to hit his head, but rather simply wanted to destroy his hands. Father didn't realize this, however, and assumed that the key issue was protecting his head. As a result, the children ended up not only mangling his hands but also injuring his head in the process. In this way they not only deprived Daro of a professional gambler, but they also ensured that Father would follow in Grandfather's footsteps and become Daro's second mental patient. Usually by the time the boy reached the shed, the children would have already dispersed, but this time, when the children began to throw sticks and empty cans into the jackfruit tree, the boy leaped down from the tree amidst a flock of fruit bats and positioned himself between the children and the fence. Several of the children tried to flee, but the boy paddled their butts with his parang scabbard, leaving them in such pain that their tears flowed like urine, their mouths puckered like the opening of a urinal, and their noses flared like chicken butts.

"If you try to run away again, I'll break your legs," the boy said, with one hand on his waist and the other on his scabbard. "Get up. I want all of you to stand up."

There were seven children in all. Morose and dejected, they stood before him in two rows.

"Do you know whose home this is?" The boy drew an oval in the air with his scabbard.

"The old duck-woman's."

"The old mute woman's."

"The gambling addict's."

"The old con man's."

The children offered several nicknames for the boy's parents.

"Do you know who I am?" The boy used his scabbard to point to his chest. The bead necklace with the boar's tooth was still hanging from his neck, giving him a slightly wild look.

"You're Shi Shicai, the son of the old woman who raises ducks."

"You're the son of the gambling addict . . . Shi . . . Mr. Shi," one older child said, with a stutter.

"You . . . You're the Dragon-killing Hero . . .," added a soft voice.

The Dragon-Killing Hero? . . . The boy stared in surprise. . . .

"It's good . . . that you know that. . . . But why do you still dare to act like hooligans standing here in front of the Shi home?"

"Mr. Shi, you . . . great men don't bear grudges against the common people," the older child with the stutter said. "We . . . we . . . we won't dare do it again. . . ."

"Do you know who's in there?" The boy gestured toward the shed with his scabbard. His father was hollering like a beast.

"We don't know. . . ."

"An ape?"

"A bear?"

"A mountain cat?"

"A boar?"

"It appears to be a . . . person . . .," a soft voice said.

"Are you still playing games?" the boy raised his scabbard again. "If you don't tell the truth, I'll use this to spank your butts. I'll spank each of you ten times."

"It's . . . it's . . . it's a person . . .," the children said in unison.

"Who is it?"

"We don't know. . . ."

"Who is it?"

"Mr. Shi . . . Brother Shi . . .," the older child said. "We really don't know. . . ."

"It's very dark inside . . . That person . . . spends all day with his head down. . . ."

"OK, I believe you," the boy said. "I'll tell you who it is. That person is the gambling addict. He's my father."

"The gambling addict?" The children stared in surprise.

"Your esteemed father . . ." the older child added courteously.

"The old con man has once again gotten us caught." Wild Ox Chen held Father's hair and repeatedly pounded his pale face into the table. Black Ox Huang then picked up a bottle of Black Dog beer and smashed it against the table, scattering dozens of glass shards across the table. Wild Ox Chen rubbed Father's cheeks into the glass, whereupon Father made a puffing sound and spat out several fingernail-size shards of glass. His chin, nose, right temporal bone and right eyeball were embedded with bamboo leaf–like glass shards. He roared and shook his head, trying to dislodge the glass impaled in his face. Blood-covered shards fell onto the table one after another, but the last piece remained stubbornly embedded in his eyeball. The fragment sliced his eyeball open, leaving him half blind.

"Old con man, last time we saw you, we spared your dog life, for Yu Jiatong's sake." Golden Ox spit into Father's face. "But this time we won't go easy on you."

"Your gambling skills leave the entire Rajang River basin in awe, but you certainly never expected you would fall into the hands of Daro's Three Oxen twice in a row!" Wild Ox repeatedly struck the back of Father's head with his right palm, and each time he did so the glass shard embedded in Father's eyeball was dislodged a bit more, until finally it fell onto the table with a thud, almost taking the entire eyeball with it. "Everyone in Daro says that your cons were flawless. So . . . what do you have to say for yourself now?"

"I hear that every time you served as banker, you would always try to carry out one of your cons. . . ." Black Ox ripped a poker card into four pieces and dumped it, along with the beer, into Father's belly. "You've always used your gambling to help put food on the table, so come eat some more. . . ."

It was said that that day Father consumed more than ten playing cards and twenty four-color cards.

"I want for you—you old con—to vanish immediately from Daro's gambling halls." Golden Ox once again spat in Father's face.

Daro's Three Oxen then took turns beating Father with a club, attempting to destroy his hands. At first Father tried to protect his head with his hands, as a result of which both his hands and his head ended up getting destroyed, to the point that he was left insane and harmless. Ultimately his wrists were broken and he lost seven fingers, and only his arms remained intact. His head was left like the red macaque butts that Junyi and the boy used to mock. Over time his wounds became filled with pus, attracting swarms of red-winged flies. His features became completely distorted, and his face was left full of scars. He would wander through the family's garden, eating with the ducks and chickens and sleeping with the cats and dogs. He viewed calendars, newspapers, and books as delicacies and would eat whatever paper products he could find. One day after his wounds had begun to heal he found several playing cards lying in a corner of the house and proceeded to devour them the way that he used to eat soda crackers while sipping red tea—a practice he had learned from his former gambling partner, the British man named Christian. Mother and the boy proceeded to burn all the house's remaining playing cards, but by that point Father had already become addicted to eating them. As long as something was made of paper, Father would view it as delectable. He consumed Yu Dafu's "Sinking," Lu Xun's "Diary of a Madman," Sartre's *Nausea*, as well as books such as *Borneo's Pagan Tribes*, *A History of Shamanism*, *A Record of Tropical Flora*, and several canonical volumes of classical literature. His primary culinary focus, however, was the boy's study, and he particularly coveted the *Landscape of Wind and Rain* hanging scroll the boy had brought back from the banks of the Rajang River. He repeatedly tried to use a ladder to climb into the boy's study through the window, but he was stymied by the injuries to his hands. After consuming several of the oil paintings the boy had completed in high school, he found that his appetite became more selective, and he developed a fondness for colorful images. The beautiful pagodas and pavilions in *Landscape of Wind and Rain* made him drool, and the half-figure color portrait of Marilyn Monroe hanging in the boy's room made his stomach rumble. Father used every means at his disposal to try to remove the living room's pictures of the birth of Christ, the suffering of Christ, the resurrection of Christ, and the Holy Mother and the Holy Child from their glass frames—to consume the first two images and hide the latter two. He was as thin as a rail, his face was like parchment, and his distended belly was as large as an urn. He had the teeth of a mouse, the movements of a cockroach, and the temperament of a beetle. His body was covered in paper fragments and wood chips, and he spoke in a language no one could understand. Eventually he ate two of Mother's five-yuan bills, whereupon Mother began furiously quacking at the boy. Mother and the boy then locked Father up inside the shed. By that point it had already been five years since the shed had been used to keep pigs, and the wooden planks were now bright and clean—making it a more appropriate place for human habitation than Father's wooden cot or the ground where he would often lie. Every day or two, either Mother or the boy would lead

Father around the garden, like an Englishman and a Chinese man who doesn't speak Chinese walking their dog in a park.

"Oh . . . oh . . ."

Large paper birds, fish, tigers, butterflies, centipedes, and grasshoppers were soaring through the air, all very colorful and aromatic. Father gazed up at the sky and made a hungry sound.

Father's sense of smell was so keen he could even smell the paper that birds used as construction material for their nests, the textbooks inside the book bags of students standing in the street on the other side of the iron fence, and the old newspapers used to wrap up the bread in the wooden box on the back of the Indian deliveryman's bicycle. The boy could tell his father was struggling to restrain himself and suppress his urge to climb the tree and grab the bird's nest or jump the fence and attack the students and the deliveryman. In his father's face, the boy saw a reflection of the expression his father used to have when his opium cravings started acting up. When his father couldn't resist rushing to the boy's study, this marked the end of his strolls through the garden.

The boy sought knowledge the way a man dying of thirst seeks water, and he was in the process of expanding the room he used for his study. The Shi family home was filled with the smell of books, including new books with the sweet scent of ink and older ones with a bitter odor of old paper. Every hour or two Father would cry out from the study. After the monsoon season ended, the boy dried out his books in the sun as his father wept like a baby. At night, when the boy was reading and writing under the light of the lamp, he would often see his father crawling through the Chinese characters like a bug, inspiring the boy to write until the page appeared full of intestines and the Chinese characters resembled tender flesh. Father preyed on printed matter until the pages were a muddle of flesh and blood, and the Shi family home was filled with book carcasses. The boy finally understood the significance of his father's cries.

"We have to move Father to somewhere there are no books. . . ."

When the boy saw from the children's uncultivated faces that they had not received any sage teachings or poetic nourishment, a wave of pity welled up in his chest. "That thing locked up in the shed is neither a pig nor a dog—it's my father. Do you understand?"

"We understand . . ." the children replied in unison.

"But why is your esteemed father locked in the shed?" The older child said.

"He is sick, very sick."

"Mr. Shi . . . we . . . are sorry." The older child patted several of the other children on the head. "Quick, apologize to Mr. Shi!"

"We . . . we are sorry," the children said stiffly.

"Which school do you attend?"

"Daro Public Middle School." The older child gestured toward two of the other children. "These two haven't started school yet. They can't read."

The younger children chortled.

"Daro Middle is actually my alma mater. It's a very good school," the boy said. "Can you sing the school song?"

"Yes!" the children replied.

"Stand at attention and sing it for me," the boy said.

The children looked at each other and giggled, then proceeded to sing.

"Very good," the boy said, "but next time you should take things more seriously."

"Oh." Oh." "Oh." The children said.

"Daro Middle School was burned down by Malays, but afterward people donated to have the school was rebuilt," the boy explained. "People donated all that money just so that you could learn to recognize a few Chinese characters, read the newspaper, and write letters. Therefore, you should study hard and learn the language well."

The children once again assented with a string of "ohs."

"You are all very well behaved, so I was obviously wrong to beat you," the boy said. "Here, I'll give you a large jackfruit."

The children climbed a tree and picked a large jackfruit, then took the fruit and departed. The boy used a flashlight to peer in at his father through a crack in the shed wall. The flashlight created a column of light, as though the boy were waving a pole at his father, to which his father responded by once again cradling his head with his hands. The boy turned off the flashlight and entered the shed, and then, leading his father by the hand, proceeded to take a stroll through the fruit orchard and the vegetable garden. Countless bird calls could be heard coming from the shrubbery and the silvergrass grove, as Father walked through hunched over with his head bowed. He passed through Fourth Brother's martial arts training arena, the swing set under the durian tree where Second Brother used to chat with his girlfriends, and the Hall of Wind and Rain where Third Brother would go to read. The Hall of Wind and Rain was now empty, but the lingering scent of books made Father hesitate briefly. He passed the treehouse where Fourth Brother and Xiaofu enjoyed their famished intimacy, and eventually he reached Eldest Brother's dilapidated cockfighting pen, where the lines *Wind and rain dark as night; the cocks crow endlessly* were inscribed on the trunk of a jackfruit tree. Father squinted at these characters for a long time, his face covered in clouds of melancholia, then he approached the tree and rubbed the characters with his wrist. It was as if he had seen the characters before, and they reminded him of his fondness for paper. With his teeth he ripped off the bark on which the characters *dark as night* were carved. Despite the boy's attempts to stop him, Father shook his head and swallowed the bark like a bird devouring a worm. He suddenly made a strange face, his veins protruding like the bark of the jackfruit tree. The boy grabbed at the fruit overhead and managed to pick three ripe rambutans, which he then peeled and stuffed into his father's mouth. Father's rabbitlike skull trembled, and the partially chewed bark became lodged between his spinal column and his ribcage. Every time Father's spine and ribcage shuddered, the bark was pushed further down into his pelvis. The rambutans—which Father had swallowed, seeds and all—also rolled down his throat until they were positioned directly over the masticated bark, like eggs in a bird's nest. Father bent over and—prodded by the bark—began coughing uncontrollably, like a rabbit eating carrots. The boy's fingers grasped Father's wrist like shackles as he forced Father to sit on a pile of firewood in front of Eldest Brother's chicken grave. The boy saw that amidst the array of chicken carcasses the spirits of Eldest Brother's bravest fighting cocks were sleeping soundly. After the massacre, the cocks' remains had been scattered in all directions, as though chopped up for food. Eldest Brother had trained many of the bravest fighting cocks in Borneo, and like a fighting cock, he too had died on the battlefield. In reality he was but a cock who had been sent into battle by Yu Jiatong. The boy saw several snakes slithering through the grave, gradually forming a vortex and then falling asleep amidst the chicken bones. The grave had become a giant snake pit. The boy noticed that Yu Jiatong kept rubbing the back of his head and moaning. Yu Jiatong took a giant gulp of the Black Dog beer that the People had donated to the Yangtze River Brigade, then took a large bite of pork that Ling Qiao had cooked. The evening he welcomed the boy in from his journey in the Yangtze River Brigade headquarters, in the book- and scroll-filled room where Teacher Shao had taught his courses, he haphazardly recounted to the boy the story of the rise and fall of the Yangtze River Brigade. On the table, apart from plates of boiled and braised pork, there were also plates of chicken and duck, as well as plates of monkey and lizard meat. The scent of cooked meat pervaded the room, which was so smoky that the books on the bookshelves and the calligraphy scrolls on the walls were all covered in oil—becoming delicacies that could be consumed with wine like the meat dishes on the table and emitting the fragrance of books and papers that inevitably would have summoned Father. "Remove the parang that the native gave you." This was the first thing Yu Jiatong said upon sitting down at the table. "It makes people nervous. . . ."

The boy removed the parang and placed it on a chair.

"Move it further away . . ."

The boy put his parang on the wooden cot in his bedroom.

"After your eldest brother's wife trained him to become a brave Iban warrior, his parang never left his hand and he fantasized that he could even use it to deflect bullets and decapitate a hundred government troops." Yu Jiatong opened a couple of bottles of Black Dog beer, handed one to the boy, and took a large swig from the other. Even as he forbade the boy from carrying a parang, his own rifles were resting on the table. "You. . . . why have you also adopted the practice of always carrying your parang around with you? Do you plan to decapitate someone? . . ."

The boy also took a swig of beer. "This parang was given to me by the clanspeople of my good friend, Dezhong. It has only been used to chop tree branches. My own parang, as well as my luggage and half of my money, were all stolen by members of your own Yangtze River Brigade."

"Yes, I heard about that." Yu Jiatong grabbed a chicken leg. "Actually, those men didn't belong to the Yangtze River

Brigade. . . . They were traitors. . . . opportunists and cowards like Wang Dada and his ilk. . . . They're only good for feeding to the crocodiles. . . . Compared to your four brothers, they aren't even as good as a dog. How much money did they take? . . ."

"My money . . . isn't important. However, my good friend Dezhong worked tirelessly for a year in a woodworks factory, only to have those soldiers come and take half his wages. . . ."

Yu Jiatong waved his chicken leg. "Eat, eat as much as you want. This is wild boar meat and is not easy to come by. In the heyday of the Yangtze River Brigade, however, we used to eat like this every day."

The boy used his bamboo chopsticks to grab a piece of meat, then gazed at his father sitting on the pile of firewood. His mother appeared out of nowhere and walked over, quacked a couple of times, grabbed a pile of firewood, then returned home. Father peered at her with one eye as she disappeared behind a grove of coconut trees.

"I view all the troops who secretly surrendered to the government as traitors. They no longer have any connection to the Yangtze River Brigade. . . . Shicai, why didn't you bring me their heads when you came to see me?" Yu Jiatong tossed the chicken bone into the hallway. A dog that had been lying in the hallway slowly walked over to the bone, sniffed it, then opened its mouth, while another dog continued lying in the hallway. "This time, however, I'll make an exception. Before you leave, just calculate how much they took, and I'll reimburse you. Fuck, those bastards are only worth feeding to the crocodiles. . . ."

The room was illuminated by a gas lamp that shone so brightly that it seemed like daytime. The titles on the spines of the books on the bookshelves could be discerned very clearly: *Songs of Chu, Conversations on Ciyuan, Remainders of Ashes, Writings from the*

Zhoushui Studio, and *Call to Arms* . . . all of these works rekindled the enthusiasm the boy had felt back when he used to practice his Chinese. For his father, however, this was an extravagant menu and included several broken and damaged antiques, like the book carcasses that Father had gnawed on. Under the lamplight the *Landscape of Wind and Rain* scroll displayed a different charm as it was transformed into a tropical landscape, like the one the boy had seen on the banks of the Rajang River, with orangutangs and monitor lizards climbing the hillside, durians and rambutans dotting the riverbanks, and longhouses and stilt houses replacing the painting's original palaces and pavilions. Meanwhile, the image of scholars and book boys climbing mountains and playing in the river was replaced with an image of young, half-naked Iban women. In this way, the entire Southern Song dynasty landscape was transformed into a batik painting perfused with South Seas sentiment. The lamp illuminated the Chinese characters Teacher Shao had left on the blackboard, some of which were so fragmented that they were difficult to decipher, while others still murkily displayed their original strokes, like a pile of carcasses of Chinese characters—like a mass grave of characters after a storm has blown through. Geckos were crawling through the characters like snakes crawling through the chicken grave. Geckos were also crawling through Teacher Shao's calligraphic rendering of the jade-faced God of War's poem "Snowscape, to the tune of Spring Garden Show." Compared to the characters in Teacher Shao's rendering of the line "When the angry lion kicks aside a stone, the thirsty stallion can then drink from the spring," these geckos appeared quite charming and delicate, like white ducks gracefully swimming through a pack of crocodiles. Countless insects flew into the lamp's glass lampshade, casting enormous shadows onto the room's walls, bookcases, and blackboard—as though the specters of the erased characters were still wandering the earth. In the mountains, the cries of nocturnal birds sounded hard and dry.

"As the leader of the Yangtze River Brigade, I must bear the ultimate responsibility for the deaths of your brothers." Yu Jia-tong picked up a rectangular piece of lizard meat. "The same way that I must bear responsibility for the death of every Yang-tze River Brigade soldier. . . . Ethnic work . . . has always been the most important aspect of our process of organizing struggle, and also our greatest failure. I always wanted to expand our organization to include native nationalities, so that we could then mobilize them to participate in the struggle. . . . Our attempts to learn native language and encourage mixed Hua-native marriages are among the best means we have of helping the natives establish themselves. Therefore, I encouraged our troops to marry native women—not to mention the fact that the brigade had very few female comrades, and I didn't want to see our troops remain single their entire lives as they fought for revolution. Shicai, your eldest brother was already quite fond of your sister-in-law, and all I did was add some kindling to the fire. I simply helped hurry things along, and definitely did not force them to marry. After the marriage, your brother and sister-in-law were like fish in water, and your brother under-went an even more fundamental transformation when he became a fierce general in the Yangtze River Brigade. Unfortunately, the hero was sacrificed before his parang had even had a chance to be stained with the enemy's blood. With my own eyes I saw your brother's blood splatter all over the faces of two artillery-men, startling them to the point that they lost all sense of direc-tion. It was only then that my troops had an opportunity to escape, thereby significantly reducing their losses. Meanwhile, your second brother. . . . Actually, let's discuss your third brother first. . . ."

Father stood up from the woodpile and slowly headed over toward Third Brother's Hall of Wind and Rain. The door was open, there were chicken and duck droppings everywhere, and Mother had already chopped up the tables and chairs for firewood. She had previously quacked to indicate that if they were ever short of firewood they would need to sacrifice the Tower of Wind and Rain. The boy, however, pointed out that this had been Third Brother's favorite place to hang out, and therefore if possible they should try to preserve it. "Furthermore," he added, "Mother, you should look after your ducks and chickens, and not let them desecrate Third Brother's sacred site." Father circled the building, repeatedly stopping and starting, as the boy followed behind him.

"Your Third Brother's sacrifice pained me the most. He was a good student and was very familiar with the history of military conflicts—local and foreign, large and small. He was my best secretary and general. Subsequent events confirmed that our decision not to cooperate with Huang Wenting had been the correct one, because otherwise not only would we have sacrificed Shiwen, we would also have lost the entire Yangtze River Brigade. . . ." After finishing three bottles of beer, Yu Jiatong opened a bottle of Johnny Walker and served it into three plastic cups. He gulped down the whiskey like a wild animal drinking water during a drought. "The night the Little Rhino Brigade troops returned Shiwen's corpse, several of us—including Wang Dada, myself, and a few others—took your third brother and got completely drunk. . . . We poured the wine into your third brother's mouth . . . and the wine . . . drained out through his neck. . . . That bastard Huang Wenting still had a conscience . . . at least he didn't smash Shiwen's skull . . . and instead he merely slit his throat. . . . That bookworm . . . that bookworm, whom Teacher Shao trained single-handedly—even on the verge of death, he had that stinking, moth-filled head of his . . ."

Father quickly lost interest in the Hall of Wind and Rain, with its piles of wind-dried chicken and duck droppings. Barefoot, he stepped onto the platform and ran around the wooden pillars. "Father, be good. Please sit down." The boy had his father sit down on one of the wooden pillars. Father panted, sounding like Third Brother turning the pages of his books up in this Hall of Wind and Rain, then relieved himself of a large glob of phlegm that was caught in his throat. He coughed several times, producing a sound like teardrops falling onto an oil-paper umbrella. Yu Jiatong brandished his rifle, aiming it out the window as Ma Guoxiong and Wu Zhaoping walked through the courtyard carrying rifles, then came to a stop under the lamp outside the hallway.

"Reporting to the commander! How can it be that we haven't seen him for two days?" Ma Guoxiong asked. "He must have gone to surrender. . . ."

Yu Jiatong lowered his rifle. "This guy is truly a thief, and it was always only a matter of time before he betrayed us. Let him go. It can't have been easy for him to persist until now. . . ."

"Yes, sir," Ma Guoxiong said. The two men continued to stand outside the door.

"Is there anything else?"

"Commander . . . you're not giving up the base, are you?"

The boy picked several rambutans, then peeled them and stuffed them into his father's mouth. His father's skin was as dry as tobacco leaves, to the point that it resembled a butterfly's wing. Yu Jiatong watched as the two soldiers disappeared across the field, then finally lowered his rifle. He took a gulp of imported alcohol, hummed the tune to "March of the Volunteers," and said, "If Shishang hadn't been singing this song before he was killed, he might have had enough breath to survive a bit longer under water. His bravery . . . was such that it even earned the respect of the Punan warriors who had come to arrest him. As for me and my brigade . . . we were hidden in the underbrush . . . mourning your fourth brother . . . and trembling in the face of the government troops' superior firepower. . . . Shishang tried twice to throw himself into the Yangtze River but didn't succeed. While alive, however, he was a Yangtze River man, and after death he was a Yangtze River ghost. . . ."

Father couldn't sit still and instead began walking in circles, as though wandering through a labyrinthine garden. Eventually he sat down on the swing Second Brother had constructed with his own hands. The swing had a back and an armrest and could support two people. Second Brother had planted grass and flowers, built a rock garden and a birdfeeder, and would often sit on the swing and recite love poems to his girlfriends. *The rush leaves are very fresh, and the white dew continues to fall. He whom I love, is at the water's edge.* The swing sets Second Brother built were enough to create a mass swing grave. It was said that Second Brother had also built several swing sets in the base area, where he managed to enjoy a few enchanting moments in the company of Qinyun, the Daro Theater ticket collector. Second Brother could have spent an entire lifetime swinging with Qinyun. . . . The boy noticed that his uncle was almost drunk and had an expression similar to the one Father had now, sitting on the swing.

"You could say your second brother's death was a direct result of my actions. . . . Actually, Qinyun liked me . . . and her decision to join the Yangtze River Brigade is irrefutable proof of this. . . . I . . . I . . . how should I say this . . . to tell the truth . . . Qinyun was jealous of my relationship with other female comrades. . . . Women . . . damn it! . . . To tell the truth . . . Qinyun certainly wasn't the only female comrade who liked me . . . but if the others could tolerate it, why couldn't she? . . . This woman . . . was full of resentment . . . and she fell into your brother's embrace. . . . When I told your brother to take your grandfather's remains back to Daro, I only assigned two soldiers to accompany him . . . but at that point the government troops had us completely surrounded, and the bounty on the head of a single Yangtze River Brigade soldier was equivalent to two years of an average worker's wages. . . . Your second brother . . . was decapitated by more than a dozen Iban . . . and because they were all competing for the bounty . . . they chopped up your brother's head like a watermelon . . ."

Father left the swing, producing a *galala* sound as he stepped on the fallen leaves from the jackfruit tree, as if his feet were being ground into fragments. It seemed as though Father's organs were as decayed as rotten leaves and were full of millipedes and flatworms. After turning around two or three times, Father found himself next to the wooden pillar where he had been loitering, where he encountered Mother, who was holding a parang. Mother made continuous duck noises and quacked a couple times to indicate she intended to chop up Fourth Brother's martial arts training arena—chop everything into firewood, then plant fruit trees in the area. Over two weeks Fourth Brother managed to chop down more than a dozen large trees. After cutting off their roots and branches, he created more than a dozen perfectly straight wooden pillars, as though an ox had dragged them back. Then he used a shovel to dig holes throughout the fruit tree grove, excavating several dozen large pits into which he could insert the several dozen poles. Then he leaped and summersaulted over the pillars, ran through them, and hit them. The boy said that no matter what, he would preserve Fourth Brother's martial arts field, just as he would preserve Eldest Brother's chicken grave, Second Brother's swing set, and Third Brother's Hall of Wind and Rain. The boy added that firewood could be collected anywhere, so why was it necessary to demolish the martial arts field? Mother said that they should demolish it to plant fruit trees. The boy replied, "Mother, for whom are you planting these fruit trees? By the time they are fully grown, neither you nor Father will be around." Mother replied, "But you'll still be here." The boy said, "Who would think about such far-off events? By that point maybe I won't be here either." Mother said, "If you're no longer here, where would you be?" The boy said, "I don't know." Mother quacked some more, and it reached the point where the boy could no longer understand her duck-speech. Meanwhile, Uncle's drunken ramblings were almost indistinguishable from Mother's duck speech.

"After your second brother died . . . you . . . you won't believe this . . . but Qinyun claimed I was . . . a murderer . . . she claimed that I had sent him to his death . . . thereby killing him with a borrowed knife . . . Her accusation . . . is there not perhaps some truth to it? . . . And afterwards, damn it, that girl actually joined the Flame Mountain Brigade, thereby giving Wang Dada a chance to mock me mercilessly. . . . Damn it, Wang Dada is only good for feeding to the crocodiles. . . . After Qinyun's breasts developed, it appeared as though she had grown a layer of cartilage like a turtle shell. . . . Her nipples were bullet tips . . . her breasts . . . I sucked and dug at them as though they were monkey brains . . . licking them completely clean. . . . She . . . she would scream and holler like a monkey having its skull opened up right on the dinner table . . ."

After quacking a few more times, Mother picked up her parang and walked away.

". . . Shicai, our revolution has failed." Yu Jiatong jumped up and grabbed the boy's shoulder with one hand while leaning against the corner of the table with the other. "However, we cannot abandon the base area. . . . If those traitors, who are only good for feeding to the crocodiles, were to reveal our secrets to the government, the base area and I would both find ourselves on the brink of destruction . . ."

Yu Jiatong released the boy's shoulder, then walked over to the bookshelf and rested his head on the back of a book. "At the time . . . I led several dozen Daro youth into the rainforest while singing 'March of the Volunteers.' At that time, socialism was like a bright flame in Sarawak! . . . When we were bidding farewell to Teacher Shao, who was staying behind in Daro, we felt we couldn't bear to part with his library, and therefore everyone took several dozen books, and in the end we were able to transfer virtually the entire library to the base area . . . En route, we protected the books with our lives. . . . Later, Teacher Shao himself joined the brigade . . . And here, right here, Teacher Shao once again lectured us on Chinese culture, helping us gain a deeper understanding of Marxist and Maoist thought. . . . We . . . when we were in class . . . Chairman Mao's greatness and talent frequently left us in tears . . ."

Yu Jiatong collapsed, and a copy of *A Study of Ancient Chinese Apparel* fell to the ground. Yu Jiatong's eyes were shut, his cheeks were red, he was breathing deeply. The boy waited next to the table for a while. The copy of *A Study of Ancient Chinese Apparel* was lying open in what appeared to be a very painful position, as though its abdomen had ruptured and its intestines had leaked out. The boy remembered his parang in the bedroom. This was the parang that Dezhong's clanspeople had given him; the parang that had been used only to peel tree bark and cut weeds; the parang was currently resting in its intricately decorated wooden scabbard. The scabbard was Fadiya's handiwork. Every time the boy pulled the blade in and out of the scabbard, he was reminded of dark, warm Fadiya. There was *xixisusu* rustling sound in the hallway, whereupon Ling Qiao suddenly appeared in the doorway.

"Are you drunk again?" Ling Qiao asked as she entered, then helped support Yu Jiatong as he left the library. The boy wanted to help, but Ling Qiao gestured him away. Ling Qiao had two rifles strapped to her shoulders and, together with Jiatong, she disappeared into the courtyard. "Son of a bitch. . . ." As the boy was leading his father back to the shed, his father suddenly uttered what had been his favorite phrase before his breakdown. . . .

Using techniques of disguised surveillance that he had learned from his uncle, the boy observed the habits of Daro's Three Oxen. He saw that the Three Oxen would leave their home every morning after ten and then would typically have breakfast and read the paper in an open-air café. They wouldn't return until one or two in the afternoon, during which there would often be visitors who would ask them for the location of that night's gambling hall. The Three Oxen had established more than a dozen real or virtual gambling dens in Daro—in the busy streets, in the countryside, in workers' bunkhouses, in the mountains, on the banks of the Rajang, in the rainforest, and in palm tree gardens. There were gambling dens everywhere, and they would often change location every few days, completely confounding the police. One morning a middle-aged man with mid-length hair, tortoiseshell-rimmed eyeglasses, sideburns, and a handlebar mustache, and wearing a batik shirt and white pants appeared in the café looking for the Three Oxen, explaining that he wanted to be their customer.

"What is the esteemed gentleman's surname?" Golden Ox asked.

"My surname is Zhao, and my given name is Guanlun," the middle-aged man said. "My friends call me Little Zhao."

"Where do you live?"

"I didn't live here before, which is why you've never seen me, Brother Lai." The middle-aged man ordered a cup of coffee and a bowl of fried noodles, then sat down at a table next to the Three Oxen. "I previously lived in Bintulu, in the fourth district. But I heard that Daro has been thriving recently, so I thought I'd come here to do some business."

"When has Daro ever been thriving?" Golden Ox asked. "The town was turned upside down by the Communist Party, to the point that it almost had to be relocated."

"But now the Communists have surrendered and Daro is free to develop," the middle-aged man replied. "Over the next several years, the government plans to invest heavily here. My fellow businessmen can't possibly be mistaken on this point."

"How do you know I run gambling sites?" Golden Ox asked.

The boy looked askance at Golden Ox. At this point Golden Ox was drinking coffee while reading the paper, Black Ox was in the bathroom, and Wild Ox was picking meat with his chopsticks while chatting with the man at the next table. The boy unconsciously stroked his fake mustache and uttered the name of one of his father's gambling partners.

"At eight o'clock tonight come to 210 Queen Street, building no. 2." Golden Ox continued drinking his coffee while reading his newspaper.

From two in the afternoon until dusk the Three Oxen would often take a yacht to the Rajang River or the South China Sea to go fishing. The boy was carrying Yu Jiatong's rifle on his shoulder, as the parang Dezhong had given him dangled from his waist. He sliced his way through the rainforest, swamps, and shrubs, to observe the Three Oxen on the yacht. Golden Ox liked to smoke opium, Black Ox often visited Daro's brothels, and Wild Ox liked to go hunting, watch cockfights, and play cricket. Apart from the time they spent fishing on the yacht, the afternoon was the period they reserved for their individual activities. The gambling halls opened at eight each evening. The first night the boy went to 10 Queen Street, building number 2, he came away empty-handed. The next day he once again went to the open-air café to see the Three Oxen. When the boy arrived, Golden Ox was still drinking coffee while reading a newspaper, and he gave the boy another address. That night the boy once again came away empty-handed. After coming away empty-handed three times in a row, on the fourth night the boy finally managed to find one of the Three Oxen's gambling halls, which was located behind a grocery store on Brooke Street. It was drizzling that evening, and the streetlights were dim since Brooke Street was located on the outskirts of Daro. On a traffic island full of large red flowers there was a bronze statue of Sarawak's first governor, James Brooke. Brooke was quite handsome, with curly hair, a sword hanging from his waist, long-toed boots, and in his tight-fitting pants his member resembled a majestic anthill. Dressed as a nineteenth-century European aristocrat, he gazed proudly down at the entire length of Brooke Street. Brooke was Sarawak's first white ruler, and he used guns and cannons to suppress the locals. He recruited Malays, Chinese, and natives to establish Sarawak's first guerilla force, and under his direction these guerillas slaughtered countless freedom fighters and Dezhong's own ancestors. The gambling hall was approximately the size of a badminton court and was filled with thick smoke and a sour stench. Several fluorescent lamps illuminated the room as though it were daytime, and twenty or thirty gamblers—most of whom were ethnically Chinese—continually wandered in and out of the hall. The boy inspected these Daro faces but couldn't make out any obvious mainland Chinese features, and only one or two of the patrons appeared remotely familiar. The boy gambled for a while and lost some money, but he didn't see the Three Oxen. At the open-air café the next morning, Golden Ox finally revealed the location of one of their permanent gambling halls. The gambling hall was in the basement of Sam Po Keng Temple on Sam Po Street, next to the wharf. It was about the size of three basketball courts and was open on Mondays, Wednesdays, Fridays, and weekends. This also happened to be a drizzly night, and the boy took an oil-paper umbrella to burn incense in Sam Po Keng Temple, then entered a stairwell leading down to the basement. The amount of incense revealed the gambling hall's prosperity and decline. The temple was dedicated to the worship of the deity Zheng He—"a magnificent Buddha with a snowy beard and childish features, bursting with energy." They completely didn't take into consideration his eunuch status, while his sideburns made him look like he was trying to camouflage himself as a local Chinese. Why did you pick a dickless eunuch to serve as your guardian angel? The temple was about forty or fifty years old, but in reality it served as the gambling hall's guard dog. In the basement the boy saw the muscular Golden Ox and Black Ox, and circulating among the gamblers there was Wild Ox and a group of burly men who were clearly the gambling hall's hired thugs. Here the smoke was even thicker, the odor was even more acrid, water didn't leak in, and everything was extraordinarily peaceful. Several large gambling tables were surrounded by gamblers who were all gazing down at the tables. The boy and a group of gamblers wandered back and forth on the outer edge of the area. . . . Approximately half an hour later there was some shouting and pushing as the Three Oxen and a bodyguard beat a young gambler who was caught trying to cheat. One gambler was slashed in the back, whereupon he screamed and lunged at the boy. In the process, he raked the boy's center-parted hair, knocking off his eyeglasses and his fake handlebar mustache. An ice-cold parang was pressed against the back of the boy's neck.

"Where is Yu Jiatong?"

That night the Yangtze River base area was similarly rainy, and the boy was sitting the library leafing through a picture album. When the blade of the parang was silently pressed against his neck, the boy suddenly remembered how, when he was running a fever, Fadiya had held her palm to his forehead.

"Don't move." An enormous hand tightly gripped the boy's left arm. The back of the boy's neck was throbbing, and he could smell the stench of blood. The parang had left a small wound in the boy's nape. "I told you not to move," the voice behind him said. "Where is Yu Jiatong?"

The boy recognized Ma Guoxiong. "Uncle Ma, why are you holding your parang up to my neck?"

"Damn it, just answer the question. I couldn't care less about your puny life," Ma Guoxiong said fiercely. "Where is Yu Jiatong?"

"Ling Qiao says that Uncle is worried about the possibility of secret plots, and therefore he sleeps in a different house every night." The boy had a surge of panic. "Ever since I arrived, he has never spent the night in this house. You should go look for him in those several dozen wooden cabins!"

"Damn it . . ." Ma Guoxiong rattled off a string of curses.

"Captain, this boy is telling the truth."

The lamp projected the shadows of two men onto the ground in front of the boy. The boy saw Wu Zhaoping standing with a rifle behind Ma Guoxiong, who was also holding a rifle. From the forest there came a strange bird cry that sounded like dry branches breaking, combined with crocodiles' loud mating calls. A rivulet of blood as thin as a strand of hair flowed down the boy's clavicle, following the bone until it reached his abdomen.

"Uncle Ma, why are you looking for Uncle?" The boy asked.

"Shut up." Ma Guoxiong suddenly shouted out through the door, "Yu Jiatong, come out and meet your fate. Your nephew's life is in my hands. . . ."

The strange bird call that sounded like branches breaking suddenly stopped and was replaced by an even more eerie sound, resembling a pair of parang blades rubbing against one another. The crocodiles' mating calls continued nonstop. The boy stared at the shadows in front of him and out of the house, alternating between feeling tense and relaxed. Laid out in front of him was Fan Kuan's famous landscape, *Travelers Among Streams and Mountains*. Because the painting's collector had been traveling (?), when he folded the scroll he left a crease that was clearly visible in the picture album. After several bodyguards led away two young, injured gamblers, all eyes in the gambling hall were fixed on the boy.

"Shi Shicai. . . ."

"The gambling addict's son. . . ."

"Yu Jiatong's nephew. . . ."

"Dragon-killing Hero. . . ."

. . . .

The gambling hall fell into an unprecedented silence, broken only by an occasional cough. The boy couldn't help thinking of the stately Triratna triad overhead. Why don't you dig a well here? You should dig a pit right here, in your dickless crotch! His face bright red, Uncle drunkenly led the boy from the library into the bedroom, then pointed to the wall where, on a nine-square graph, was written the "Divination Song" that the jade-faced god of war had composed in memory of Dipa Nusantara Aidit, the former leader of the Indonesian Communist Party. Enviously, Uncle told the boy one of his greatest wishes for after he died: "Aidit was a mere foreigner, yet after his death the Chairman wrote a poem commemorating him. After I die, will the Chairman similarly compose a "Divination Song" poem or something commemorating me? . . . Shicai . . . please remember . . . if the Chairman writes a poem in my memory . . . please copy out the poem . . . and burn it in front of my grave. . . ."

"Welcome Mr. Shi." Golden Ox Laiya walked up to the boy and said, "Mr. Shi is someone we admire. Is the reason you've come in person to visit our illegal gambling site because you're afraid that if word got out it would stain your reputation? If so, then you can rest easy. No one here will say a word about this."

The boy couldn't remember whether it was he who first extended his hand or whether it was Golden Ox who initiated the awkward handshake. With a frown, the boy stared at his father's enemy, as though staring at a saltwater crocodile in the Rajang River and a nearby boat full of prey. At that point all the boy wanted to do was to take a rifle and aim it at one of the Three Oxen, and in that way he could easily eliminate an enemy. In the end, however, he couldn't bring himself to pull the trigger, the same way that he later would stare at Uncle's neck but wouldn't bring himself to pull his parang from his scabbard. . . .

"Ma Guoxiong, you can deal with me directly. There's no need to take the boy as a hostage."

The sound of Yu Jiatong's voice drifted in from outside.

"Yu . . . Yu Jiatong, come out. Come out and face death." Ma Guoxiong put down his parang, then gripped his gun with both hands. In the darkness, the boy could see that the gun's muzzle was pointed at his own head. "Otherwise, I'll destroy your nephew's head with one shot. . . ."

The bird songs and crocodile mating calls abruptly stopped, and all that remained was the sound of insects chirping and frogs croaking. In the darkness, the boy could clearly see that Ma Guoxiong's chin was dripping with sweat, and Wu Zhaoping was looking all around. A breeze was blowing in from outside, rustling the picture album and startling the three people in the room. As the breeze flipped the pages of the picture album, one towering peak after another flashed before the boy's eyes.

"Ma Guoxiong," said Yu Jiatong from outside, in an even louder voice. "Throughout my life I've been threatened by countless people, but I've never yielded. Do you really think that I would sacrifice myself for the sake of this youngster?"

"Regardless, I'm ready to go all in." Ma Guoxiong aimed his gun at the back of the child's head. It was because of you that the Shi family's four sons lost their lives, so now it's time for you to repay your debt to the family. You inhuman thing, show yourself now!"

"Ma Guoxiong, you loyally followed me for many years, but in the end you still betrayed me. You are no different from those we feed to the crocodiles. . . . You must be doing this for the bounty?"

The drops of sweat on Ma Guoxiong's chin dripped down even more rapidly. "I joined the Yangtze River Brigade when I was twenty-four, but apart from killing several government troops I haven't done a thing since then. Instead, I've been holed up in a native territory teaching natives to read and write, so poor that I can't even purchase a wooden shack. The bounty on your head would be enough for me to purchase a foreign-style house in Daro, with enough left over to buy several imported cars, hire several servants, find a wife, and have several children. That way I would be set for life."

There was a period of silence outside the house. "My head is right here. Why don't you come and get it? But if you harm a single hair on my nephew's head, I swear I'll feed you to the crocodiles."

"If you don't present yourself, I'll decapitate your nephew."

"Would you dare . . .?"

In the shadows, the boy saw Ma Guoxiong holding a gun in one hand and a parang in the other, while behind Ma Guoxiong he saw Wu Zhaoping also holding a gun, the muzzle of which was slowly redirected toward Ma Guoxiong's back. Just as Ma Guoxiong was about to raise his parang, the sound of a gunshot resonated throughout the entire base area. Outside, the two dogs yelped in surprise. The boy spun around as Ma Guoxiong collapsed in a pool of blood. A bullet had entered his back and exited through his chest. Smoke was seeping out of the muzzle of Wu Zhaoping's gun. Wu Zhaoping dropped the firearm and, his eyes full of tears, immediately knelt down beside Ma Guoxiong, crying like a child. "Captain . . . I'm sorry . . . captain. . . . Although Zhaoping is a fool, he is nevertheless loyal to his leader. . . . Captain . . . we've already betrayed our motherland, but we can't betray the Yangtze River Brigade . . . you claimed that Zhaoping hasn't killed a single enemy his entire life, but now he has finally killed one . . ."

The boy rode his bicycle along the Daro's asphalt road. The sun was shining brightly, and several groups of Englishmen and Chinese working for oil companies passed the boy in their jeeps and all-terrain vehicles on their way to go hunting in the rainforest and fishing in the Rajang River. In the boy's imagination, in the Yangtze River Brigade's base area it was always night filled with the sound of drizzle, strange bird songs, and crocodile mating calls. And it was only in this climate and during this season that Yu Jiatong would gather several cans of Iban rice wine or foreign liquor that Daro's townspeople had previously given him, take them to the library, and then would proceed to tell the boy endless stories about the history of the Yangtze River Brigade. After the boy appeared at the gambling site behind Sam Po Keng Temple, a rumor began circulating that the boy intended to exact revenge on the Three Oxen. The Three Oxen asked someone to give the boy's mother a ten-*liang* necklace made from pure gold and a pair of jade bracelets that also weighed ten *liang* each. The boy continued to appear in Daro in a variety of different disguises, though by this point he was no longer doing so to protect himself from the Three Oxen, but rather to avoid the complicated looks that the people of Daro would often cast in his direction. The boy urged his mother to boil a bird's nest, then eat half of it with her husband and give the other half to a neighbor. The gold was exchanged for cash, which was stored in a biscuit tin in the mother's closet. After Father stopped eating books his health didn't improve, but neither did it deteriorate further, though his cries of hunger from wanting to eat books noticeably diminished. In the silvergrass grove the boy encountered the children who had tormented his father and asked them what they were doing there. The children replied that they were looking for coucal nests. The children's gazes and voices were filled with awe. The boy asked them if they had found any, and the children replied that there were not many coucals left, so their nests were hard to find. Yu Jiatong would suddenly appear in the library, and once he told the boy that he should simply finish reading the books in the library and then leave the base camp. The boy replied that that was indeed his intention. Uncle asked him what he planned to do after reading all of these books. Both sides of the street were lined with newly built stores and foreign-style houses, and in one location they were building a restaurant and an entertainment facility. The government had decided to develop Daro into a tourist destination. The boy pedaled faster and faster, leaving the town center and heading toward the front of Sarawak's first crocodile observation park, which had been established with government support. On the right-hand side of the road there was a swamp, and a monitor lizard was lying on a piece of dead wood and gazing up at the boy. Behind the marsh there was rainforest, and several monkey-eating eagles were flying back and forth above. Dark clouds descended, like a beard. A group of natives were on the side of the road selling tourists local products and handmade art. Rambutans. Jackfruits. Pseudomonas. Sweet potatoes. Taro. Bamboo baskets. Hats. Shields. Blowguns. Parangs. Wood carvings. Jewelry. . . . Countless fish hanging from a bamboo pole, with the small ones the size of a foot and the large ones as long as a person is tall. Some were still gasping for air. A black boar as big as a hippopotamus had been carved into ten pieces, which were being sold in a street-side stall. Black skin, meat dripping with blood, it looked like a Bible that Father had preyed on. The boy and several tourists lined up at a ticket booth in Daro Crocodile Observation Park to purchase tickets. The ticket-seller was graceful and poised and looked familiar. As the boy was hesitating, Dai Qinyun, the former ticket-seller at the Daro Theater, recognized him.

"Shi Shicai!" She exclaimed, with a look of pleased surprise. "Oh, it's you?"

After she finished selling her tickets, Qinyun left the booth and led the boy into the park.

"Honored guest, what a pleasant surprise!" Qinyun said as she walked. "Dada will be so pleased to see you. From the day we opened, Dada has been awaiting your arrival."

The crocodile park was filled with tropical plants to the point that it resembled a man-made rainforest. Over the walkway there were all sorts of specimens of local fauna. Monitor lizards. Pythons. Clouded leopards. Mountain lions. Asian rhinos. An elephant only as tall as a man's abdomen. Another walkway was decorated with an array of different-sized crocodile specimens, with labels specifying the location and date of each animal's capture. One specimen after another had its mouth wide open, as though it were smiling. On the wall there was a rectangular bulletin board on which were posted an assortment of newspaper clippings in English, Malay, and Chinese—all of which were announcements about incidents of crocodiles eating people: "Daughter of Australian Filmmaker is Eaten by a Crocodile." "Biologist Morris is Eaten by a Crocodile for Breakfast," and "Angler Ends Up in a Crocodile's Belly." . . . Qinyun laughed brightly as she showed the boy around the park. She had experienced countless vicissitudes over the years, but her earlier reputation of being Daro's greatest beauty was still evident. In Yu Jiatong's eyes, her beauty was rivaled only by that of another Yangtze River Brigade comrade, Chen Yili. When he was drunk, Yu Jiatong would often regale the boy with stories about his carnal relations with Chen Yili. Once, during the early period after the Yangtze River Brigade was first founded, Jiatong and seven or eight other soldiers found themselves surrounded by more a hundred government troops. One of Jiatong's comrades was severely wounded and was lying on the ground waiting to die. Government troops gunshots and shouts could be heard coming from all directions. Bullets and cannonballs whizzed by. Grenades exploded. Jiatong had no choice but to order a retreat. "Comrades, run! Escape! We'll see meet up in the base area! But if you are truly unable to escape, however, then just fight them here." At that point Chen Yili had recently graduated from high school, after which she had taught for half a year in a preschool attached to the Daro Primary School. She was nineteen when she joined the Yangtze River Brigade. Yu Jiatong led her to a burrow located beneath the roots of a silk-cotton tree. The burrow was dark and humid and was just barely large enough for the two of them. Originally it may have been the burrow of a Malayan sun bear or a Malayan cat. They stood face-to-face inside the burrow while outside the sound of gunfire continued without pause, and they could feel the ground tremble every time a cannonball landed. With each impact they would lean closer together, and Jiatong would get harder. The government troops kept patrolling the area around the tree, and the slightest sound would have led them to toss a barrage of grenades into the burrow, like a troop of pig-tailed macaques in a tree picking fruits and hurling them at people down below. Jiatong and Yili were drenched in a river of sweat, as though they were soaking in mud. Jiatong whispered to Yili, saying, *Do not move or shout, because otherwise we'll both go to prison.* Then he caressed her body and kissed her lips. The government troops fired warning shots and used a loudspeaker to urge them to quickly surrender. The sound of fighting came from nearby, and the Yangtze River Brigade troops began to return fire. Jiatong ripped open Yili's black shirt and pulled down her black pants. When Jiatong ejaculated, two Yangtze River Brigade troops were fleeing toward the silk-cotton tree, and beneath the tree they were hit by hand grenades and machine gun fire to the point that they couldn't even be recognized as human. Their blood saturated the mud like rain falling on drought-parched land, staining the burrow and tree roots red, as their blood mixed with Yili's virgin blood. *Why is he telling me this?* The boy's lips trembled. Jiatong gulped down a can of rice wine, then stared out the window at the rest of the base area enveloped in darkness. He suddenly changed the subject. "Shicai, you came here to kill me, didn't you?"

It had already been a week since Ma Guoxiong was killed. The boy's heart began to pound, as his face turned red and purple.

"Shicai . . . you came here to kill me, right? . . . " Yu Jiatong repeated.

The boy stared at the dishes of cold food on the table. Chicken? Duck? Pork? Everything was a blur.

"The first time I saw you in the base area, I immediately knew your intention." A warm smile appeared on Yu Jiatong's lips. "No one is more entitled than you to chop off my head. . . . and no one is more entitled than you to collect that bounty. . . ."

A stream of tears rolled down the boy's cheek and onto the table.

"Exchange my head for that bounty, which while help compensate for the debt that I owe the Shi family. . . . I face death without any regrets. . . ." Jiatong stared at the boy. "Shicai, you can proceed whenever you like. I won't resist. . . ."

The boy stared at the dining table. His limbs were ice-cold, and his mind was a blank. The ridges on the table resembled a crescent moon and reminded the boy of the design that Fadiya had carved on his parang scabbard. It was as if the scabbard were sitting on the table, camouflaged as the ridges in the wood, while his parang was hidden within the ridges. His parang was like an object bobbing in the water, and the wooden handle poked out like an elbow. His parang sliced back and forth through the table's flesh, as though he wanted to dismember it. Before Wang Dada led more than four hundred Flame Mountain Brigade troops to surrender to the government, he first dug a giant grave in the rainforest, where he buried his troops' two hundred parangs. The location of this parang mass grave became a hot topic in the media and among explorers. One soldier returned to the rainforest after surrendering and slit his neck in front of the grave, after which a clouded leopard consumed his corpse.

"Making love with Yili in that cramped burrow was like wrestling with a crocodile in a mud pit. . . . It was as though a giant python were squeezing us together, in order to devour us. . . . No matter how hard I tried, I couldn't move at all, and I ejaculated almost the instant I entered her. When the government troops departed I again wanted her desperately. Later, during countless expeditions, Yili and I would temporarily leave the brigade . . . Her breasts were pale, translucent, and very ample, like a pair of jellyfish with their tentacles extended and floating on her soft and plump chest. . . . She excitedly cried out in a very odd manner, like a solitary manatee emerging from the bottom of a river . . . her tongue . . . was like an anteater's tongue entering my inner organs, licking clean the lustful ants inside me. . . . Shicai, you're still a virgin, right?"

Did he even care whether I was or not?. . . . The parang scabbard remained camouflaged on the table. The boy's thoughts were muddled, and in the table's ridges he saw Fadiya's dimples. A group of white tourists resembling proboscis monkeys walked past them. In the walkway there an enormous statue of a nude Iban woman. Her breasts were coarse and pockmarked, like a coconut shell that had been stripped of its outer layer. Her genitals resembled an olive, and her body was covered in tattoos. The boy was again reminded of Fadiya.

"I hear you got along quite well with the younger sister of that native when you were staying with his family. . . ." Jiatong rolled his empty bottle on the table as though he were kneading flour, and in the process making a sound like a pig snorting. "Hua-native marriages are just one option. . . . You're the last descendent of the Shi family. You shouldn't let dirty native skin taint your pure yellow skin. . . ."

In the shed, the chickens and ducks started making a commotion. Several chickens cried out, as though someone were cutting their turtle-like necks. Their wings flapped loudly. Jiatong picked up his rifle and a flashlight and walked over to the shed. The boy could see the flashlight beam waving back and forth in the darkness. He was reminded of the time those two black-shirt soldiers led him to the base area, and of that strange animal watching him from the silvergrass grove. From the shed there came the sound of a gunshot, combined with chickens squawking, ducks quacking, dogs barking, and pigs oinking. The boy heard the sound of someone chewing paper coming from the study. Chalk writing on the blackboard. Geckos scurrying across the *Landscape of Wind and Rain* scroll. Outside, someone was walking quickly. Someone was standing in the courtyard, with a parang hanging from his waist. There was a human head carved into the parang handle. The person's shadow seemed to be camouflaged as a tree shadow. Uncle emerged from the tree shadow and proceeded toward the study, dragging a dead monitor lizard by the tail with his left hand. Uncle had shot the lizard in the abdomen, and a dead chicken was protruding from the animal's ruptured stomach. Uncle returned to his seat and proceeded to peel some peanuts and jackfruit seeds, then put them in his mouth and chewed them. "That damned lizard ate two of my chickens! Tomorrow I'll feed it to the crocodiles. Shicai, have some wine." Yu Jiatong lifted his wine glass. "Do you have the guts to do it? Shicai . . . you . . . since you were young, you've always been a coward, and the moment you entered the rainforest you immediately started running a fever . . ."

The boy stared into the dark courtyard outside the window. Was it a person camouflaged as a tree shadow? Or a tree shadow camouflaged as a person? Wang Dada had chopped down several thousand trees to build a crocodile observation park, in the center of which he had erected a tree grave, and every year he would come offer a sacrifice. "Shicai, before I die, I have a wish. . . ." Jiatong proceeded to relate his wish that the Chairman compose a poem for him after his death. His second wish, meanwhile, was that he be buried in Daro's Chinese cemetery.

"Finally, Shicai, I hope you'll accompany me into the rainforest for one last elephant hunt. . . ."

Wang Dada was wearing a batik shirt was as bright as a fighting cock, and his ample posterior was covered by a pair of dark red beach pants. From behind a desk as large as a ping-pong table, he lunged at the boy like a boxer and hugged him warmly. "Hero! Hero!" With his head on the boy's shoulder, Wang Dada emitted a deafening laugh. "Welcome to the crocodile observation park!"

Like Wang Dada himself, the office was colorful and full of vitality. Flowerpots with all sorts of tropical plants were everywhere, making the office resemble a fruit and vegetable market. Some were hanging from the ceiling, like soaring birds, while others were hanging from the walls, like insects. Some were sitting on the ground, like reptiles. The leaves and branches were lush, and the fruits and flowers were abundant. Sunlight shone into the room from all directions through the curtained windows, reminding the boy of how in the rainforest canopy there was a flower garden that had become a world of its own. Uncle and the boy selected the largest silk-cotton tree they could find and spent two days building a rudimentary observation tower in the treetop. Then they waited twelve days, using binoculars to search for the legendary elephant herd. After twelve days they moved to a different silk-cotton tree, where they built another rudimentary observation tower. Altogether they built three towers, but in the end they had to return empty-handed. While Yu Jiatong was watching from the tower, sometimes he would chatter nonstop, but other times he would go for long stretches without saying a word. Most of the time the boy was silent. A fiery-red golden parrot was screeching in the corner, and several carnivorous tropical fish were swimming around in an aquarium as large as a coffin. In a glass container resembling a cooler there was a purple spider as large as a man's hand, which resembled a chopped-off furry ape paw. On the desk there were several elephant tusks of different lengths. *Why did he call me a hero?* The boy accepted the coconut juice that the waitress handed him and finished it in a single gulp.

"From my office decor you can tell how much I miss life in the forest." Wang Dada led the boy over to a sofa that was camouflaged as a giant stone. "I particularly miss my deceased comrades. . . ."

It was raining. . . . Although the raindrops were very abundant, they were unable to penetrate the silk-cotton tree canopy. The observation post wasn't touched by a single drop of rain. Jiatong painfully rolled around in the observation tower, and several times he almost rolled out of the tower entirely. The boy tightly held him down until the pain subsided. Once, during the final days of the Yangtze River Brigade, Yu Jiatong and troops from the Flame Mountain Brigade fought together against the government troops, and in the tumult Yu Jiatong's head was sliced open behind his left ear. The blade almost penetrated his skull, and although he managed to escape with his life he was left with serious complications. In the observation tower, Uncle remarked in a nonchalant tone that even by that point the bounty on his head was already sky high, and he didn't know whether the person who attacked him was friend or foe. Perhaps it was his companion Wang Dada. The boy asked, *Why is it that no one tried to chop off Wang Dada's head?* Uncle replied disdainfully, *Huh, how could his head be worth anything?*

"We kept everything that was worth keeping . . ." Wang Dada said, while gazing at the two pairs of elephant tusks on the table.

"Are these from elephants you shot?" The boy asked.

"Yes, when I was with the Flame Mountain Brigade."

"Who killed more elephants, you or Uncle?"

"You uncle did . . . however, he sold most of them, in order to. . . ." Wang Dada stood up from the sofa. "Let's let bygones be bygones. Shicai, it was not easy for you to come here today. Let's go. I'll show you around."

It was raining. . . . It was an afternoon thunderstorm, and the rain pelted down to the point that all scenery more than two meters away was cut off like a dismembered body. The boy and Uncle sat on a tree stump and watched the rain. These thunderstorms would begin everyday between one and two in the afternoon, completely washing away any tracks and dung the elephants might have left behind. Based on Jiatong's more than a decade of experience hunting elephants, he knew you needed to find the tracks or dung before the thunderstorm starts, because otherwise even a hunting dog with the most sensitive nose in the world would have no choice but to bark futilely into the rain. Thunderstorms also brought endless hope. The elephant herd usually traveled at dusk, when it was cool, but the thunderstorms often forced them to push up their travel time to the afternoon. At the same time, the rain functioned as a natural screen. Walking slowly through the rain, the elephants seemed to be camouflaged as short trees. Yu Jiatong was carrying two rifles and a parang, and the boy was also carrying a rifle and a parang. They tried to avoid walking in the rain to protect their gunpowder and to keep their rifles from jamming. Two weeks earlier, when Jiatong was passing a Punan longhouse, he hired a young Punan hunter to serve as a guide. The Punan are excellent trackers, and two weeks later the hunter used a combination of his own language and hand gestures to indicate that if there were some kind of animal on the island that was able to remain undetected after having been tracked by a Punan for two weeks, that must mean that it belonged to a species that was either critically endangered or already extinct. Without accepting any compensation, the Punan hunter disappeared into the rainforest like a ghost. This was their fifth week hunting elephants. After having already spent years moving through the rainforest, Yu Jiatong's knowledge of the rainforest was not any way inferior to that of the Punan. Accordingly, the departure of the Punan hunter did not affect Yu Jiatong's confidence in the slightest. He led the boy along a secret path that the Yangtze River Brigade had previously followed, through a site where the brigade and government troops had fought a bloody battle, past the route that the Yangtze River Brigade troops took when they fled following their defeat by government forces, and they safely avoided the still-live traps that Yangtze River Brigade troops had placed in the area. The body of a government soldier with an indeterminate skin color was impaled to a tree with several wooden stakes. The corpse had obviously been consumed by wild animals, its bones were scattered around on the ground, and the only thing that could still be clearly identified was the soldier's dark green camouflage steel helmet. A brown-shirt soldier from the Little Rhino Brigade had hanged himself from a small tree. Vines covered the skeleton like a death shroud, like a man-eating plant seizing its prey. Sometimes Uncle and the boy slept in a tent, and other times they slept in one of the small wooden rooms that Yangtze River Brigade troops had erected in the forest to rest or hide. One of these hard-to-find wooden rooms would appear every day or two, and sometimes they would have a small flag with a black dragon against a red background. Bones from two corpses—an adult's and a child's—were scattered across the floor of one of these rooms. The tattered clothing and long hair clearly indicated that the adult had been a woman. The child's skull had been smashed open. To save bullets, Yu Jiatong hunted with a bamboo bow and arrow.

"This is where I killed my first elephant."

Jiatong pointed to a silvergrass grove. Most of the elephant bones had already sunk into the mud, and the ones lying in the grass resembled metallic parts from some machine. The second and third elephants Jiatong shot had been sleeping in a pond, and the bones lying in and outside the water were now all covered in moss and algae, like some sort of ancient bones. The fourth one was killed in a marsh. After the bull elephant that had been separated from its herd was shot several times it ran into a dead tree, then entered a marsh that was so deep it couldn't touch the bottom. Its bones and a pair of enormous tusks remain buried there. Jiatong killed his fifth elephant under a fig tree, after the young bull elephant had just finished mating with a female, and to this day their bones remained neatly arranged, kneeling below the tree. The sixth and seventh were killed in a plain. They were two bulls that had been fighting, and their bones still faintly retained their standoff stance. The eighth was a calf with a pair of small banana-like tusks. Terrified, it tried to hide behind a pair of adult females, and the bones of all three animals remained entangled in a field that recently was burned by wildfires, leaving the bones unevenly charred, like the remains of a wooden house.

"Including a hundred and thirty-seven baby crocodiles that were born just yesterday, this park currently has five thousand six hundred and twelve crocodiles," Wang Dada said as he walked. "Apart from a couple hundred that are either on display or are used for performances, the rest are all reserved for commercial use."

The boy followed Wang Dada into the sales department of the Daro Crocodile Observation Park. The sales department was enormous, and on display there were all sorts of goods made from crocodile skin, including handbags, wallets, suitcases, shoes, belts, watch bands, gloves, sofas, notebooks with crocodile-skin covers, and crocodile specimens of different sizes. . . .

"Most of the goods produced in this park are intended for export. What you see here is only a small part of the total." Wang Dada casually selected one of the most expensive wallets and belts and told the attendant to pack them up. "Shicai, here is a small gift. I hope you don't find it too shabby."

When they left the sales department they followed a winding cement path, and in the park filled with all sorts of different tropical plants they strolled past several hundred crocodile pens. The crocodiles were assigned to each pen based on their age. The pens were made from waist-high cement walls that formed small ponds. Some were positioned under the sun, others in the shade. In the pens, the crocodiles were packed in like sardines. When the large crocodiles saw someone they wouldn't move a muscle, while the small crocodiles would quickly scurry away.

"Shicai." A dark-skinned worker greeted the boy.

"That is Minhao, a former member of the Flame Mountain Brigade," Wang Dada said. "There are many former members of the Flame Mountain Brigade who now work in this park. As they say, you shouldn't let your own fertile wastewater flow into someone else's fields. These troops followed me loyally for many years, so now I have a responsibility to look after them."

The boy grunted in agreement.

"Although these crocodiles were all hatched and raised in this park, we also have some wild-caught specimens, which are extremely fierce." Wang Dada pointed to a large crocodile that resembled a living fossil. "Don't be deceived by its lack of motion. Many workers have learned that the hard way." Wang Dada showed the boy the scars on his arms and legs. "This is their handiwork. The injuries I received during the decade or more that I spent in the rainforest are no match for the ones I've suffered working in the park this past few years."

Yu Jiatong led the boy to the various locations where he had previously killed elephants, and the two of them stayed in each location for up to three days, hoping to see the elephant families that might have survived the earlier attacks by Uncle and his subordinates. The sites of the elephant hunts were now overgrown with weeds and trees, and no fresh tracks were visible. The boy spoke very little, to the point that he resembled his mute mother. He quietly absorbed the hunting techniques and rainforest survival skills that his uncle imparted. He would periodically go into the forest alone to hunt, and if his luck was good, he might be able to bag himself a wild boar or a muntjac; but most of the time he returned home empty-handed. Every time the boy left Uncle his courage always seemed to grow. Several times he wandered too far afield and got lost, and he would develop an urge to run away, but his feet would invariably hesitate, and like a baby rhinoceros he would inevitably end up returning to his uncle's side. Once he had already gone quite a way when he realized he had forgotten both his rifle and parang. The rainforest was like an enormous machine that operated around the clock, like billions of hatchlings milling about. The boy heard a low rumble coming from somewhere off to his side. He looked up and saw a leopard-like mountain lion perched on tree branch a yard in front of him, staring at him with its fangs bared. . . .

Will it attack me? The boy felt a surge of panic.

"You don't look like you were just hunting," Uncle said when he saw the boy return. "You look like Beethoven searching for inspiration."

That night when the boy went to the tent to sleep, he dreamed of an animal with a long trunk. Government troops surrounded him and Uncle. A red-hot bullet burning like a Molotov cocktail slowly entered his abdomen, like a beehive firecracker. Blood stained the lower half of his body. The bullet suddenly became a boar's tusk, slicing his inner organs into jam. A grenade exploded in Uncle's chest, and as the wound erupted into a fireball, the shrapnel reassembled to form an enormous blossom. A herd of long-trunk animals scattered the government troops, then used their trunks to pick up the boy and place him on a large stone on the riverbank. They used their trunks to caress his wound, suck at it, and spit out the bullet—or was it a boar's tusk? The animals used their trunks to pick several different kinds of medicinal herbs, kneaded them with their hoofs, then applied them to the wound. . . .

"It's ten-thirty." Wang Dada looked at his wristwatch with the crocodile-skin band. "It's feeding time. Let's go and watch the excitement."

The enormous open-air crocodile shed was as big as a soccer field, and in the center there was a man-made pond where more than forty crocodiles were being fed. In four tall observation towers, numerous spectators were watching as crocodiles swam around in the water. The crocodiles on land were motionless, and most of them had their mouths open, revealing the deep white interior of their mouth cavities, like wild lilies. Two workers lowered more than a hundred live chickens and ducks from the observation tower as the spectators watched in awe. Inside the park the birds ran around squawking desolately and fleeing nimbly. The crocodiles, by contrast, appeared slow and clumsy, but in less than five minutes they had already devoured their prey. All that was left was a fat cock standing on a dead branch, trembling. The crocodiles must have already been full, and therefore paid it no heed.

"Visitors always love this part," Wang Dada said with a smile. "The crocodiles also have a tame side. Let's go. I'll take you to have a look."

Uncle and the boy spent three and a half months retracing the path to the enormous piles of elephant bones that Uncle had discovered during his hunt a decade earlier. The pond was once again filled with water, submerging elephant skeletons that were either in the process of drinking or playing in the water. Kingfishers, brown swifts, and dragonflies flitted back and forth over the water. Schools of fish gulped down food. How was it that these ponds, which had previously completely dried up, now had so many fish? The first time the boy saw a pile of elephant bones he carefully counted them and found that there were sixty-eight in all, one of which was still hanging from a tree. From the condition of the overgrown vegetation, it was clear that in the more than ten years since the hunting expedition left, no humans—or elephants—had returned here. The boy sat on a log and imagined how, centuries earlier, sixty-eight elephants must have lived and played in these fields, and he listened as Uncle told him how, on the day Shicai was born, a herd of long-trunk animals had trampled his mother's vegetable garden and part of her fruit orchard.

"The evening you were born, your father was still at the gambling hall. My mother and I went to your house to help out. . . . At around nine that evening, the sound of wild animals could be heard coming from the vegetable garden, and your family's dogs kept barking in that direction. Your maternal grandmother, Shinong, and I took flashlights and went to investigate. There was a herd of elephants resembling the shadow of a wooden house—like enormous snails that were either crawling around or standing in place. They were using their trunks to uproot mango trees and to consume bananas, corn, and vegetables. They extended their trunks into the wells, then spurted water in all directions, splattering droplets onto the roof of your house. We were so terrified we didn't even dare to breathe. Half an hour later, the animals slowly wandered away. The next day, the vegetable garden had been reduced to a mud pit and there were bucket-sized hoof prints everywhere. Someone organized an elephant-hunting expedition to follow these hoof prints and kill those long-trunk animals. However, it then rained hard for two days straight, which completely washed away their traces and scent. It was said that the elephants had known it would rain hard the next day, which is why they dared appear where humans lived in the first place. . . ."

Jiatong lit an imported cigarette that he had been saving for a long time. "Shicai . . ."

"What?"

"When the elephants appeared in your family's vegetable garden . . ."

The boy waited for a long time, but Uncle didn't say anything else.

It was like a stage in a theater in ancient Greece. There were four or five spectators watching the performance, and Wang Dada and the boy sat in the first row. A waist-high railing separated the spectators from the stage. The stage was a cement oval, and half of it was filled with water. Twelve crocodiles, their stomachs bulging from having eaten so much, crawled through the water or over the cement ground. Two dark-skinned trainers were standing on the stage, and one of them was holding a microphone and explaining crocodile habits to the audience. When the performance began, the two trainers performed countless tricks, like kissing the crocodiles, lying with them, riding them, pulling their tails, dancing with them, pretending to copulate with them, and inserting their torso into the crocodiles' mouths. . . . Probably because their boss Wang Dada was present, the two trainers worked very hard. The audience clapped nonstop, but the boy was not amused.

"Visitors just love this!" Wang Dada exclaimed.

In the park's air-conditioned and luxurious restaurant, Wang Dada treated the boy to a large meal of crocodile meat. Using his knife and fork to gesture at the eight dishes on the table, each of which featured crocodile meat cooked in a different way, Dada said, "Although this park primarily produces crocodile-skin products, it's a shame to simply throw out all of the meat.

Therefore, I'm in the process of promoting crocodile meat to the world. If it catches on, then this park's business will become a lot easier. . . ."

Using a bowl and chopsticks, the boy devoured all eight dishes. Crocodile meat resembled lizard meat, monkey meat, and snake meat and was even like chicken or duck meat. After they were done, Wang Dada seemed reluctant to leave. He shook the boy's shoulders with both hands, like a sun bear shaking a fruit tree. Dada personally accompanied the boy to the exit. As they were walking down the walkway decorated with crocodile specimens, the boy saw, hidden in a corner, an old, yellowed newspaper clipping. In large Chinese characters the headline read: "Crocodile Attack in the Rajang River, Daughter of the Shi Family is Devoured." . . .

Qinyun escorted the boy back to where he had left his bike. As the boy was getting on his bicycle, Qinyun, her eyes bloodshot, suddenly said quietly, ". . . is it you?"

The boy's heart lurched.

"Is it really you?"

The boy remembered the old cock standing on the log, trembling, and wondered whether it was still alive.

"Were . . . were you really able to do it? . . . " Warm tears streamed down Qinyun's face.

Hualala. For more than four months, the sound of water had filled the boy's ears. Entering these sunless days, in the belly of the rainforest and cut off from the world, the sound of water became his only connection to the outside world. *Zilala. honglonglong. pingping. paipai.* Sometimes the sound resembled a sounder of boars crossing a river, sometimes it resembled a symphony of birds and insects, and sometimes it resembled a wildfire burning through the rainforest. The louder the water, the more frequent the animal sounds. Each of the animal sounds followed a different pattern, with some always coming from the same place, some alternating from one side and another, or from above and below. The boy had an astonishing familiarity with these sounds, and based on the sound alone he could tell that a sun bear was defecating, a pig-tailed macaque was nursing, or a pair of monitor lizards were copulating. It was as if his own butt, nipples, and penis had sprouted ears and could detect the sound of other species' lust. The boy once again left Uncle and entered the sunless rainforest. He stepped on old leaves, decayed branches, and muddy ground, as though walking barefoot on something living. There was no visible trace of any animals, birds, or insects, but in this kind of place, shapes and images are not at all useful. Instead, the boy had to use his sense of hearing to tell things apart. At this point, sound was more tangible and real than visual images—it was more corporeal, and lent itself to the boy's ability to feel, smell, lick, and chew his counterparts' skin, bones, blood, feces, and saliva. All wind and sunlight were completely cordoned off by the rainforest's canopy, the vegetation was unusually peaceful, but in this kind of place, plants were even more animalistic than animals themselves. The boy could sense that the plants had fat like bears, fangs like boars, beards like mountain lions, horns like rhinos, and trunks like elephants. . . . There was a loud and clear cry, mixed in with the churning of flowing water and the cries of birds and insects. The boy stopped, and the animal emitted another cry. . . . Was it them? Or was it "them?" The sound seemed to be coming from somewhere far away—somewhere with abundant water and vegetation. Was it coming from the south? From the north? The boy slowly moved in the latter direction. Ten minutes later, he heard the sound again. Was it them? It must be them. . . . The boy was ecstatic. The second sound seemed to be coming from a different location from the first. The boy hesitated but ultimately decided to head toward the second location. About twenty minutes later he heard a faint call. This sound was even more murky and more distant than the earlier one. Could it be that he was moving further and further away from them? *Xixi susu.* A sound behind him was surging toward him like a flood. The boy grabbed his rifle. A cluster of wild orchids and nepenthes had been crushed and the crowns of trees were trembling. What *was* it? The boy's pulse quickened, as the hand with which he was gripping the rifle became soaked in sweat.

"I heard it!"

A parang sliced through several vines as Uncle emerged from the foliage, his forehead, neck, and hair covered in leaves and spiderwebs. He excitedly shouted to the boy, "I heard it! Did you, Shicai?" The boy nodded. Then, hand in hand, they went in pursuit of the sound. An hour later they heard several shouts, each one clearer than the last. The sound was so loud that it resembled a planet exploding. By evening, however, the sound had stopped. Had they escaped? Had they fallen silent? The red setting sun gradually sunk behind the weeds. The boy and his uncle set up camp and cooked some food, but they didn't hear anything more. Night was precisely when they were usually most active. Jiatong climbed a fig tree and used his binoculars to look around until the sky was completely dark. Over the next two days they had to search relying only on their sense of touch. It was not until the morning of the third day that they finally heard the sound again. The boy and his uncle searched the nearby pond, river, field, and bushes but found no indication that anything had passed through or stopped there. Could their hearing have been mistaken? Could the sound have been an illusion? Or maybe it wasn't them at all? On the sixth day, there was an enormous, clear sound. It seemed as though the source was only about fifty meters away, but when they rushed over they found nothing there. Uncle repeatedly climbed a tree to look around. He smelled the air, the earth, and the branches and leaves. He placed his ear to the ground. Their fleshy hoofs made no sound when they walked, but their appearance might cause a disruption among other animals. The spare batteries of Uncle's and the boy's flashlight had already been used up, which significantly limited their sphere of activity after sunset. In Uncle's face the boy could see his earlier passion and tenacity, to the point that he fully resembled the young Yu Jiatong that the boy remembered from Teacher Shao's lecture hall more than a decade earlier.

"Shicai. . . ." Two weeks later, the boy and his uncle were setting up camp in a field, and as Jiatong was using a stick to prod the fire, he suddenly called out to the boy.

The boy yawned.

"Have you ever wondered what might happen if the revolution succeeds?" Jiatong's vigor had not diminished in the slightest over the preceding five months, especially after they heard the elephant calls. He slept remarkably little every night. "I've never thought about it, because I know better than anyone that this revolution will never succeed. Less than three months after the Yangtze River Brigade was established, I realized that this was the case. . . ."

Still groggy from sleep, the boy looked up at Uncle.

"I always knew that this day would come. . . ."

The boy still didn't say anything. Every day he followed Uncle through rivers and forests, and every night he would collapse from exhaustion. . . .

"I know what you're thinking. . . ." Uncle paused. "Sooner or later, someone will carry out the revolution. . . . Shicai . . ."

. . . The boy yawned. Was he dreaming? Or was Uncle talking in his sleep? . . . Uncle's moanlike speech drifted into the boy's ears.

". . . . I'll always remember how, amidst the sound of gunfire and comrades screaming . . . at that point I'd give up everything to pursue that sound. . . . Ling Qiao . . . she was my final lover in the Yangtze River Brigade. . . . She had voluptuous breasts, a firm butt, and would scream with excitement . . . like . . . how strange . . . it was just like an elephant's call . . . sometimes it was low and far away, while other times it would be ear-piercingly loud . . . sometimes it would be gentle, and other times coarse. . . . It would make my entire body feel buoyant, as though I wanted to point a gun at her head and pull the trigger. . . ."

The boy once again rode a dream beast to collect the bones of his elder brothers and younger sister. The dream beast broke up countless chicken graves, walked among the legendary elephant graves, stomped on the riverbank's crocodile bones that resembled thornbushes, and sniffed at the skulls in the hallway of the longhouse. Fadiya was washing her hair in the hallway of the longhouse and was baring a pair of breasts that were pink and trembling like a pair of avian air sacs—resembling enormous stemless and leafless parasitic mushrooms. Like a white fungal puffball, the boy's member emitted mistlike spores. Uncle's description of the voluptuous breasts of his Yangtze River Brigade comrade resonated in the boy's ears all night. It was as if Uncle were describing an extinct species of insect or snail.

The boy didn't return to the tent, and instead spent the entire night sleeping while leaning against a cliff wall. At five the next morning he was awakened by a loud noise. He opened his eyes and saw a rainbow. It was low and faint, like a reflection in the water or like a chameleon's camouflage color that was about to fade away, and was floating in the hazy sky above the hazel bushes. About a hundred meters away, four elephants were playing in a pond. The lower halves of their bodies were submerged, and they used their long trunks to suck in water and then spurt it onto themselves or into the air. The air above the pond was full of water vapor, and rainbows obscurely streamed through it. Of the four elephants, one was a bull, and its curved tusks were like blades. Its trunk was like a water snake, and its back was like a whale. It was as though a chain of islands were floating in the water. In a field to the right of the pond there were another seven elephants, including one calf and six adults. Two were male and the other five were female. They were picking grass and leaves from small bushes with their trunks. The elephants standing in the grass resembled an array of flowers in a sea of algae, and several birds were hopping back and forth along their backs.

Jiatong was sitting cross-legged next to the boy, intently watching the elephants. A pair of binoculars was hanging from his neck, and his rifle was lying next to him. How long had Uncle been staring at the elephants? Why didn't he pick up his rifle? Jiatong glanced at the boy, then continued watching the elephants.

A large elephant, a cow, stepped out from a forest to the right and joined its companions in the field looking for food, thereby increasing the total number of elephants to twelve. The calf walked between the legs of the adults so that only its back, head, ears, and trunk occasionally surfaced out of the tall grass, and from a distance it resembled a baby bird in a nest. Eventually the calf emerged from the grass and entered the pond to play in the water. The adults standing on land had their posteriors oriented toward the boy and stood motionless for a long time. Jiatong handed the boy the binoculars, through which the boy saw that the distant elephants' posteriors were as still as stone. He shifted his gaze to the elephants grazing in the field. A cow facing the boy was picking leaves from branches overhead. The boy observed carefully as the elephant picked several leaves and placed them in its mouth. Then he shifted his gaze and turned to the next elephant. He continued in this way until he reached the fourth elephant. This one had its side toward the boy, and on its back there were two clusters of dark red flesh, like a satellite image of burnt sections of the Amazon rainforest. The boy switched to a larger lens and saw that the dark patches were actually gaping wounds. A patchwork of indentions and depressions covered virtually the animal's entire back. They were dripping with blood, and some had formed scabs while others were open wounds revealing exposed bones and were covered in flies and gnats. Even from a hundred meters away, the boy could almost hear the *wengweng* sound of the insects. The birds perched on the elephant's back pecked as they walked back and forth, periodically turning their heads and twisting their tails. These were the sorts of wounds that you normally would only see on a carcass, and it was unbelievable that a live elephant could have such large craters on its back that it resembled a Bactrian camel. The boy looked at some of the other elephants in the field and saw that they all had similar wounds on their backs, abdomens, legs, and even their heads. Some of the wounds were large and others were small. Some elephants had only one or two, while others might have four or five. There was a bull that, apart from its head and legs, seemed to not have a single square inch of intact flesh. The boy shifted his gaze to the elephants in the pond. Aside from the calf and two of the cows, the cow that had already come ashore and the two bulls that were still in the water all had wounds. A sharp elephant call cut through the field, but it was unclear where exactly the sound was coming from.

The boy put down his binoculars and glanced over at Uncle. Uncle was still staring at the herd. The boy picked up his binoculars again. These contusions did not resemble gunshot wounds, but rather it looked like the animals had been attacked by a sharp object or some sort of infection. There were no animals on this island capable of attacking an elephant. Was this the work of humans? . . . The boy put down his binoculars. Several eagles soared through the sky. A flock of birds flew out of the field, as though someone were casting a web. The web fluctuated in size, appearing alternatively tight and loose, and after spreading for a while, it eventually covered the entire field. The elephants playing in the water gradually slowed down as the rainbow became weaker and weaker, until eventually it disappeared altogether. The gray sky turned light red. The dawn light gushed forth like water, the clouds became an odd shade of emerald, as the eastern sky appeared to be covered in fossils of flatworms and brachiopods, like slugs in amber. One bull elephant walked quickly through the field, and as it passed by it rammed an enormous tree and produced a bitter cry, while the others remained as quiet as tortoises. After the bull rammed the tree seven or eight times, it bellowed and ran through the field until eventually it turned around and rammed the tree again. The tree was like a mountain, and next to it the elephant appeared puny, like an ant trying to shake a stone. Perhaps it was a wound that was troubling the elephant? Eventually the bull calmed down, whereupon a cow began running and bellowing and, as if the two animals were in a relay, also began ramming the same tree. The other elephants were unable to calm down, and soon the entire herd was bellowing while facing the cow. Was this an expression of appeasement? Of sympathy? Of lamentation? . . . Two other elephants suddenly left the herd and also began ramming the same tree. . . . Was this "them?" The enormous herd of legends? During the many years Uncle had spent hunting elephants, the largest herd he had personally observed on the island consisted of only six elephants, and even elderly native hunters had never seen a herd with a double-digit number of elephants.

"Shicai," Jiatong suddenly said, after half an hour. The boy was still staring at the disturbance among the elephants. "Apart from your Shi family and my Yu family, very few people know what happened the night elephants appeared in your family's vegetable garden. Because Mother didn't want the elephants trampling your family's vegetable garden, she grabbed a flashlight and rushed over to shoo them away, whereupon one of them trampled her to death. . . . To be killed by wild animals in one's home is decidedly inauspicious, and therefore this incident became a taboo topic for both of our families. . . ."

It was unclear when, precisely, the elephants' bellows suddenly stopped, and the herd once again became as silent as tortoises. The elephants in the pond came ashore and gathered together with the elephants in the field. Led by the enormous cow, they headed toward an overgrown field to the right. At the back of the herd was another large cow. The herd slowly proceeded forward, one after another, head to tail. Through the binoculars, their mottled wounds could also be seen stretching from head to tail, like the glow from the setting sun. Uncle, relying on his astuteness and experience, was the first to realize that a gigantic animal was nearby. He looked back, as did the boy, and they saw an enormous female elephant standing two meters behind them. Its body was as dark as a rainy sky, its skin resembled ammonites, and its ears resembled a burnt war shield. Its eyes were like a whale's, its nose resembled a rocky peak, its legs resembled totem poles—forming an enormous panorama that exceeded the limits of the Uncle's and the boy's gaze. They stood motionless, so quiet that they could even hear each other's hearts beating. There was a light morning breeze as the morning sun shone down on the elephant's back and head, like a wildfire burning through a crack in the earth. Except in his dreams, the boy had never been so close to a wild elephant before.

The elephant stood perfectly still with an angry and cautious attitude, as though poised to attack. It only needed to take several steps forward and it could easily trample their rifles, crush their organs, and shatter their skulls. A sharp sound came from the elephants that were lazily walking back and forth in the field. The cow faced the boy and his uncle, then began to retreat. Each time it took a step back, its body would lean slightly to the right, as though it were standing on a giant concave surface. After the cow had retreated about fifteen meters, it turned around and, with its back to the boy and his uncle, returned to the herd. What the boy and his uncle saw in the field no longer resembled elephants, but rather ambulatory pieces of decayed flesh. A wound shaped like a giant wave covered the elephant's buttocks and extended to its entire left rear leg. The animal's left leg was almost completely rotted, its bones were visible, and it walked with a prominent limp. The elephants in the field came to a halt and called out once again, as the female elephant with the wounded hindquarters struggled to pick up the pace.

Mother stood in the doorway of their house, quacking and gesturing anxiously to her son. It was three o'clock in the afternoon, and the boy had just returned from the crocodile observation park, his belly full of crocodile meat. He had just gotten out of the car when his mother pulled him into the study. The study, which used to be very neat and orderly, was now in a state of complete disarray. Half of the books that had been the bookshelves looked as they had been preyed on, and now some were lying on the floor fully intact, while others had been torn apart and dismembered. The *Landscape of Wind and Rain* scroll hanging on the wall was unharmed, but a reproduction of a batik painting and a calendar featuring a set of famous renaissance paintings had disappeared without a trace. Compared to the delicate pavilions in the *Landscape of Wind and Rain*, the color-ful, nude-filled Western paintings appeared even more exqui-site. The boy and his mother stepped on one book carcass after another, producing a *zhilagada* sound that seemed as if the books were moaning and crying for help. The desk's drawers had been pulled out, the drawer openings were stuffed with ripped-up paper, and the day's newspaper on the desk was in tatters. Father was sitting in a corner, his legs extended and his hands dangling down. His digestive track, from his throat and esophagus, down to his stomach, was completely stuffed with colorful, chewed-up paper. His stomach was protruding as though he had con-sumed an entire boar. His head was raised, his eyes were half-closed, and he had a colorful map stuffed in his mouth. That was an octavo map of Borneo, of which the hot and humid southern portion of the island had already disappeared into Father's stomach, and the northwestern coast that abutted onto the South China Sea was soaked with his saliva. Very few peo-ple in Daro knew that Father had died from gorging himself on books. How Father and Grandfather had managed to break down the shed door remained an unsolved Shi family mystery. . . .

There was a torrential downpour. Rain pounded down on the galvanized iron sheets and the courtyard trees of the Yangtze River Brigade base camp. The two dogs were still lying in the hallway, like a pair of small crocodiles. The bird calls were filled with human flavor, resembling the sound of carpenters, metal-lurgists, and loggers. In the rain, Ling Qiao was slicing the throats of chickens and ducks as elegantly as though she were clipping her nails, and she was plucking the birds as daintily as though she were doing embroidery. She was singing while chop-ping up the birds, and when she brought out several dishes of steaming chicken and duck meat, she was still singing the same song. She put down the dishes, opened her oil-paper umbrella, and ventured out into the rain. This was the sixteenth day after Jiatong, and the boy returned to the base camp following their elephant-hunting expedition. Jiatong had not gone out to hunt for more than ten days, and the livestock in the shed were rapidly decreasing. All the leftovers were used to feed the pigs and the two dogs. There was nothing left to feed the crocodiles, and therefore they all headed either upriver or downriver, but each day at sunrise and sunset they would still gather beneath the suspension bridge. During this period the crocodiles' stomachs were mostly filled with mountain boars, mountain deer, and monitor lizards, but they were also capable of devouring a sun bear. They were camouflaged as stones, driftwood, scum, mud, and the reflection of trees or the suspension bridge in the water. If you looked down from the bridge, it would appear as if there were no crocodiles at all. "1970, evening, rain. While marching along the Rajang River with the soldiers under my command, we saw a bull elephant being attacked by a group of crocodiles while trying to cross the river." Jiatong drank one can of rice wine after another, and his face became as slick as a salamander as sweat poured down like rain. "The elephant repeatedly bellowed in agony, and rushed toward the shore, disappearing into the rainforest. Although the elephant eventually succeeded in escaping, it lost a lot of skin in the process. I didn't have a chance to get off a shot, and instead could only watch as the elephant escaped. There were too many crocodiles in the river, and I didn't dare try to ford it."

The study was hot and humid, and raindrops noisily dripped into the hallway. On the bookcases covering the three walls, the books—most of which the boy had already read—seemed to rise and fall, as their contents flashed before his eyes and resonated in his ears. If the boy were to open one of them, the sound of that book would become extremely loud. Uncle leafed through an old notebook, on the cover of which there were four characters in old seal script written in ballpoint pen: *Elephant Hunting Journal.* After drinking, a hoarse voice read a portion of this text. The journal briefly recorded the time, location, and circumstances of the eight bull elephants that Uncle killed, and the one bull elephant that he had let go free. Uncle was holding a ballpoint pen, and he hesitantly prepared to record this last elephant herd sighting. "July 12, 1974. Clear skies. Five a.m. The border of Sarawak's third district and Indonesia's Kalimantan, near the Zhilong River. We see Borneo's largest elephant herd from this century standing in a field, grazing and playing in water. Twelve adults and one calf. Three bulls. The calf and two of the cows appear healthy, but the rest are sick or wounded, their skin peeling off and hair falling out, and open sores all over their bodies." Uncle read aloud what he had written and made a correction. First he wrote, "Within half a month, the sick elephants had died . . ." Then he erased this and wrote, "Within a few months, the entire herd was extinct. . . ." But then he erased this as well. Eventually he stopped writing and closed the notebook. He carefully placed the notebook into a metal box. Then he closed the box.

There was a torrential downpour. The boy and his uncle loudly chewed chicken necks and duck wings, and it seemed as though the chickens' necks were still squawking and the ducks' wings were still flapping in the water. The boy had experienced this power of rice wine during his stay in the longhouse. Two cans of wine entered his belly, as the roasted suckling pig began to appear as charming as a woman. He saw Fadiya's fragrant and tasty body. Dezhong's clan had used this kind of rice wine when receiving guests and dancing a warm welcome guest dance or when dancing a bloody warrior dance or a foul-smelling sacrificial head dance. The rice wine transformed their bellies into bamboo baskets used for storing skulls. Small insects repeatedly flew into the lamp shade, leaving enormous, fractured shadows on the bookcases, the ceiling, and the blackboard—like diseased spirits of elephants roaming through the rain forest. Beneath the lamp there were several dozen insects, some of which were still flapping around, and even though a mosquito candle was burning on the table there were still an astonishing number of mosquitoes in the room. *Pai.* If Uncle and the boy repeatedly slapped themselves, their hands would come away with numerous blood splotches. When the female mosquitoes flew close to the lamp, the human blood in their bellies glowed such that they resembled fireflies. The pile of chicken and duck bones on the table continued to grow, and Uncle and the boy finished most of the vegetable dishes. The cut-up chicken and duck heads remained on the serving plate.

After burying his father, the boy returned to the study, opened the desk's bottom drawer, and removed a metal box that was hidden beneath a newspaper. He opened the box, releasing a rusty smell, and the black cover of *Elephant Hunting Journal* resembled an intact corpse sitting inside. "Now that your father has died, you can look through these records." Uncle placed the box on the table littered with chicken and duck bones, next to the boy's hand. The boy opened the journal. After the rain the stream exploded, and the bottom half of the silvergrass stalks were under water, while beneath the water wild taro, wild water spinach, and various other wild plants could be seen. Monitor lizards extended their snakelike necks and heads and waved their legs and tails in the water. Coucals were sitting in shrubs preening their wings. The sound of the boy turning pages accompanied the sound of the water, birds, and frogs.

The boy lay half-asleep with his head on the bone-covered table, the rice wine rising up from his belly like some sort of water bird, passing through his esophagus, his throat, and then hiding inside his skull. He slowly opened his eyes. The chickens and ducks began making a commotion. Several hens squawked, as though someone were cutting their turtlelike heads. The pigs also began making a ruckus. Was it another monitor lizard? A snake? The table began to rock back and forth, as Uncle grabbed the corner of the table and tried to stand up, holding a parang in one hand and a rifle in the other. "Dead lizard . . ." In a haze, the boy saw Uncle take his rifle, turn on his flashlight, then march down the hallway toward the base camp in the rain. The boy saw the source of the flashlight beam shaking in the darkness and was reminded of the night Ma Guoxiong had first led him to the Yangtze River Brigade's base camp. He was reminded of that strange animal that had been camouflaged in the silvergrass grove. The boy once again rested his head on the table, closed his eyes, and then fell asleep. The cut-open chicken and duck heads fused together to form a strange new head, and the limbs on the plate also began to fuse together, forming a weird chicken-duck hybrid that began pecking at the human head resting on the table. The chicken consumed half of his lips as the duck swallowed his eyeballs. The chicken and duck began struggling with one another, whereupon the boy woke up with a start. The sound of chickens and ducks fighting in the pen drifted over. The boy rubbed his eyes and looked around. How long had he been asleep? Maybe it had just been two or three minutes? The boy saw someone standing in the courtyard, in the dark rain. The person had a parang hanging from his waist, with a human head inscribed on the handle. The shadowy individual appeared camouflaged as a tree shadow and was hidden among several other tree shadows. In the darkness there was the sound of urgent footsteps. The shadowy figure took the parang hanging from his waist, held it in his hand, then disappeared into the darkness. More chicken, duck, and pig sounds emerged from the shed, and dogs could be heard barking in the courtyard. The boy heard someone chewing paper and flipping sheets in the study. He heard Teacher Shao teaching and the students reciting their lessons. He heard the sound of chalk on the blackboard. Geckos were running across the *Landscape of Wind and Rain.* Three enormous heads were making hiccuplike moaning sounds, and the skulls in the bamboo basket were trembling. Why hadn't Uncle returned yet? The boy took the parang and flashlight that were sitting on the chair, then crossed the courtyard toward the animal pen.

The floodwaters quickly receded. Several two-spot gourami and climbing fish were swimming through the verdant grass. A white-bellied crake was standing on a jackfruit leaf and swaying in the wind, and occasionally an enormous reptile would pass through the silvergrass grove, making a *hualala* sound as it searched for prey. The thick journal was mostly filled with empty pages, but the front portion contained records pertaining to the elephant hunt. Then, after many empty pages, in the latter portion of the journal there was a passage the boy hadn't noticed before: "On December 20, 1954, Shicai was born. I went with Mother to Sister's house to help out. That night wild elephants entered the Shi family garden. Mother went out alone to drive the elephants away and was trampled to death by a female elephant. The next morning, Father and Brother-in-law collected some food, tents, guns, and parangs, and headed out in pursuit of the herd. It rained for two days straight, and after ten days, Brother-in-law returned to the Shi family home, while Father pursued the elephants alone. Father never returned."

The chickens and ducks appeared terrified under the flash-light's beam. Five pigs bowed their heads and hid in the corner, as though they had done something wrong. Where did Uncle go? The boy was about to call out, when there was another loud commotion in the chicken pen. The boy became light-headed. He felt an after-effect from the rice wine, as though millions of ants were biting his nerves, and almost fell over. The chickens spread their wings, like rubber balls bouncing around. The shed's iron fence door was already ajar, and a large green monitor liz-ard was crouched in the doorway eating a small hen. As the hen emitted a terrifying death howl, the boy rushed over to the liz-ard, hacking wildly with his parang. His flashlight fell to the ground, and the boy gripped his parang with both hands and continued hacking. A cacophony of sounds could be heard com-ing from the shed. Chickens were squawking and ducks were quacking. Pigs were squealing. There was the sound of metal striking metal. Footsteps. Someone or something was crying out. . . . The boy hacked with his parang until his hands were numb, whereupon he leaned against a tree trunk to catch his breath. He picked up his flashlight. The parang was covered in blood, and his hands, feet, clothing, and even his feet were also splattered with blood. The lizard was chopped into bits, and the hen in its mouth was also chopped into paste. A person com-pletely covered in blood was lying on the ground next to the liz-ard. That person was covered in knife wounds, and his face was drenched in dark blood. The boy was so terrified that he dropped his parang. Another figure holding a parang was standing next to the lizard and the dead man, facing the boy. The other figure held up his blood-covered parang and, with a *huo* sound, chopped off the dead man's head. The other figure then leaned over, grabbed the decapitated head by the hair and lifted it up, as a stream of blood flowed to the ground like an earthworm.

Uncle's head had been separated from his body and was now swaying back and forth in midair. Uncle's eyes were closed, and his tongue was slightly visible, as though he were sound asleep. The boy shone his flashlight on the figure holding the head.

"Dezhong. . . ."

"My friend," the blood-covered Dezhong held up the head. "We finally killed him. . . ."

A bowl-sized water turtle and a spoon-sized field turtle were swimming together through the water, as a kingfisher camouflaged as a green leaf stared at the fish in the water and at a small green snake camouflaged as a water plant with tender leaves. Mother went out into the garden wearing plastic sandals. The floodwaters reached up to her calves, and some of the melon sheds and bean racks had been destroyed by the storm. Mother waded through the water to inspect the garden and rescue the inundated sprouts. "There are two opinions on where Father may have gone. One is that he was killed in the rainforest, and the other is that he has already become a master elephant hunter. Legend has it that Father hid the tusks from the elephants he slaughtered deep in a mountain cave, then erected terrifying traps all around the cave, which led people who later tried to recover the tusks to die horrible deaths. I am convinced that the second version is the correct one. One morning about half a year after Father disappeared, a pair of elephant tusks was found next to the Shi family's back door. After this, every few weeks another pair of tusks would appear next to the back door. Although Father-in-law was an opium addict and Brother-in-law was a gambling addict, by relying on these tusks that appeared by their door every few months, the family was somehow able to get by. Eventually Father-in-law managed to escape from the pig shed, and legend has it that this was also Father's doing. . . ." The boy shuddered, as the sound of chickens and ducks drifted over from the garden. More than a dozen ducks ran out of the pen and began swimming in the garden while pecking at fish and vegetable sprouts. Quacking loudly, Mother shooed the ducks away. ". . . After becoming the leader of the Yangtze River Brigade, he was constantly searching for that legendary cave. Father probably passed away when Shicai was eight. From that point on, elephant tusks never again appeared by the Shi family's back door. . . ."

There was a torrential downpour. Rainwater surged into the chicken coop like a river, washing away Uncle's and the lizard's blood. In addition to the lizard that the boy killed, there was also another that had been chopped to death in the chicken coop. The boy and Dezhong carried the latter carcass to the animal shed, then took Uncle's severed head and placed it in the hallway outside the study, where they covered it with five or six black shirts. The two dogs that had been chopped to death were lying in the courtyard. The rain washed away the bloodstains from Dezhong's and the boy's bodies and their parangs. Rainwater mixed with blood flowed into the boy's mouth, and he detected a sweet, acidic taste. Even after the boy entered the study to wipe off his body, this taste still lingered. Tears also flowed directly into his mouth. Dezhong stood in the hallway, leaning against the window with his back to the study and the parang hanging from his waist. The boy squatted in the doorway with his head bowed, trying to reconstruct what they might had said to each other in the shed. Small insects were still flying into the lamp shade of the gas lamp, and occasionally the sound of them bumping into the lamp shade would be loud enough to cut through the sound of the rain and reach the hallway. Every minute or two the sound of birds like dry branches breaking would emerge from the courtyard, as two nightingales that were probably perched beneath one of the rafters exchanged odd calls. Sounds of disturbances continued to emerge from the shed. Had another monitor lizard appeared? "Why . . ." The boy finally spit out a few indistinct words in a soft voice but was almost drowned out by the rain. Had Dezhong heard him? . . .

Maybe he had, and maybe he hadn't. A long, long time . . . The hallway still echoed with Dezhong's ghostly whisper. It seemed as though he were answering the boy, but it also seemed as though he couldn't resist defending himself.

"It was after we were robbed by those communists on our way from Daro to Kapit that I first came up with idea of killing your uncle . . . particularly since I knew you already had the same plan."

"How did you know that? . . . "

"After you got drunk in my house . . . you discussed it several times . . ." Dezhong fell silent. *Gagaga.* The sound of bird cries like dry branches breaking. *Gugugu.* Lovesick nightingales. "You told me: I want to kill Uncle. . . . Sometimes you said: I want to chop off his head. . . ."

" . . . "

"I heard it, and my family heard it too. Fadiya heard it and viewed you as a hero. . . . She congratulated you, gave you a parang, and danced the warrior dance for you. . . . She even planned to perform a victory dance for you and prepared a celebration. . . . Everyone saw Fadiya prepare that boar's tooth for you, to serve as a protective amulet for a head-hunting warrior about to embark on a mission. . . ."

"How did you find . . .?"

"After you left that night, I followed you . . . and then stayed nearby the entire time, except from those months when you went to hunt elephants. . . . I was waiting for an opportunity. . . . Actually, I had many opportunities . . . but wanted to give you a chance first. . . ."

The boy remembered that night when he noticed a strange animal watching him from the silvergrass grove. Perhaps . . ."it" had actually been Dezhong? . . . Now, however, there was no point in focusing on these details. . . .

"Was this for . . . that bounty?"

"Yes. . . . It will be very useful for my people. That is certainly one factor. Also, the Communist Party encouraged my people to join the insurrection and serve as their human shield, but the party only offered us with very inferior equipment. . . . Party members married our women, to satisfy their ambition. . . . More than once, your uncle placed his neck under your blade. Why did you lose your will?. . . ."

"Dezhong . . . I'm brave enough to leap into the river and wrestle with crocodiles, to stare a mountain lion in the face, or chop off the head of a wild boar . . . but I don't know why . . . when I saw Uncle's neck looking as fragile as a tender bamboo shoot, I . . . simply couldn't follow through . . ."

"My friend, I've never killed anyone before either, but my ancestors' heroism courses through my veins. The parang hanging from my waist collects their bravery and strength. My ancestors and I took the first cut on your behalf . . ."

"I didn't kill Uncle . . ."

"We killed him together, my friend."

"I didn't . . ."

"Like your uncle, you were discombobulated by the rice wine, which obscured your vision. After your uncle killed a monitor lizard in the animal shed, he left the shed in pursuit of another lizard. . . . When you entered the shed, you, like your uncle, were drunk from rice wine, and the hand with which you were holding your parang was trembling like a dog dick that can't find a bitch. You swung your parang and chopped a lizard. Your uncle heard the sound and came to look for you. . . . I hacked him from behind, and he fell at your feet . . . Later, we chopped him together. . . ."

"I only killed a lizard. . . ."

"Well said. It was indeed just like killing a lizard."

"I didn't kill Uncle . . ."

"My friend . . ."

"I didn't . . ."

"You became brave after drinking, but I didn't. I was very lucid—as lucid as an eagle nabbing its prey in midflight. I saw everything very clearly. . . ."

Mumbling. Murmuring. Whispering. . . . Every word was like a needle piercing the boy's tongue. The rain was still pouring down. The two strange birds continued singing through the night. The boy wept in the rain.

The ducks ambled around like arrows. In groups of two and three, they wandered through the silvergrass grove and the collapsed melon sheds and bean racks. Two ducks were about to follow the stream away from Shi home. Mother quacked continuously while trying to shoo the ducks away with a bamboo pole. The boy put down the journal and went outside to look for a bamboo pole, then proceeded to the garden to help his mother. The boy first shooed away the monitor lizard hiding in the silvergrass, then went in search of two ducks that had run away from the Shi home, by which point Mother had already taken more than a dozen ducks back to the pen. The silvergrass was making a *sisishasha* sound, and some of the blades had been flattened. A piece of driftwood slowly floated out of the silvergrass as the current carried it toward the garden until finally it ran aground next to a vegetable bed and became completely motionless. Mother returned to the garden. The boy was about to enter the house when he saw Mother pointing at the driftwood and quacking nonstop. Mother picked up a small bamboo pole and extended it toward the piece of driftwood. When the pole landed next to the driftwood, the driftwood began to move. A saltwater crocodile. . . . By the time the boy had gone into the house to get Uncle's rifle, the crocodile had already disappeared without a trace. The boy spent the rest of the morning at his mother's side, holding the rifle and a parang.

A little after five the next morning . . . the boy was standing on the suspension bridge with his rifle, shooting furiously at the crocodiles in the river below. By the time the boy had fired his third shot the crocodiles had already retreated to a safe distance, but the boy continued shooting at anything in the river that bore the faintest resemblance to a crocodile. In the end, he shot all two hundred of the bullets that Uncle had painstakingly saved up. How many crocodiles did he hit? Maybe he didn't hit even a single one. He certainly didn't see any carcasses. The three rifles were as hot as burning coals, the boy's eyes were bloodshot, his brow was furrowed like chains, and the tips of his hair tickled his shoulders like bird feathers. His chin had sprouted whiskers like fish bristles. In the reflection of the suspension bridge, there stood a familiar figure. Was it Uncle? . . . The boy glanced back and saw that there was no one else on the bridge. That reflection glimmered in the current, it was holding three hot rifles. . . . The boy returned to the base camp and began packing his things. He couldn't bear to leave the books, so he loaded as many as he could onto the sampan. After filling the sampan, he gazed at the four-fifths of the books that remained on the bookshelves and couldn't believe that he had this inclination. He liberated six pigs and several dozen chickens and ducks. Then he and Dezhong fashioned a rudimentary stretcher and carried Uncle's dismembered corpse to another sampan. The corpse was still covered in black shirts. When Ling Qiao received news of Jiatong's death early the next morning, she did not appear overly upset. Instead, she calmly looked at the corpse beneath the black shirts, then stared at Dezhong and the boy. During this period she had gained considerable weight, and every night she slept like a pig. Her eyes appeared to be full of poetry, like a pond full of tadpoles. Her lips were full of emotion, like a nepenthes pitcher in the process of digesting a dead insect. What was she thinking? Without saying a word, she returned to her room to begin packing her bags.

Several sampans were moored on the bank of the Rajang River near the base camp. The boy and Ling Qiao boarded one of them and used a rope to haul another filled with books. Dezhong rode in a third, to accompany Uncle. The three sampans proceeded one after the other, with Dezhong and Uncle leading the way, followed by the Ling Qiao and the boy, and the sampan loaded with books at the end. When going with the current they didn't need to row, and instead simply needed to control the direction of the sampans. If they hadn't had to worry that the sampan loaded with books might capsize, they could have proceeded even faster. When they encountered a strong current, they focused most of their attention on the books, with Uncle becoming the equivalent of a pile of firewood that wouldn't be missed if it were lost. They reached Kapit by evening. Under Dezhong's direction there was no welcome ceremony, no banquet, and no laughter. Instead there were only Dezhong's clanspeople whispering and peeking. The boy saw Fadiya again, and he immediately became as awkward as when they first met. They hadn't seen each other for eight months, but Fadiya was wandering between two chaotic zones: dark night and bright day, ocean and sky, dog and wolf, green and mature. Her eyes were full of longing, like coucals cooing. Her lips were trembling, like the snake- and lizard-infested marshland. The boy noticed that she was staring at the boar's tooth hanging from his neck.

The boy cracked a grin, as though the corpse did not exist, but then immediately wiped the smile from his face. Fadiya also smiled faintly, her smile positioned between water and fog. After dinner the boy and Ling Qiao slept in separate rooms. The boy was exhausted and was overcome with drowsiness, and he tossed and turned at the edge of sleep. Suddenly he saw a female elephant standing in front of him, and as it extended its trunk to caress his body, his member grew hard. He opened his eyes wide, and in the darkness he saw a woman standing in front of his sleeping mat. She had already removed her shirt and proceeded to throw herself onto him, licking his face, his neck, and his strong chest. Holding his boar's tooth in her mouth, she kissed him, as the boar's tooth moved back and forth between their mouths, like a fang poking out of their lips. She removed her undershirt and underwear and began rubbing her body against his, ultimately receiving the most magnificent ejaculation that he had produced in his entire life. As she lay on top him, panting, there emerged a sound that seemed to be between human and animal, bitterness and pleasure. If it wasn't a dying monkey, a solitary rhino, or stampeding elephants . . . then what was it? Maybe she was struggling not to make a sound, in this well-ventilated longhouse with cracks in all the walls. Then she got up, put her clothes back on, and quietly left the room.

The next morning the boy carefully examined both Fadiya and Ling Qiao. Which of them had it been? Who had it been? Neither of their faces revealed the slightest clue. The woman's ample breasts and expert movements made the boy suspect it had been Ling Qiao; however, her breath and charm had been more similar to Fadiya's. The boy smiled like a tombstone. Who was it? Fadiya or Ling Qiao? Or someone else entirely? The boy was not interested in investigating. When he was ten, he had begun intermittently giving some furry creatures. Then the boy bid farewell to Fadiya, Dezhong bid farewell to his clanspeople, and Ling Qiao bid farewell to the longhouse as the three of them continued their journey downriver. Two hours later they encountered some government troops who were searching for residual communist soldiers.

After Wang Dada received the news, he and four subordinates rode a truck to the Shi family's garden. "It's a good distance from here to the Rajang River." He used his binoculars to survey the river's silvergrass grove in the water. "How could there be any crocodiles here?"

Wang Dada's four subordinates lowered the truck's two large sampans into the water. The boats were loaded with several rifles and equipment for trapping crocodiles. The four men boarded the two sampans and took turns rowing out to the silvergrass grove. The grass was very dense, and the sampans could only advance very slowly. Wang Dada became very excited. "Crocodiles are almost never seen in the lower part of the Rajang River anymore. I'm most interested in this sort of wild crocodile, and therefore we must endeavor to capture one alive."

"Do you want my help?" The boy asked.

"No need, no need. You go do your thing. When I find my crocodile nemesis, the animal will surely be out of luck."

Wang Dada climbed a jackfruit tree and continued using his binoculars to survey the silvergrass grove, while shouting down orders to his subordinates. The boy also used binoculars to look around. A submerged freshwater crocodile shaped like half a sampan was virtually invisible, becoming part of nature. Wood, mud, silvergrass, floating light and passing shadows—they could all be transformed into crocodiles. The large sampan frequently got stuck in the silvergrass and bushes. Someone would have to get out of the boat and wade through the chest-deep water, get several thick bamboo poles from the boy to serve as push poles, and then wade back to his sampan as though there were no crocodiles nearby. Wang Dada climbed one tree after another. Mother slaughtered two chickens and a duck, then squatted in the kitchen doorway to pluck them. She wanted to prepare a lavish dinner with meat and fish to fete the crocodile hunters. The boy went up to his mother and said that if a crocodile appeared in their garden, it would automatically belong to the Shi family, and therefore if the hunters captured it there that would be the equivalent of the family giving them the crocodile—so what need was there to also give them a meal with meat and fish? Mother quacked twice in response. The boy squatted down to help her, but she just quacked some more and waved him away. With the aid of the push poles, the sampans were able to make their way through the silvergrass, rocking from side to side. With oars on either side and the push poles at the end, each sampan seemed to have two limbs and a tail. Wang Dada climbed to the top of the oldest jackfruit tree, where he swayed back and forth as though leisurely searching his belly for grasshoppers and caterpillars. The boy had no choice but to return to the study.

After returning to Daro from his trip back down the Rajang River, the boy spent six months without leaving his home. Instead, he remained locked in his study reading the books he had brought back from the base area. The only two occasions on which he left the house were both for Uncle. One time was to bury Uncle in the Chinese cemetery. After Dezhong collected his bounty from the government, he fulfilled his promise to return Uncle's entire body to the family, and he also wanted to give the boy part of the bounty. The news media referred to Dezhong and the boy as "dragon-slaying heroes." At the funeral the boy denied to the news media that he had helped kill Yu Jiatong. Reporters examined the boy in a series of article with titles like "After Executing His Own Kin for the Sake of

Righteousness, Does He Harbor Any Regrets?" When the boy declined his portion of the bounty, this was assumed to be a reflection of a murky sense of morality and an obligatory gesture of compensation for Dezhong's family. Reporters repeatedly visited the Shi home, parking themselves in the family's doorway and refusing to leave. Mother quacked as usual, while Father slept during the day and went out at night. The boy, meanwhile, resembled a silverfish buried in a pile of paper and text, steadfastly refusing all visits. Reporters took countless photos of the Shi family compound, and the same morning that the governor of Sarawak publicly praised Dezhong and the boy, the boy disappeared and spent the day wandering alone through the rainforest. After he grew tired, he climbed a silk-cotton tree and spent the rest of the afternoon perched in its branches. Each of the tree's fuzzy seeds had a pair of appendages, and as the seeds were blown in large groups from the tree, they spun around in the air, flying up and down, forward and backward, and sometimes hovering in place. The seeds appeared reluctant to leave the tree, but at the same time they seemed to recognize that they needed to find somewhere to land and put down roots. One cluster of seeds was picked up by a strange wind and proceeded to circle the mothertree, unwilling to depart. The mothertree was unmoved by this and continued swaying in the wind to release more seeds, as though saying, *Quick, before the birds notice you—go find some fertile soil and grow!* The seeds resembled millions of windmills circling around in the sky above the rainforest, as urgent as sperm racing toward an egg. Munbirds, turtledoves, parrots, swallows, and assorted other wild birds that the boy didn't recognize all rushed over to devour the seeds. The birds soared through these clouds of windmills, and each time they seized a furry seed in their mouth and perched on a branch to slowly eat it, it looked as though they had sprouted a gray beard.

The mothertree shuddered even more violently, as though in agony. The tree understood, however, that even if the birds devoured the seeds, they would not be able to completely digest them, meaning that there would still be many seeds that would be expelled into uncultivated land, where they could take root and sprout. The boy couldn't resist the urge to pleasure himself against the mothertree. His semen spurted into the air and splattered all over the succulent leaves. The boy then hugged the tree trunk, feeling a thrill as though he had just copulated with the tree. His sperm spouted furry wings and soared off in all directions. The Japanese had hired some natives to serve as guides and coolies and were using video cameras to record the rainforest's ecology. They had several pieces of heavy equipment and a small square screen, but several weeks passed in the blink of an eye, and what could they possibly record? They didn't even notice the interspecies love affair between a tree and a modern human that was unfolding overhead. Someone had dug up Uncle's grave and left the bones in a strange configuration, so that at first glance they resembled some sort of bizarre animal. The bones were splattered with animal blood, and there were several amulets, as well as cat and dog skulls. It was rumored that this was a form of Malay shamanism, which cursed Uncle's soul to be forever bitten by insects and insured that if he were to be reincarnated it would also result in the death of both the mother and the infant. This was the boy's only public appearances during that six-month period. *I swear I'll chop off the hands and feet of whoever desecrated Uncle's remains*, the boy told the reporters and observers who had gathered around, as he repaired his uncle's grave. *By this point it has already been five months since Uncle's death, but the political leaders on China's southern coast have not even sent a short expression of condolence, much less the kind of eulogy that the Chairman had written for Comrade Aidit. We'll just have to wait until the Chairman himself is willing to send something.* Uncle's death had created ripples in many neighboring Southeast Asian countries, but in distant China everything remained undisturbed. The homeland resembled an ancient well, dug deep in the interior and cut off from its surroundings by mountains and rivers, and even a much larger storm wouldn't have created any waves there. The boy even found himself wondering whether the news of Uncle's death had been transmitted into the old well at all. Given that by that point Wang Dada had already brought an end to the insurrection and encouraged his followers to surrender, Uncle's death therefore had even less significance. But why hadn't Teacher Shao uttered a single word? Was he even still alive? Earlier Teacher Shao had sent troops to attack Wang Dada, yet now he was too stingy to even send a note of condolence following the death of his prized student? Six months after Uncle's death, meanwhile, Father was beaten senseless in a gambling hall by Daro's Three Oxen.

"When Father and Father-in-law were young, they were quite close. When they were seventeen or eighteen, they were assaulted and kidnapped on a dark road and were taken to the bottom deck of a thousand-ton sailboat, where, together with several hundred other 'piglets,' they were sold to Java to serve as Chinese coolies. This was during the late Qing, and this was when Father took up gambling in sugar cane fields, coffee gardens, and public squares, while Father-in-law developed the opium habit that he never managed to shake. When their coolie contracts expired, Father and Father-in-law took a boat to northern Borneo to work as loggers and get married.

"Most of Father's and Father-in-law's children died before reaching the age of two or three. After Elder Sister survived a serious illness, she was left deaf and mute. She was incredibly beautiful, and had it not been for her disabilities, her suitors would surely have been more numerous than maggots. Father loved her dearly, and once I took her to play in the rainforest, but when we returned Father beat me to the brink of death.

"After the outbreak of the Pacific War, Father was worried Sister would be forced to serve as a military sex slave, and therefore he quickly arranged for her and Brother-in-law to get married. At the time, Brother-in-law was in his twenties and had already learned some impressive carpentry and gambling skills from Father. After the humiliation of the arranged marriage, however, Brother-in-law spent three straight days relieving his frustration in the gambling hall, and on the fourth day he returned home and slept the entire day.

"Before the sun came up on the fifth day, Sister was in the animal shed feeding the ducks when several Japanese soldiers arrived. Brother-in-law heard them and immediately rushed over. He was seized and tied to a jackfruit tree as Sister was gang-raped. As the soldiers were leaving, they sliced off Brother-in-law's member and Sister's left breast."

Several quacking sounds could be heard coming from the silvergrass grove, as a pair of fat ducks—one white and one black—with tail feathers like lances ambled through the reflections of the blue sky and white clouds. The ducks themselves resembled a pair of clouds, one light and the other dark. The climate of the silvergrass and the bushes was transient, and the atmosphere was strange. Wang Dada offered the boy's mother a high price for a pair of ducks to serve as bait. It was unclear where exactly Wang Dada and the two sampans were hidden. Ducks quacked, coucals cooed, and fish gulped. White-bellied crakes and green frogs made a loud racket. The *hualala* sound of running water pervaded the house's rear garden. Mother was in the kitchen chopping up chickens and ducks, making a *dedede* sound resembling a wooden fish knocking in an ancient temple.

The ducks did not detect any danger, as though they were hovering at the gates of hell, with the bottom halves of their bodies extending into the water to eat fish. The two ducks saw the wild grass covering the river bottom, through which two-spot gourami, climbing fish, and peacock fish were swimming, as fighting fish spit out bubbles to build nests. The ducks dove to catch fish, and each time they caught a two-spot gourami, they would return to the surface to eat it, and then would dive again. Again and again they would catch a fish, resurface, then dive again. A pair of small eyes were shimmering underwater like fluorescent mushrooms, as the fanged mouth opened and bit down on the duck. The water splashed as two sampans appeared out of nowhere like a pair of arrows. A variety of curses could be heard coming from the sampans. There was a monitor lizard, and someone pulled out a rifle and shot the lizard in the head, then placed the carcass inside the boat. The white duck had already entered the lizard's belly. The silvergrass grove suddenly became dark. What about the black duck? The silvergrass became silent, as birds and animals all fell silent at the sound of the gunshot. The monitor lizard and the white duck had attracted everyone's attention, and even as dusk approached no one noticed where the black duck had gone.

"We have already placed a vast net beneath the silvergrass grove, and if the crocodile dares to make an appearance, we'll definitely be able to catch it alive." As he ate his dinner, Wang Dada cursed nonstop. "This thing is extremely cunning; it must be an old crocodile. It must have eaten that black duck, and if it doesn't leave before the floodwaters recede, you will temporarily be unable to return to the river. You must be very careful."

The boy asked Wang Dada for advice on how to trap a crocodile.

"You have a gun, so just shoot at it when necessary. Tomorrow I'll ask several more people to come."

After seeing off Wang Dada and the others, the boy returned to his study and continued reading the latter portion of the journal. With each page the journal became increasingly damp and moldy, filled with pen stains, ink stains, coffee stains, oil stains, and alcohol stains. Uncle's handwriting was a messy scrawl, and his characters were as large as a dipper. Every character looked like a blood-filled leech occupying the journal, like an anchor covered in algae and parasites. Wilted characters, covered in fat and tender parasites, and sentences made of scattered bones, overgrown with twisted and gnarled algae. A first-person narrative entangled in mud, and a humid and stifling reading environment. As though engraving a tombstone at the bottom of a river, the boy went underwater until his breath was like gossamer strands, but all he saw were ineffable sentence fragments struggling to reach the surface. Among terrestrial animals, only crocodiles and monitor lizards would be able to read this writing. But the sound of the pages turning was so dry, it was as though he were crushing one origami mandrill after another.

". . . Only the Yu and Shi clans know this. Nine months later, Sister gave birth to a Chinese-Japanese mixed-race son, Shinong. Afterwards, Brother-in-law completely abandoned his irregular carpentry job and instead became a professional gambler, frequently accumulating enormous debts. Was it Brother-in-law who noticed his creditor's desire, or was the creditor the first to make the proposal? One encounter between Sister and the creditor repaid all of Brother-in-law's debt, and nine months later Sister gave birth to Shishu. Brother-in-law repeated this process of symbolic repayment several times, until finally Sister give birth to my niece Junyi.

"... At first, it was only gambling debts that were being repaid, but over time this practice evolved into a means of procuring additional money for gambling. Father and Father-in-law initially reacted with anger and violence, and eventually they acquiesced and acted as though they hadn't seen or heard a thing. Perhaps they had completely succumbed to the torment of debt and an imperative of ethnic reproduction? And Sister? Did she attempt to resist, or did she welcome this arrangement? In the dark, was she able to see the men who assaulted her? Did she feel the need to surrender? When she gave birth to Shicai, I saw an odd smile on Father's face, as though he were trying to suppress his desire to snuff out this monstruous birth.

"I deliberately forgot those men and didn't even ask them their names. Brother-in-law borrowed some gambling money from Teacher Shao, for which Teacher Shao sold two landscape scrolls he had brought over from the motherland. Shiwen, that pedantic bookworm, went in and out of Teacher Shao's home as though it were his own, and whenever he had free time he would enter the studio filled with the scholarly odor Teacher Shao had prepared for him—like an infant who still smells of milk entering the crotch of father's pants that are saturated with the stench of semen.

"After Junyi was born, elephant tusks mysteriously began to appear by the Shi family's back door, which helped address the family's food expenses as well as Brother-in-law's enormous gambling debts. Had it not been for these tusks, Sister would have needed to continue selling her body to satisfy Brother-in-law's greed, and the Shi clan's 'later generation' would have continued appearing. Were the tusks a gift from Father? By why didn't he simply return home? Was he consumed with guilt for having wanted to extinguish this monstruous birth?

"The head of the longhouse told me that when Father-in-law initially took refuge with them, he was carrying two pairs of enormous elephant tusks covered in moss and algae, which looked as though they had been submerged under water for a very long time. Where did these two pairs of tusks come from? After Father-in-law escaped from the animal shed, why did Mother-in-law drown in the well?

"I always suspected that if we had somehow managed to find the cave full of elephant tusks sooner, the revolution might well have taken a different turn, and it is entirely possibly that it might have ultimately succeeded. . . .

"I suspect that Sister knows this all too well . . ."

The journal abruptly broke off. The remaining several dozen pages were drenched in ink, leaving them blue, wrinkled, crisp, and swollen. Like a marsh, a flattened roach carcass was wedged between two of the pages. Like a blue sky, a dead butterfly, which had mostly turned to dust, was stuck to another. Like a shady rainforest, an enormous leaf from some unidentified tree covered an entire page. Like on a blackboard, a gecko had been crushed to the point that it resembled a miniature crocodile skeleton. Had an inkpot gotten overturned? Or had the tip of a ballpoint pen touched the white paper while he was in the throes of creation? The boy leafed back and forth through the journal, reading it over and over. The first half was blank, the middle portion was filled with an overgrown mass of wild characters, in which many birds and animals were sitting, as beetles and trilobites were chewing and eating the characters. The latter half, meanwhile, was wet and muddy, containing countless unknown mysteries and unforeseeable futures. Was he about to float away into that emptiness, just as he had previously passed his days in blissful ignorance? Or was he searching for clues in the overgrown mass of wild characters? Or was he dredging the muddy marsh that had subsequently developed there? And why had Uncle left this journal behind in the first place? Were its contents merely idle graffiti, like prehistoric cave paintings? Or was it intended only for the boy's eyes?

The lamp illuminated the books on the bookshelves and the *Landscape of Wind and Rain* on the wall, making it appear as though they were shrouded in a layer of gauze. Aside from the haze, the *Landscape of Wind and Rain* was full of sound and fury, as though there were a hermit surrounded by a gentle breeze and flowing water while instigating a bloody battle far away. In the books, millions of characters hatched as though from eggs, using their beaks and feathers to represent the primal form of the characters' meaning. Father's book consumption was inefficient and disgusting, like a sun bear that disappears into a cornfield while scattering kernels all over the place. Many books had been tossed aside after Father had consumed only a page or two, resulting in an immense amount of damage. The boy reluctantly returned the books to their original positions on the shelves, where, under the light of the lamp, their bones and flesh were clearly visible—reminding the boy of the critically ill elephants he had seen in the field. By this point more than a year had already passed. Were those elephants still walking? Were they still together? Or had disease already thinned their herd to the point that only two or three individuals were left, all alone and waiting to die? The eight hunting expeditions recorded in the journal, together with the countless times the boy's maternal grandfather had hunted elephants that were not recorded, all flooded the boy's memory like a tidal wave, together with the sound of the gunshots that would scare the house dog shitless, the roar of the elephants that would drive the livestock to break out of their pens, and the sound of the elephants collapsing that would stir up the thick, putrid surface of the swamp. . . . Outside the window, there was a seasonal northeastern wind that enabled countless sailboats to sail south from ancient China, and which was blowing the journal pages such that they made a *paleipalei* sound. The moon resembled an egg waiting for a sperm, as its dusty hue lustily lit up and disturbed the journal and enticed countless men and beasts to launch their semen toward the moon. The boy saw that the first half of the journal had already disappeared into the sky, the several dozen pages in the middle that were full of Chinese characters scattered across the wasteland, and the soggy latter portion had sunk into the marsh.

Early morning. The boy woke to the sound of quacking. Was it mother speaking? Was it a duck quacking? The journal was still lying on the table. Dejected, the boy lay in bed. He was twenty years old. He couldn't continue spending the entire day hiding in this enclosure surrounded by bookcases, like a living person buried in obituaries along with the dead. After his bath he sat down at the table and ate some noodles. After Mother finished feeding the chickens and ducks, she squatted down in the bathroom to wash clothes. She quickly washed the clothes, then went outside to hang them up to dry. Next she filled a pot of water and put it on the stove to boil. The boy finished his noodles and used hand gestures to communicate that he would watch the stove for her. Mother nodded and proceeded to the fruit orchard, where she used a sack to wrap up a jackfruit that had already begun to smell, to prevent birds and insects from eating it. She opened another sack and lightly patted another jackfruit that was already as large as a pillow. She listened to the sound like a doctor conducting an exam, palpating the fruit up and down. Then she went to the kitchen to get a parang. The boy followed her, then squatted down and held the bottom portion of the jackfruit. Mother used her parang to slice off the fruit's stem, as the entire weight of the jackfruit fell into the boy's hands. She put down her parang and helped the boy carry the jackfruit to the kitchen. Next she returned to the tree to retrieve the parang, then leaned over and effortlessly chopped the fruit into six pieces. She used hand gestures to tell the boy to give five of the pieces to the neighbors. The boy asked, *Mother, do you plan to go into the field?* By that point the floodwaters had already fully receded, and there could very well could still be some crocodiles hiding in the silvergrass grove. Mother ignored the boy's question and, wearing a bamboo hat and plastic sandals, went out into the garden. The boy wrapped the jackfruit in some straw rope and hung it from the handlebars of his bicycle. The five pieces of jackfruit swayed back and forth, as chunks of jackfruit flesh hung down with white juice dripping from them, like five freshly decapitated human heads. The neighbors' houses were positioned in a circular array around the Shi home, and therefore the boy had to make a full loop around his house to complete his assignment. The road was very quiet, with the silence broken only by the dull thud of the jackfruit pieces bumping against one another. A troop of pig-tailed macaques were chasing each other around a tropical willow that didn't have any edible fruit. Chickens and ducks pecked at one another, and wild dogs bit each other. Two housecats were facing off on an iron railing covered in vines, as though performing stunts. Creeping forward on four legs, with their fur standing on end, the cats resembled giant caterpillars. The boy used a slingshot to shoot some birds, and stones filled the air. Dead and almost dead birds were carried in his tender, young hands. The boy picked up some birds that had been injured by stray stones, which made a *ding-dingdangdang* sound as they landed on the corrugated roof of a house. One of the boy's elder brothers hid behind the iron fence, snickering. The house's owner picked up his stick and left, whereupon the brother also departed. The boy fell to the ground.

Eldest Brother? . . . Second Brother? . . . Third Brother? . . . Fourth Brother? . . . Who had it been? Whoever it was, he turned and carried the boy toward the vast wilderness. The brother's bright laughter wandered into the heart of the boy carrying the dead bird.

Three of the men under Wang Dada's command again boarded a sampan to patrol the silvergrass grove. Carrying a rifle and a parang, the boy went to the garden to help his mother clean up the melon sheds and beanpoles. The sampan was covered in weeds and branches, to the point that it had become camouflaged by the silvergrass. The men told the boy that one of the traps had already been completely destroyed. "This crocodile," the man said, "can destroy our sampan with a flick of its tail." The man quickly left and returned, then tossed a more accurate and durable trap into the silvergrass. That evening the man returned to check the trap. At night there was the sound of large fish jumping in the water, enormous reptiles entering the water, coconuts or mangos falling into the pond, and there was also the scream of some sort of enormous bird that sounded as though it was flying out of a mountain cave, or a miserable whistling sound of a storm with no point of origin blowing toward an old house full of open windows. All these noises distracted the boy from his book or woke him from his dreams. As he stared out the window, his book was like a barking dog writing the earth, and as he lay in bed listening, his dream was like a pack of wild boars roaming the earth. The sounds were abrupt and appeared to be unrelated to him. At the same time, however, they also seemed to contain a hidden response to a kind of desire buried deep in his heart— some sort of long-suppressed canine or porcine characteristics. At times the sounds appeared extremely unrealistic, as though they were some sort of association from a book or were emerging directly from a dream. The crocodiles' pleasure, the elephants'

death, the skulls' discord, Fadiya's foreign speech, Junyi's . . .
Gegege. Leileilei. Was this the hanging scroll knocking against
the wall? A cat scratching? A bird bumping against a screen
window? A snake strangling a chicken? The boy put down his
book and glanced up at the clock. 11:50. The rear garden was
pitch-black. The boy emerged from his study, passed though the
living room, then stood in the hallway. A dark shadow opened
the Shi family's iron gate and left. A flashlight beam swayed back
and forth in the darkness in front of the shadowy figure.

Carrying a heavy sack on her right shoulder and holding a
flashlight in her left hand, Mother slowly left the house. The
flashlight was turned off more than it was turned on. Obviously
Mother was very comfortable following this path in the dark.
The boy didn't have a flashlight, and from a distance he followed
the *geleigelei* sound of snails being crushed underfoot. Mother
avoided the streetlights, heading instead into the darkness. One
hour later, after completing a long loop, she entered a brightly
lit two-story concrete Western-style house downtown. She
knocked on the door with a code that she had clearly already
practiced. Christian, the Englishman, answered the door and let
her in. For the past decade Christian had been trading in
restricted goods, leaving him with fat cheeks and a large belly,
and he was already one of Daro's rich elite. The boy climbed a
tree, and through the window he could clearly see his mother
remove a pair of elephant tusks from the sack. Christian examined the tusks, then handed Mother a wad of bills. Mother
counted the bills, took the empty sack and the flashlight, and
returned along the same path she had come. The boy remained
perched motionless on the tree branch for a long time. Why did
Mother have these elephant tusks? Was Grandfather still alive?
Mother and Christian both acted as though they had already
been engaging in this sort of exchange for some time. Mother . . .

what was she hiding? The next day, the boy opened the biscuit tin where Mother kept her money and saw that not a single bill was missing from the money she had made selling her jewelry. Mother remained as busy as before, completing all the housework without fail, and sooner or later she'd prepare the boy a sumptuous meal.

The floodwaters receded, leaving the vegetable garden and silvergrass grove covered in mud, but without any crocodiles. Wang Dada explained that most of the crocodiles must have already returned to the Rajang River, since they couldn't possibly remain in the small creek in the Shi family's rear garden. After directing the soldiers under his command to go retrieve the crocodile traps, he drove away. The boy continued helping his mother clean up the garden. A week later the boy noticed that in the creek there appeared a long floating log, on which there were some weeds and a water bird. The log occasionally sank into the water, leaving the weeds and bird on the surface. When the log resurfaced it acquired even more weeds, and the same bird landed again on it. It was a crocodile. The boy went inside to get his rifle, but by the time he reemerged the crocodile had disappeared. This time the boy did not notify Wang Dada, and instead he went into the street and caught a wild dog. He tied a rope around the dog's neck, then tied the other end to a small tree in the silvergrass grove. Next, he climbed a large tree, selected an optimal position, then cocked his gun and waited. Two days later the dog had disappeared, and all that remained was the rope tied to the tree. A week later, the boy tied another wild dog to another tree, and after nightfall he took the dog back and tied it to a coconut tree in the rear garden. Within a week this second dog had also disappeared. The boy caught yet another wild dog and tied it to a wooden stake next to the creek, but several days later the dog mysteriously disappeared. Within a space of only three months the boy lost five dogs in succession, yet didn't manage to glimpse even half of crocodile's claw. The boy realized with a start that he had unwittingly been feeding the crocodile for three months.

The sun was shining bright, and there wasn't a cloud in sight. Shadows of monkey-eating eagles appeared over the cracked riverbed. Birds and insects were eating fish and shrimp, as turtles, crabs, snakes, and frogs hid in deep burrows. Thanks to the sadistic wildfires plants were destroyed, and animals were burned alive. In June, July, and August fire became seeds, bones became earth, and ashes became fertilizer, and fruit rotted. The creek, marsh, and silvergrass groves all disappeared without a trace, leaving behind an occasional patch of dry or scorched earth. Coucals flew back to the tree to look for their nest, and monitor lizards returned to the rain forest. But where did the crocodile go? Despite using emaciated wild dogs and noisy chickens as bait, the boy never saw the crocodile come eat. The duckweed-filled pond behind the pigpen had already dried up, and the water level of the well had dropped. One day the boy went over to the well, peered inside, and noticed with surprise that a cluster of cylindrical objects were dimly visible beneath the water's surface. They were white and green, pointy at one end and round at the other, as though a cluster of tender, edible thorns were growing in the water. The boy leaned over to look more closely. A climbing fish swam into a crevice in the pile of cylindrical objects. It was a pile of tusks . . .

How many tusks were hidden at the bottom of the well? Perhaps thirty or forty pairs. . . . or even fifty or sixty? The tusks were of different lengths and were covered in moss and algae. The portions sticking out of the water were bone-dry and were bundled together in pairs with string, piled haphazardly on the bottom of the well. A passage that the boy had read millions of times suddenly appeared in his mind, like the elephant tusks appearing at the bottom of the well: ". . . elephant tusks covered in moss and algae, looking as though they had been submerged under water for a very long time. . . ." Grandmother's corpse, which years earlier had fallen into the well, also resurfaced. The journal's withered characters rose up proudly, as though they had been teased, and this long-hidden secret was now clearly revealed. Perhaps Grandfather, when he was placed under house arrest by Grandmother, not only robbed the grave but also stole the tusks in the well. Perhaps while he was locked in the animal shed, he discovered the secret in the well . . . but had been blocked by Grandmother when he attempted to retrieve the tusks? . . . Had Grandmother been killed by Grandfather accidentally? Or deliberately? Did she drown in the well? Did Grandfather then take away two pairs of tusks. . . .

Like Mother, Grandmother also kept the well's secret close to her bosom. . . . It turns out that the boy's maternal grandfather never stopped supplying the tusks, but instead he began hiding them inside the well to serve as an endless supply of wealth for the Shi family. Was that legendary tusk-filled cave none other than this well? The family had three wells in all. . . . The boy walked over to the one outside the bathroom. The water level had already dropped as much as that of the other well, but nothing was visible inside. The boy used a bamboo pole to prod the bottom of the well. Something uneven. Hard. He struggled to hook the object onto the well wall. A pair of tusks. . . . The boy used the same method to examine the well in the garden, and there, too, he found pair after pair of elephant tusks. So, the elephant tusks Mother sold to Christian came from here. Father . . . did Father know? The boy remembered how one night many years earlier, Father and a tall man left through the back door and rode away on bicycles. Based on the sound, the boy had always assumed that that man was leaving from Mother's room. . . . Did Mother continue using her body to repay Father's gambling debts even after Junyi was born? Why didn't she use the tusks to resolve those outstanding debts? Or perhaps she wanted to keep the tusks a secret, to prevent Father from selling them? . . .

In November the drought finally broke, and it began raining heavily for several hours every afternoon. The water level of the creek rose, and the silvergrass grove once again became a marsh. The crocodile that had been missing for many days once again passed through the bushes. After the crocodile moved in, the monitor lizards and other large reptiles disappeared without a trace. The boy had already lost interest in trapping the crocodile, particularly given that for more than half a year the animal had not done anything bad, and instead it merely needed to eat periodically. Every week or two the boy would go into the street, catch a wild dog, and tie it to a small tree. These wild dogs bred at an astonishing rate, to the point that every several months the local health bureau would need to use poison to cull the herd.

As the June drought was still raging, however, some news was brought over from the Rajang River by either natives or local Chinese. This news spread like algae and reproduced along the road until it finally reached the hot and dry town of Daro. The news was full of fat, and it appeared in Chinese announcements in the form of succulent, enchanting, and strange Chinese characters, thereby revealing the astonishing nutrition it had absorbed on the road. The news was that, adept at disguise, the former leader of the Yangtze River Brigade, Yu Jiatong, was still alive and was gathering his scattered troops. The boy froze in shock. Uncle was still alive? . . . The boy and Dezhong had chopped up the corpse to the point that human and lizard flesh were completely mixed together. They had seen with their own eyes that the body was completely destroyed, the head was chopped off, and the brains were splattered everywhere. But had they been actually hacking at the lizard? Or at Uncle? The boy was reminded of how wild dogs would curl up into a ball when being attacked. The government troops had confirmed the body's identity based on the boy's and Ling Qiao's testimony, a rifle with a dragon and a crocodile engraved on the handle, and Uncle's colonial-era ID card. Was Uncle really still alive? He had survived hundreds of battles. . . . Dezhong told the news media that the back of Uncle's skull had previously been wounded and would periodically start throbbing. Uncle happened to have one of these migraines that night, which is why the slaughter proceeded so smoothly. . . . No, it simply wasn't possible. . . . The boy had confirmed that the head Dezhong was holding was in fact Uncle's. . . . A former Yangtze River Brigade soldier named Wu Zhaoping was recruiting soldiers and equipment to reconstitute the Yangtze River Brigade, but behind the scenes he was actually being directed by Yu Jiatong. . . . Shao An, the founder of the SCP, who remained strong even into his eighties, snuck back into Sarawak, where he prepared to raise again the Communist Party's red tide. . . .

It was just a rumor. . . . A fatty rumor, and even if people stopped feeding it, it could continue burning its stored blubber for at least another year and a half. In August, Daro's Black Ox and Wild Ox disappeared into the rainforest, and it was rumored that they had found a cave full of tusks.

Hualala. The sound of a large object falling into the water. Had a coconut or a mango fallen into the pond? The sound was somewhat dulled, as though there had been an attempt to stifle or cover it up. The boy looked out the window at the garden. There was someone wearing long pants, a short-sleeved shirt, and a cloth hat. The person had dark-red skin and was in the process of placing a pair of elephant tusks inside the well. *Hua-lala*. The boy immediately rushed over to the garden. *Hey, who is it? Who are you?* That person had already disappeared into the wilderness, his shadow flickering through the silvergrass. The boy pursued him, but the other person was very skilled and seemed to know the way like the back of his hand. After a couple of turns he easily left the boy behind. The boy pursued him until he was panting like an ox, and thought to himself, *I'm just twenty, and am running as fast as I can, yet I still can't keep up with that figure's shadow; could that figure be a specter?* The figure entered the rainforest, and as the boy was falling further and further behind the figure stopped, turned around, and looked at the boy—or was he looking at something else? There was a dark shadow beneath the brim of his hat, his features were indistinct, and there was a trace of a smirk in the corners of his mouth. He was of average height and was slender but with large bones. Hanging from his waist there was parang in its scabbard. Was it the boy's maternal grandfather? Uncle? Wu Zhaoping? Dezhong? Teacher Shao? . . . Who? Who are you? Hey! Wait. . . . The boy loudly shouted, but his voice was quickly drowned out by the cacophony of birds and insects, and by the sound of running water that seemed to come from all directions, like thin August clouds that quickly dissipate under the searing heat of the sun. That person always managed to find a faint path through the dense jungle, or to extract a narrow trail through the fields. He was like a mountain lion in the rainforest, and all the areas he passed through were ones that were almost uninhabited, or animal routes where humans had previously never set foot. At several points the boy almost wanted to give up, but the other person always seemed to realize it and would go to an elevated or open area and beckon to the boy with his shadow, attracting the boy like a traveler trapped in quicksand who sees a helping hand. In the dense jungle, where it was as dark as the middle of the night, that person's eyes flickered like a crocodile's. He pulled his parang from his scabbard to hack at vines and weeds, as his blade flickered in and out of sight like the luster of a half-finned large fish at the bottom of a well. Pursuit . . . escape . . . escape . . . pursuit . . . Was it a pursuit? Or an escape? That person did not seem to be avoiding the boy, but neither did he appear to want to face the boy. Was he trying to lure the boy to get lost in the jungle? Or direct him out of the jungle? How long could this type of pursuit last? The boy stopped twice to eat some fruit to slake his thirst, wash his face in a creek, and even release a load of urine. The other person waited for the boy to rest and collect himself, then beckoned him again from a distance. *Who? Who are you?* The boy wanted to shout, but either because he had already gone hoarse, or because the gaps in the jungle's vegetation and stones devoured his voice to the point that it was left completely boneless, the boy discovered that when he opened his mouth no words came out, and instead the sound resembled a silkworm spitting silk. During this pursuit, the two of them sometimes went through dark regions and sunny areas, they forded rivers and climbed mountains . . . eventually the boy came to a stop in front of cave. The cave was as large as a pigpen. It was as deep as a well and was full of sharp stakes. There were a couple of two human skeletons, one facing upward and the other facing downward, and they were impaled by the stakes like a needle through cloth. The stakes penetrated their entire body. Some of them went through the bodies' eye socket, while others went through their neck, torso, and limbs. The skeletons were still completely intact, like withered melons on melon racks. It was a trap, and all that was left behind were tattered shirts, rifles, watches, water bottles, and shoes—like assorted burial objects. The watch hands were still silently moving . . . and a rifle was resting on the ribcage of one of the skeletons, with the character for "ox" inscribed on the handle. . . . Black Ox and Wild Ox? Why did they die here? The shadow . . . that spectral shadow . . . was waiting for the boy up in front. The boy walked around the perimeter of the cave, pursuing the shadow, before coming to a halt in front of a rock face covered in tropical plants. The rock face was steep and precipitous, like a cracked riverbed full of fish bones and shrimp shells, like a battlement hidden in the morning mist, or like a human wall. There was graffiti on the rock face, but it was unclear whether it contained text or pictures. Numerous faces that appeared to be neither human nor animal resembled . . . that person? In front of the rock face there was an almost dried-up stream that approached the gully, with water so clear that you could see the bottom. In the stream there were several fish that resembled rusty iron, like a shipwreck. They struggled to rise to the surface, only to sink back down to the riverbed, where they were slowly covered in sand, like . . . the specter of that person hiding in the bushes? A skinny monkey was perched on a vine growing up the rock face, and when it saw the boy it slowly climbed, in a completely unmonkeylike manner, to a higher position. Its figure and affect closely resembled . . . that person? A hornbill with enormous tail feathers that draped over its entire body stopped on an old tree in front of the rock face . . . and a large, dark butterfly perched on a bush and was camouflaged as a dead monkey face with its eyes closed, while another perched on a tree and was camouflaged as the face of an owl in a tree hole . . . and their expressions both resembled . . . that person? Apart from the vines crawling up the rock face, the nearby vegetation was not particularly verdant, and much of it had already begun to wither, as though it had been scorched by a wildfire. A thin, midsized lizard slowly crawled into a crevice in the rocks, like a blade entering a scabbard, and its leisurely decadence also resembled . . . that person? The ear-piercing bird cries and insect sounds could no longer be heard, and the sudden stillness made the boy rather uncomfortable, like the silence of that person full of the smell of decay . . . from the stillness there occasionally emerged one or two imposing and stinging dripping sounds, and the sound of flowing water like the sound of someone chanting while in the middle of the creek while dying of thirst, as though that person were hiding somewhere, sobbing. . . .

Where did that person go? Why had that person led the boy here? That person . . . did that person really exist? Or was he just the boy's optical illusion? From the point when the boy started to reminisce after hearing the sound of something falling into the water, he suddenly discovered that he couldn't remember that person's movements, and instead all he could remember was that dark face that appeared as though it had been tattooed, and that strawlike fragmented shadow. . . . Whenever the boy glimpsed a being with even vaguely human features, he seemed to assume he was related to them, and the entire area seemed pervaded by foul odor from that person's nose and mouth and the stench of semen emanating from his crotch, as though the boy and all the birds, fish, insects, and animals had become millions of sperm anxiously swimming toward an old woman's depleted ovaries. . . . The boy proceeded several dozen steps down the creek and noticed a sampan-like object. He approached and saw that it was a boat coffin containing an intact human skeleton lying on its back and staring up at the sky. The skeleton's head seemed to have a helpless expression, like . . . that person? The bow of the boat contained a carved animal head with its mouth open and fangs bared, like a crocodile. The sides of the boat were carved with dragons. The boat was slightly tilted, and its base was buried in sand, as though it wanted to proceed up that almost-dry creek bed. Next to the boat there was a cave filled with countless elephant tusks—so many tusks that they spilled out and were scattered in front of the stone wall, half-buried in the sand. Apart from the tusks, there was also a collection of old artifacts such as Chinese porcelain and urns. It turns out that the legendary cave full of elephant tusks was actually a deadly trap . . . Was it Grandfather's body in the coffin? The boy looked around, but couldn't find any of Grandfather's personal effects, aside from those elephant tusks and that crocodile-dragon totem that seemed to have some connection with the Yu family.

On his way back, the boy discovered with surprise that the road appeared very familiar. He barely hesitated in finding his way, and in only three hours he was home. He felt as though the previous pursuit had lasted a century. On the way home he noticed several dozen enormous elephant footprints. The prints sank deep into the dry, hard earth, as though a spectral herd of elephants had passed through. It was as though they were clues that the boy had left when he first came through, or else were signs leading the boy to the boat coffin and then back home. The coucals were still making their love-filled *gugu* calls, a skinny dog produced a terrifying howl, and an enormous crocodile observed with a flickering gaze. The boy opened the *Elephant Hunting Journal* and proceeded to ejaculate into the oil-, alcohol-, coffee-, and ink-stained pages of the latter portion of the volume. The boy couldn't remember whether he had buried the boat coffin and the skeleton. He began to unpack and inspected his parang and rifle. The next day, he might purchase a sampan and head back up the Rajang River to revisit the Yangtze River Brigade base camp, and pursue that fat-filled legendary creature, and carry hidden within his heart the tusk-filled wells and caves.

GPSR Authorized Representative: Easy Access System Europe, Mustamäe tee 50, 10621 Tallinn, Estonia, gpsr.requests@easproject.com